breathe

Grenton PD *One*

L. Setterby

Chapter One

A DARK FORM HUDDLED ON THE snowy bench overlooking the lake, underneath sweeping pine boughs. Ray Waller. Fifties, with a graying patch of stubble and shabby clothes. All the guys at the station, including Simon, took turns picking Ray up for public intoxication and letting him sleep it off in the holding cell overnight.

Simon stopped beside the bench, ankle-deep in snow, and frowned at the thin sleeves of Ray's sweatshirt. "What're you doing out here, Ray?"

"Old lady kicked me out again."

"Where's your coat?"

"Forgot it."

With a sigh, Simon sat down beside him, ignoring the way Ray's bloodshot eyes widened in surprise. "You can't stay out here," Simon said. "You're gonna get hypothermia."

Ray shrugged. He looked worse than usual, like he didn't care if he got hypothermia or not. Slouching forward, Simon rested his forearms on his knees and gazed out at the frozen lake, its vast expanse as white as the sky.

At the sound of crinkling paper, Simon glanced over to see Ray uncapping a bottle half-hidden inside a paper bag.

"You can't drink that out here, buddy," Simon said, suddenly very tired.

"You gonna book me again, Labelle?"

He was off-duty today, if only because the Chief had insisted. Though being off-duty didn't necessarily make much of a difference. "No."

Ray nodded, his face pinched. "When're you gonna solve that case? The bombing?"

"Dunno." Never, since the State's Attorney had decided there wasn't enough evidence to pursue it. God damn it.

"Here." Ray offered Simon the paper bag. The just-opened bottle of cheap whiskey smelled utterly benevolent. The bag trembled slightly in Ray's hands. His gloveless fingers were pale with cold.

"I'll trade you." Simon stood, unzipped his coat, and tossed it onto Ray's lap. "Go see the pastor. He'll let you sleep in the church basement. Promise me you'll get out of the weather."

Ray gazed down at Simon's coat. "You're giving me this? Why?"

"Merry Christmas," Simon said, sitting back down on the bench. "Get yourself cleaned up. I'll take that." He took the booze from Ray and stuffed the bottle into the bank of snow at his feet.

Ray slid Simon's coat on over his thin frame. "Thanks, Labelle."

He wandered away, back toward the town. For once, Ray hadn't argued with Simon about confiscating his booze. Simon should've been glad. Instead, he stared at the frost glistening on the bottle's mouth and thought about the bombing case: the same endless rounds of thoughts he'd had for months. The Chief kept telling him the case was cold, that Simon had done his best and now he needed to take some time off and decompress. But when Simon went home, he lay on his couch or in bed and stared at the darkness, and peace felt further away than ever. At least when he was working, he could keep up the pretense of doing good.

Simon's gaze drifted away from the bottle and back toward it again. He rubbed his knuckles over his jawline, his heart racing. No one was around. No one had to know. That wasn't why he'd taken it, but…

He pulled his phone free from his jeans pocket and dialed the station. Keene's direct line.

"Bryan Keene." The man shouted every damn word he said.

"Keene, do me a favor."

"God damn it, Simon, what the hell is your problem? You're supposed to be taking the day off, for fuck's—"

Simon interrupted Keene's ever-present stream of cursing to ask him to check on Ray, make sure he got to the church all right. Keene immediately agreed, before launching back into his lecture. "So now what, you're gonna keep running yourself into the ground as fucking penance—?"

"I told you, I'm fine," Simon insisted. "Seriously. See you tomorrow." He hung up and jammed his phone back into his pocket.

Quickly, before he could change his mind, he leaned forward, snatched up the bottle, and took a swig. The whiskey flooded his body with warmth, banishing the cold from his fingers. A sense of relief rendered him momentarily breathless.

Fuck, it was cold out. He should go home. At least he, unlike Ray, had a home to go to.

Stuffing the bottle back into the snow bank, Simon

slid his palms over his wool hat. He imagined the long walk home, the empty afternoon, the night. Days like this, the future was a crushing weight of unmet expectations.

What if he didn't go back? What if he just stayed here?

"Simon? Or should I say Officer Labelle?"

Shit. Dragging the back of his hand across his mouth, he glanced back across the field of snow to where Leona fucking Chaisty was standing just off the hiking trail that looped around the lake. She wore black running pants and a black coat that hugged the long, slim lines of her body. Her fair skin glowed with exertion.

She hadn't spoken to him in so long, he'd sometimes wondered if she'd forgotten his name. Not easy to do in a town of five or six thousand, especially since there were, including him, only six cops. But Leona had kept to herself even when they were kids. Now he hardly ever saw her, unless he was walking by her artsy little shop on his beat.

It figured the one time they ran into each other, he was at his worst.

Leona glided toward him, hardly indenting the snow under her feet. With her long black hair and ever-present smirk, she had always reminded him of a fairy—an evil one, who might curse you just for fun, or steal your first-born child if you forgot to leave a saucer of milk out one night. That smile, he'd always thought, was dangerous.

"You all right?" she asked, one eyebrow arching.

"Fine." It was all he ever said these days. "I'm fine."

"Why don't you have a coat?"

"Gave it to Ray Waller."

"Why?"

"He didn't have one."

"But now *you* don't have one." Her wide, expressive mouth quirked. "You see how that works."

"I get it, thanks." His tone was acidic, but his heart thudded hard as she moved closer to him, her hips swinging. She sat down delicately beside him, crossing her legs.

"That your whiskey?"

His neck burned under the soft collar of his fleece. "No."

"All right." Leaning forward, she plucked the bottle out of the snow and took a swig, her white throat arching.

"Leona." Simon couldn't contain a sound of hypocritical disapproval.

Her unrepentant gaze turned toward him, assessing him, as if she could unspool his soul from his body and examine it in her hands.

"I've never seen you like this," she said.

"Like what?"

Instead of answering, she took another deep swig of whiskey. There was something obscene about watching her drink, the way she swallowed—it set his blood on fire. Every time he'd seen her over the last ten years or so collided together in his mind in a carousel of erotic imagery. That old longing burned in him.

She handed him the bottle, and its scent struck him again, as difficult and as thrilling as Leona's presence. He set it down on the bench between them with a *clunk*.

"First of all," she said, raising a finger, "I hardly ever see you out of uniform. And even when I do, you're always…I don't know. Helping little old ladies cross the street or something. Right now you're practically loitering."

"I am not *loitering*," he snapped.

"What are you doing, then?"

He opened and closed his mouth, then shook his head, frustrated. He no longer knew. That was the problem.

"What are *you* doing?" he managed finally.

"Well, I *was* jogging, but now…" She shrugged. "Loitering, I suppose. You must be corrupting me."

"You don't need my help with that," he said, and immediately regretted it. He knew nothing about her personal life and never had. She was intensely private, even secretive, which had always just made her more interesting to him.

"I'm sorry," he said. "That was rude."

"You're right. It was." Her gray eyes glittered with amusement. "But it's also accurate."

Falling snow had begun to stick to the whiskey bottle's brown paper bag, and to the sleeves of Simon's blue fleece.

"It's getting dark," she said. "You should go home."

"I'm fine," he said automatically.

"Are you?" With a quizzical tilt of her head, she leaned in close and traced one gloved fingertip down his cheek like a tear. It was the first time they had ever touched, even by accident. His cold, numb skin sparked, and he couldn't look away from her eyes, luminous in the fading daylight. This close, he could just catch the sharp, gingery scent of her perfume, mingling with the scents of whiskey and new snow.

She drew away suddenly and stood, brushing snow off her chest and arms. "Well, you might be immune to the cold, but I need to go home."

Disappointment flashed through him. The one time

she spoke to him—

"You should walk me there," she said.

"What? Why?"

"Because you're a compulsive do-gooder and I'm a little buzzed."

"Jesus," he muttered. So much for feeling flattered.

"On your feet, soldier." She reached for his arm as if to help him up, but he brushed her away. He didn't need her help. He was only going with her because she was right about him—he didn't like letting anyone walk off alone into Vermont snowfall, even when it was still relatively light snow like this. He couldn't even call Keene to check up on Leona, like he could with Ray.

"Come on," he said gruffly. Picking up the whiskey bottle, he made his way back toward the trail. All the outdoor enthusiasts he'd passed earlier had gone home to their wood stoves and hot chocolates, leaving him and Leona alone in a world of snow and gathering darkness. Even dressed for jogging, she was a fairy queen, presiding over a twilit netherworld.

"How do you jog in all this snow?" he asked, when she joined him on the trail.

"Sometimes I have to put spikes on my sneakers," she said cheerfully.

"And you're not freezing?"

"Not when I'm moving."

"Fair enough," he grunted. For him, standing had only highlighted just how cold he'd become, sitting on that bench. Not just his hands or his feet, but deep in his joints.

They passed a trashcan and Simon chucked the bottle of whiskey into it. Good riddance. He should never have opened it in the first place. If anyone else had caught him with it, apart from Leona… At least she didn't care enough about him to think less of him.

They followed the trail through the pine forest to a road on the outskirts of town. Soon, they reached tiny downtown Grenton, where the Christmas lights lining Cascade Street cast a gentle glow across the covered bridge, the handful of art galleries, and the retro chrome diner. Only Piper's Pub showed signs of life, with a gentle buzz of activity behind its warm, golden windowpanes.

"Where do you live?" Simon was pretty sure she rented an apartment on the main drag, not far from her shop, but he didn't want to admit he knew even that much about her.

"Up there, on Cascade. Above the ice cream shop. But I actually have to stop by the liquor store," she said, with a innocent glance at him.

He rolled his eyes. He'd be helping her with her grocery shopping next. "Fine."

They left Cascade Street for the even darker, quieter Pine Road. Leona peered into the forest lining the road, smiling to herself.

"Aha!" She stopped at the entrance to Simon's driveway. "This is yours, isn't it? I thought I remembered seeing a police car parked here. And here it is." She pointed up the long, dark driveway to where Simon's cruiser was parked in front of his duplex. He let his tenants use the garage, so he parked his cruiser outside when he brought it home.

Leona looped her arm through his, dazzling him, once again, with her scent and her closeness. His elbow bumped her ribs, the underside of her breasts. He ought to move away—but he wanted to pull her even closer. Touching her was both impersonal and intimate, disorienting and addictive.

"I thought you had to—" he began, trying to stay focused.

"It was a ploy, Simon. It takes a lot more than a sip of whiskey to get me buzzed."

She led him up the driveway to his front porch. His tenants must have strung white Christmas lights along their door sometime while he was out this afternoon, casting that same soft glow across his porch as in downtown. The light shimmered on Leona's black knit hat, her glossy black hair, her sinful mouth.

"Go inside and warm up," she told Simon, releasing his arm. "I don't want you dying of hypothermia. Then the town would have to hire a new cop. What a pain."

"I can't believe you tricked me."

She patted his cheek. "You're only human, darling." She turned away, glancing back over one slim shoulder. "Good night."

This time of day, light caught on the baubles hanging in the shop's bay window and spattered rainbows across one cream-white wall. Leona secretly loved it; she would never have admitted it to Paul, but she'd hung the baubles there precisely to catch that light.

"How about this one?" Leona unearthed a handthrown clay lamp base from a shelving unit along the wall and straightened back up, blinking rainbows from her eyes.

"It's beautiful." Her favorite customer, Mrs. Jacobs, leaned forward to admire the intricacies of the glazing. "It's perfect, Leona. You always know just what to pick out."

"Always a pleasure to help. Let me wrap it up for you. You said you wanted the set?"

"Yes, please, dear. I know she'll love them. She loves everything you help me find."

Leona had never met Mrs. J.'s erstwhile granddaughter, but she'd heard a lot about her over the years. Mrs. Jacobs had been coming to Grenton Fine Crafts since it had opened twenty years ago. She, like Leona, was a creature of routines.

Back at the counter, she wrapped the lamps thoroughly in tissue paper, placed them in the shop's signature teal-blue bags, and handed them across the counter to the older woman, who beamed at her. "Anything special planned for the holidays, my dear?"

"You're looking at it, Mrs. J." Being in the shop *was* special to her. There was nowhere else she'd rather be, even if she was surrounded by constant reminders of her least favorite holiday—her least favorite *day*, if she had to choose just one.

Mrs. J. frowned, glancing at the door leading into the back room, where Leona's boss, Paul Bouchard, was unpacking a new shipment with their only other full-timer, Margie. "Surely Paul is giving you time off? Paul, you're not making poor Leona work too hard, are you?"

Paul poked his head out through the doorframe, grinning and running a hand through his short gray curls. "Are you kidding? You try getting this girl to take a day off."

"I'm very hard to get rid of," Leona agreed. "Like a fungus. Anyway, I had yesterday off."

Paul still scheduled her off every other Saturday, whether she asked for it or not. Leona and her best friend, Iris, had started their tradition of Saturday runs when Iris had still lived in the States and had been, theoretically, working a nine-to-five job as an administrative assistant. The routine had hiccupped periodically, when Iris had changed jobs or travelled, but they'd always come back to it.

After Iris went to Europe six months ago, Leona was left to carry the tradition on her own. And she had, because that was how she was—until yesterday.

She hadn't been able to help herself; she'd been drawn into the strangeness of seeing Simon Labelle sitting alone on that bench, in a wool hat pulled low enough to brush the line of his jaw and a navy fleece that had hugged his muscular back. She almost hadn't recognized him like that—out of uniform, alone, clearly lost in his thoughts. And when she'd sat down next to him, she'd seen something in his pale blue eyes she'd never seen there before. Sadness, perhaps. The sight had unsettled her more than she cared to admit. She'd never imagined Simon feeling anything other than a sort of official annoyance.

The idea that there could be a little more depth to him fascinated her. He'd always been good-looking, in his clean-shaven, buttoned-up way, but that hint of vulnerability had shaded his good looks into something else. Something so…tantalizing.

The door to her shop opened, bringing in a cool breeze that soothed her flushed cheeks.

Simon Labelle walked inside. He took in the entire shop in a matter of seconds, then fixed his gaze on her, his eyes intense and serious. Whatever she had seen in his expression yesterday was gone today, but her memory of it had steeped into her blood, warming her from within.

Deliberately ignoring him while she collected her

thoughts, Leona said a protracted good-bye to Mrs. Jacobs. Simon prowled around a display of blown glass Christmas ornaments, his gaze never leaving her.

After Mrs. J. left, Leona made a show of looking around, searching for anyone else who might need her help. The shop usually did steady business, especially around the holidays, but it was now completely empty apart from Simon. He walked up to her counter and stood in front of it with his big arms folded across his chest. He was in uniform today, with a gun at his belt. His sensual mouth flattened into its usual annoyed line.

"Yes?" She smiled toothily at him. "May I interest you in a wooden box carved in the shape of a frog? It's the perfect size for holding matches, if sir is a smoker?" She could go on like this all day. "Or, for a lady friend, might I recommend a hand-quilted handbag? We have a very nice selection of colors, just in from—"

"Leona." His handsome jaw clenched. "I do not want a handbag."

He said it with such perfect seriousness that she dissolved into laughter at her counter and had to lean on the cash register to collect herself.

"I actually just wanted to thank you. For yesterday," he continued, with stubborn, if irritated, determination. "And apologize. I might have been kind of a dick."

She caught herself before she could show her surprise. "Are you allowed to say 'dick' on duty?"

"My shift hasn't started—and also *yes, obviously*. For the love of God, Leona Chaisty, I'm trying to ask if I can buy you dinner."

This time, she couldn't manage to suppress her astonishment. Why would Simon Labelle want to buy her dinner? Whatever wormhole had merged their sepa rate universes yesterday had surely vanished back into the ether by now. He had no reason to talk to her; they could not have been more different. They had always been impossibly different.

She met his eyes for a moment, wishing she understood, and glanced away at the Christmas decorations artfully arranged all across the shop.

People did sometimes get weird around her during the holidays, if they suspected she spent them by herself. She wouldn't put it past Simon to make up some excuse to take her out in a horribly misguided attempt at Christmas charity.

"Is this, like...a pity date?" she said finally.

"What? No. Why would it be?" He sighed. "Doesn't have to be a date at all. Just dinner. Up to you."

Leona tapped her fingernails on the counter, her pulse a little restless.

Dinner with Simon did have a certain appeal. He was beautiful, she was curious about him, and she was...well.

The truth was that since her best friend had moved away, the last few fragments of Leona's life outside of work had crumbled, too. Saturday runs, by herself, were all she had left—just the merest memory of friendship. She didn't care at all about being alone on Christmas, but she was tired of being friendless.

"When would you want to go?" she asked.

"I don't know...tomorrow night?"

"All right. I'll drive." She grinned. "Pick you up at seven?"

"What?" He rolled his eyes. "All right. Fine. You know where I live."

"Yup." Her grin widened. He turned away, and she

watched him leave her shop, all austere, masculine authority. He made regulation polyester look damn good.

Chapter Two

LEONA WAS LATE, WHICH SIMON found especially irritating since they lived two streets apart. When his buzzer finally rang, he went outside to find her on his front porch in a fitted black pea coat, a black knit hat, and black, lace-up, high-heeled boots. He wondered if she ever wore colors. Yesterday in the shop she'd been wearing a black sweater with a neckline that had almost touched her pale white throat. It had distracted him completely.

"Hello, darling," Leona said. "You look as lovely as a rose."

Simon gave her a leveling stare. "Same to you." Unlike Leona, he actually meant it. A black rose, with frost clinging to the petals.

He shook his head. What the hell was wrong with him?

Last night, as he'd lain in bed, staring at the ceiling, he'd thought about the way she'd traced her fingertip down his cheek, about her laugh and her scent and her strange, hypnotic hold on him. He wondered if anyone else would've convinced him to go home, the way she had. Or if he would've stayed there all night without her, contemplating the lake.

"This is Lulu." Leona stepped aside to reveal the car

parked next to Simon's cruiser. Simon's jaw dropped.

"Is that a Mustang?" In the wan glow of the Christmas lights, he could just make out its cherry-red paint and white racing stripes. The car practically preened. "I didn't know you were into cars." He couldn't remember ever seeing her drive.

"I'm into *this* car," Leona said, opening the passenger-side door for him and chivalrously gesturing him inside. "I got Lulu after she was in a *tiny* accident and the then-owner was too chicken to keep her."

"Oh, God." Simon buckled his seatbelt. "So, in the snow, she's…?"

"Terrifying," Leona replied, as she slid into the driver's seat. "Fortunately, it's not snowing."

"Great," he said sarcastically. "I feel really safe."

Leona laughed as she started up the car. Its engine roared to life. Simon had to restrain himself from feeling up the dashboard.

"So, where are we going?" she asked, as she put on some mellow, instrumental music, which was, once again, not what he'd been expecting.

"I made reservations at that Italian place in Montpelier."

She nodded. "Is that where you take all the ladies after you've been—what did you call it? 'Kind of a dick'?"

"I'm not usually a dick at all."

"I feel so special."

God, she got under his skin. "I had a bad week," he insisted. "I swear I'm not an asshole." At least, he hoped he wasn't. Sometimes he wondered.

"Oh, I bring assholery out in people," she said airily. "I'm well-aware of that. It's a life-long habit."

He shot her a concerned glance. "Don't say that."

He'd heard some rumors about Leona while they were still in high school. Her childhood. Her parents. He didn't want her to think she ever deserved to be treated badly.

"You don't need to worry about my tender little feelings, I promise." She cast him a slight sidelong smile. "I'm surprised you remembered where I work," she added, after a moment. "I've never seen you in the shop before."

"Small town," he grunted.

"So you haven't been secretly admiring my beauty through the shop window all these years?"

In spite of himself, he laughed. "Actually, a few weeks ago, I saw you standing in the window, making some kind of display. You looked like an extremely cranky mannequin."

"Yes—the hummingbird mobile!" She whacked her steering wheel. "Fifteen insanely breakable, hand-blown hummingbirds. My nerves were shot. I'm sure your job is stressful, but until you've had to hang fifteen glass hummingbirds in a rickety bay window, using only bits of plastic that refuse to turn into proper knots, you don't know what stress is."

Simon laughed again. "I believe it. I would not be able to do that." He wasn't clumsy, but the sheer breakableness of Leona's shop was nerve-wracking. "You seem like you like it there, though." He hadn't missed the loving, proprietary way she'd laid her hands on the counter yesterday. She cared about her shop the same way he cared about the town as a whole, as if it were a living, breathing thing.

"The shop is the best," she said, with a big smile. "So is Paul, and the merchandise. I even like most of the customers, and I'm nothing if not a misanthrope."

She'd always been so gleefully self-deprecating. He'd never been able to tell how much of it was an act.

"How about you?" she asked. "You like being a cop?"

"Yes. It's...it sounds lame, but it's my calling." Too bad he sucked at it.

"Your dad was a cop, too, right?"

"Chief. Thirty years in the force."

"Following in your old man's footsteps."

"Yup." Simon had always idolized his dad, and he still did, mostly. He'd grown up enough to realize the man wasn't perfect, but he was a good dad, and he'd been a great cop before he'd accepted early retirement at the age of fifty-five, thanks to a bad back. Now Earl Labelle spent most of his time hollowing out canoes, fishing, and being handsy with Simon's mom, Audette.

"Is this it?" Leona asked. "*Veni, Vidi, Vino?*" He nodded and directed her toward the parking lot. She rolled her eyes. "Thanks, Officer."

They walked inside to opera and candlelight. He told the host about their reservation and glanced at Leona when the host asked if he could take their coats. Her eyebrows rose, but she shucked off her pea coat without comment. Underneath, she wore more black, of course. Her short dress had see-through black lace at the neckline and shoulders, teasing the smooth column of her throat. "You look—really nice," he managed.

She frowned at him. "Thanks."

The host led them to their table, which was set back in a quiet corner, partially hidden behind cascading ivy.

"This is nice," she said, as they sat down. "Best random dinner ever."

"You haven't tried the food yet."

"Is that a warning?"

"More like a promise." He had no idea where that

had come from, but she didn't seem to mind. She brushed her long hair back from her neck, smiling to herself, her lashes smoky smudges. Her fingernails were painted cherry-red, like her car, and he wondered what her pretty hands would look like against his skin if she touched him again.

A waiter came by and asked for their drink orders, tearing Simon away from his thoughts,

"I'll have a cabernet sauvignon, please," Leona told the waiter. "And the gentleman will have, I assume, whiskey?"

"Uh, no. Water's fine." He had a feeling it was time to lay off the booze again. He thanked the waiter and turned back to see Leona, as usual, smirking at him.

"Not planning on indulging tonight?" she asked.

"No."

"Darn, I was hoping I might get another dinner out of this." Her smile widened.

"I'll have to make an ass of myself some other way."

"Oh, good, I love surprises."

He bet she did.

"So," she continued, picking up her menu, "there's no girlfriend to be driven wild with jealousy at the sight of you with a strange woman?"

"Not even with a woman as strange as you."

She arched an eyebrow at him over the top of her menu. "Cheeky."

Their drinks arrived, and they each ordered pasta courses and entrées. She was, unsurprisingly, decisive about what she wanted and a lot more adventurous than he was.

After the waiter left, she fixed him with that appraising stare again. "Seriously, though—how can you not be hitched? Practically everybody else in town paired up in high school."

It was a strange card for her to play: he couldn't remember ever seeing her dating anybody. She'd always seemed to be somewhere else—taking off right after class, skipping proms and socials. "*You're* not hitched," he pointed out.

She made a face. "Well, no, not *me*, obviously. But *you*—you're a catch. For the right kind of girl, anyway. A nice, submissive girl."

"'Submissive'? What's that supposed to mean?" Like he was some kind of bully?

"You know, big macho cop, likes to give orders…"

"Maybe I like strong women. You really have a bad opinion of me, don't you?"

"Not at all." She grinned at him as if he were missing out on an inside joke. The tips of his ears burning, he glowered at his water glass, wishing he'd gotten a drink after all. He had always tried to be the kind of man who had a plan for every situation, but apparently that did not include a single interaction with Leona Chaisty.

Sometimes the best defense was a good offense. "What about you?" he demanded. "Why aren't you with someone already?"

Slowly, deliberately, she licked a drop of red wine from the lip of her glass with the very tip of her tongue. Simon's stomach tightened. "I've been with lots of guys," she said. "But so far, no one's kept my interest."

"Lots of guys." He realized he was gripping the tablecloth in his fist and forced his fingers to relax.

"*Lots.*" Her voice pitched low and husky.

"How many is a lot?" he ground out.

She leaned back in her chair, still holding her wine glass in one slender hand. Candlelight shimmered across her lace neckline, highlighting glimpses of her skin. "Does it matter?"

It didn't matter—of course it didn't. It was none of his business. But he still wondered who she'd been with. If he knew them. What she'd done, what she liked.

The waiter returned to their table, set down their plates of pasta, and scuttled off, leaving them alone in their quiet corner once again. Simon's pulse was pounding so hard he would've bet Leona could hear it.

"Let me guess," she drawled, "you've had a small number of long-term girlfriends, who were all basically lovely. And you dumped them all, eventually. Why, though, I wonder? Too clingy?"

Simon stared at her. She had known where he lived; she might have noticed him around town more than she'd let on. "How did you know that?"

"It was a guess? Have you heard of guesswork? I imagine it's a pretty big part of policing."

Fair enough. "Three," he admitted begrudgingly. "Three long-term girlfriends. And a couple of flings. And yeah, I always ended things." As soon as they complained about how much he worked, or looked upset when the Christmas gift turned out to be earrings instead of an engagement ring.

He couldn't imagine Leona doing either of those things. But then, Leona was different—a maneater, if there ever was one.

"I love being right," she remarked.

"No kidding."

Simon's phone vibrated inside his pocket. He grimaced. The one time in his life he didn't want to be interrupted by work. "Hold on." Pushing back his chair, he went to take the call somewhere more private.

Watching Simon walk away, Leona debated whether he'd only pretended to get a call so he could escape from her line of questioning. But no, Simon Labelle would never fake a phone call. He was too decent.

With a sigh, she ate another forkful of pasta. Interrogating Simon about his love life wasn't the nicest thing to do. But Leona wasn't nice. Everybody knew that. And Simon was fascinating. He'd always been so dutiful and responsible, he was practically the poster boy for the town of Grenton—except for the fact that he, unlike everyone they went to high school with, wasn't married with two kids.

Why was that, really?

She poked contemplatively at her pasta with her fork, searching for scallops. He was busy, she was sure of that. Work would always be his first love. But he would still be thoughtful. He even seemed to care about Leona's feelings, and she'd never understood why anyone would care about those.

The waiter came by with their second courses. A moment later, Simon slid back into his chair across from her, immediately distracting her from her entrée. What a strange thing, to be at a proper dinner with a man. Especially this man. He was wearing a button-down and khakis, as if Leona were a respectable girl. The pale blue shirt brought out his eyes.

"Sorry about that," Simon said. "I'm training the rookie and he had a question about some paperwork."

"Oh, yeah, Jack, right?"

"Jack Miller."

"I've seen him around. He has the hots for my fashion protégé."

"Yeah?" His mouth quirked. "Who's that?"

"Emma Pinette. She works at the shop part-time. We're keeping it fresh, you know."

When Simon smiled, his whole face lit up. His eyes actually twinkled. Leona had always thought that was just an expression. He had such a stern face, normally, but suddenly he looked so approachable—the kind of man you could tell anything to.

"Paul wants to sell me the shop," Leona blurted out. She immediately regretted it and wished she had said absolutely anything else. More intrusive questions about his love life, sob stories about her childhood, anything.

Simon's eyebrows shot up. "Okay."

This is not how you make friends, Leona, she told herself sternly. *You can't just say things at random.*

"What did you tell him?" Simon asked.

"I asked him to let me think about it." And she'd done nothing else but think about it, obsessively, since he'd asked her a week ago. "He offered me an outrageously low price for it, too. He wants to retire."

"And you've been working there for, what, a decade?"

"I started when I was sixteen, so…thirteen years."

"Wow. And you love it there?"

"Yes."

"So what's the problem?"

She didn't know how to explain the abyss that opened up inside her at the thought of Paul retiring. She had never felt anything like it before. Paul had always been there. The world could never be that dark for her, as long as he was there.

But even she knew that an internal abyss was not proper dinner conversation. "Don't you ever want to leave Grenton?"

"I know a lot of people do."

"But not you?"

"Not me. I like it here."

"You want to work your way up to Chief, like your dad?" She hardly needed to ask; she knew he did. He was that kind of guy: ambitious, but only because he wanted enough responsibility to do a good job. When he nodded, she said, "Must be nice—to know what you want, I mean."

"Yeah, I guess."

Leona set about decimating her veal, which was even more delicious than the pasta had been.

"You should go for it, Leona," Simon said quietly.

"Do you mean the last slice of bread? Because if so, you are absolutely right."

"I obviously mean the shop. Look, I saw you in there yesterday. You looked…"

"Cross-eyed?" she suggested. "I swear it was the lighting."

He gave her an exasperated look. "I was going to say *happy*."

"Ah. That." She *was* happy there. For now, she was happy.

They finished their entrees, and he asked for the check. "Thank you for dinner," she told him as they walked out of the restaurant, shrugging on their coats against the bitter night. "It was really delicious."

"That place is one of my favorites," he said, which made her wonder where else he had taken his three long-term girlfriends and various short flings. "I really am sorry about the other day. I don't—"

"Oh, no need to worry about that with me." She waved a hand as they crossed the parking lot toward

Lulu. "You had a shitty week. I get it." She'd had the occasional drink or joint by the lake herself. It was peaceful there. "I kind of liked it," she added, both because she knew it would make him crazy and because it was true.

"You liked what?" He stopped and turned toward her. Just behind him, Lulu's paint shone under the streetlight, but Simon stood in shadows, his face hidden by darkness. They were so close together she could have reached out and touched him.

"I liked seeing you a little out of control," she said quietly, her skin prickling. *Lose control with me.*

He made a low, rough sound, deep in his throat, as if he'd intended to speak—to chastise her, she had to imagine. She could see his shoulders rise and fall with each hard breath, silhouetted by the streetlight. Desire crackled off of him.

He might have asked her out as Christmas charity, but he wanted her, too, whether he would admit that to himself or not.

It would be so easy to take his thick wrist in her hand and draw him in toward her. Right now, he would let her; she could sense it.

"Did I shock your delicate sensibilities?" She kept her tone light and teasing.

"You're constantly shocking me," he growled. "I get the feeling you enjoy it."

"I really do."

If she took one step forward, she could cup his face in her hands. What would he do? Would he let her kiss him? What would it be like?

Her foot edged forward. Her whole body seemed to be straining toward him, wanting him—but at the last moment, she shook herself and tore herself away.

She didn't know what this was. She had never done anything like this before. She couldn't act, even if she wanted to.

She got into Lulu's driver's seat and, a second later, Simon climbed in beside her. Her heart skipped a beat. *Stop it,* she told herself. This was all hopeless. She should never have accepted his invitation to dinner. She didn't do candlelit Italian dinners with nice local boys; she did play parties and hook-ups and various and sundry dirty things.

Though it had been a couple years since she'd done any of that, truth be told. She had gotten old and dull.

Taking a deep, fortifying breath, she started up Lulu and pulled out of the parking lot.

"Leona…you want to do this again sometime? Hang out, have dinner?"

"Is that code for fucking?" she asked in a rush, desperately relieved.

Simon actually flinched. "What—no!"

"Ah," she murmured, stung. "Sorry… I misread the signs. It happens." This must have been just a pity date after all. Charity from the upstanding officer.

Simon ran a hand through his short hair. "I'm not saying I'm not attracted to you. I was thinking we could try out a couple dates."

"Oh." Some of her lovers had asked her about that over the years, but she'd always turned them down. She preferred to keep things simple, cheerful, with clear-cut rules and expectations.

"Forget it," he said. "You're not interested, it's fine, I'm sorry I asked."

"No…" She stopped at a red light and snuck a glance at the shadows outlining his cheek and jaw, his eyelashes, the straight bridge of his nose.

She had left the scene two years ago because she was tired of it, and she had no desire to go back to it now. She wanted something else…something more. Something she didn't know how to possess.

"I'm interested," she said, trying to keep her voice steady.

"Okay." He took a deep breath. "Jesus."

They drove back to town in silence. Leona felt…raw. Exposed. She glanced at him again. He was staring out the window, as if he wanted to escape. She couldn't blame him.

Chapter Three

BACK IN HIS DRIVEWAY, SIMON listened to the low rumble of Lulu's engine idling in the quiet night and tried to figure out what to say. Leona hadn't even put the car into park.

"Thanks again for dinner," she said, her tone calmer than usual, even detached.

"Sure. I'll…" What? 'I'll call you'? He didn't have her number. After their conversation on the drive home, the thought of asking her for it left him completely flummoxed. He settled for a gruff: "I'll see you later."

She nodded, he got out of the car, and it was over, just like that.

Inside his apartment, he fixed himself a whiskey soda, figuring he could lay off drinking starting tomorrow, and turned on the television. With a sigh, he stretched out on the couch, still in his khakis and button-down shirt. All he could think about was Leona's expressive mouth, her long-lashed gray eyes, the low purr of her voice. He wished he had kissed her good night, even if it would've been like kissing a cactus. He wished he'd handled absolutely every aspect of their drive home differently.

Strange to think Leona might've liked seeing him a little rough around the edges. A little out of control, as she'd put it, when he'd been loitering by the lake.

Then again, it was strange to think she might like him at all.

Restless, he sat up again and put his head in his hands. *Is that code for fucking?* she'd asked, with that sinful smile, and he'd said no, like an idiot. If he'd said yes, she might be up here with him right now, stripped down to a black bra, her skin glowing pink under his touch.

The thought made him instantly hard, even though he felt a little creepy for thinking about her like that. He didn't want to objectify her; she was more than a sexual fantasy. She was more than *his* sexual fantasy— the fantasy he'd had since they were fourteen, when he'd seen her in a black leather miniskirt at a kegger, doing shots and looking like trouble and sex. There had always been something about her: an energy, an appetite. One dinner with her and he felt like a rabbit caught in a snare.

He knew she would smile during sex, and he wanted to see it, wanted to feel that smile pressed against him. He wanted to know what she'd taste like, how she'd feel, tight around him, the way she'd cry out when she came.

She had to be a screamer. She wouldn't care if anybody heard her.

His hand crept to the fly of his khakis before he remembered he was sitting right next to his living room window. He stumbled to his feet and into his bedroom, tugging his fly open and taking his cock in his hand before he could make it onto his bed. Bracing himself with one hand on the mattress, he imagined her underneath him, her pretty eyes squeezing shut as she panted his name. She'd tilt her face to one side, expose her elegant neck to him so he could run his thumb up her throat and along the graceful line of her jaw. He'd slide his fingers into her black hair, and she'd gasp, like she wanted it as much as he did.

That familiar mix of excitement and shame curled inside him, and he came hard and fast, his cock jerking against his hand.

Afterward, as the tension left his muscles, he should've felt relieved. He only felt more ashamed.

◆

He woke up the next morning hard for her again. A cold shower helped, but not enough. He needed to see her, figure out what they were doing, if anything. There was a right way to do everything. There had to be a right way to ask Leona out again, properly this time, without scaring her off.

Since he still had a few hours before his shift started, he dressed in street clothes and walked over to Leona's shop before he could second-guess himself.

She was alone in the store, standing on the top step of a rickety stepladder with her back to the door. "Shouldn't someone be spotting you?" Simon asked, with a wary look at the ladder.

Glancing over her shoulder, she raised a single eyebrow. "Where's the fun in that? I love heights. Paul had to take away the bigger ladder."

Surprising himself, Simon smiled. "You're an odd duck, Leona Chaisty."

"Me? You're the one who showed up here ten minutes after we opened. You must really want to look at one of our brand new Sea Dream Sea Salt Shakers. Which is a great idea, because they are very reasonably priced and are hand-made by a local—"

"Actually," he interrupted, steeling himself, "I'd like to look at your handbags."

She cast him the biggest, most delighted smile he'd ever seen.

"*Not* for me, just so we're clear," he said. "For my mom. For Christmas."

"Ah, yes, the perfect Christmas gift for a discerning female relative!" Leona hopped down from her stepladder. She was holding a gigantic purple feather duster that formed a startling contrast to her slim-fitting black pants and drapey black top. Even from a few feet away, he imagined he could smell her ginger perfume, and it made him want to be closer to her, to kiss her hello, as if they were a couple, instead of… whatever they were. Nothing.

"So, I really like these." Leona crossed the store to a display on the far wall and pointed at a couple of bags with her feather duster, as if it were a fairy wand. "But they are maybe too…hippie-ish? What kind of stuff does your mother like?"

"Uh…" Simon looked at the bags on the wall. They were blue and had lots of things hanging off them. He thought about his mother, who was small and plump and perennially cheerful. "She might like those. She likes…" He racked his brain for things his mom liked: his dad, gardening, potted plants… "Sunflowers."

"Oh!" Leona clapped her hands together. "That is actually helpful!"

He laughed. "No need to sound so surprised."

She rummaged through a drawer underneath the display. "I haven't put many of these out yet, because I've been saving them for spring. But…here, hang on…"

He liked watching Leona work, and not just because he liked trying to sneak a peek down the back of her pants when she was bending over. She really did seem happy here.

With a flourish, she pulled out a bag made of big blocks of blue and green, contrasting with yellow sunflowers. "Hey, yeah, that looks right," he said. "Wow."

"Can you imagine her wearing it?" She slid the bag over one shoulder and struck a pose, pouting her lips and sticking out her ass.

"Not like *that*," he said, flushing. "Thank God. But otherwise, yes."

Leona tilted her face up toward his, her eyes curious. "You're *actually* here to buy your mom a handbag, aren't you?"

"As opposed to…?"

"I have no idea. Trying to be smooth, I suppose."

"I don't need to *try* to be smooth."

This got another one of those laughing fits that Simon secretly treasured, even if it was at his expense. She'd been famous, or maybe infamous, in high school for that laugh—first made fun of for it, then feared because of it.

He cleared his throat. "We never did pick a time for another date, though."

Wiping her eyes on her sleeve, she smiled warily at him. "That's true."

What was with this girl? She'd been with all these guys, but asking her out was like pulling teeth. It didn't make any sense.

Maybe she hadn't been with as many guys as she'd implied, or…something. He didn't know.

"What did you have in mind?" Her wary smile curled upward. Her eyes glinted with a leisurely, predatory interest. That look sent tendrils of fire winding through his entire body.

She had asked him a question, he reminded himself, about what he wanted to do on their second date. Besides getting her naked and wet in his bed.

"Dinner?" he suggested, struggling to compose himself. "Tonight or tomorrow?"

"All right." Still holding the sunflower bag, Leona gestured with her feather duster for him to follow her to the cash register. She set the bag down on the counter and rang it up.

"There's a new Thai place I've been dying to try," she said, as she wrapped the handbag in tissue paper, her movements neat and efficient, and slipped the package into an extremely girly handled shopping bag. "We could have a drink at my place first. Get some Thai. See how it goes. That sounds like a date, right?"

He raised his eyebrows, puzzled by the question. "Sounds like one to me."

"Good. Tonight at seven?"

He nodded, said a flustered goodbye, and left the shop more ensnared than ever.

Paul came in around five looking worn out from a day spent Christmas shopping. "How did it go today?"

"Busy in the afternoon, but fine." Leona set down the pen she was using to write out price tags at the counter and smiled up at him. "Margie called out again tonight, but Emma said she could come in for a bit if you needed her."

Paul loosened his scarf, his brow furrowing. "What do you think is going on with Margie?"

"No idea." Leona hesitated, thinking about how worried Margie always looked now, when she thought no one would notice. "She hasn't been herself lately."

"I could say the same thing about you, Jellybean." Paul chucked the underside of her chin gently. "You still pining for Iris?"

"You know I don't pine. How was shopping?"

"The usual." He smiled wryly. "Everything is badly made and overpriced and Mellon is impossible to buy for."

Henry Mellon was Paul's longtime partner, now husband. Although Mellon was the most mild-mannered and amiable man on Earth, Paul always agonized over the best ways to spoil him. Even Leona thought it was cute.

"What did you end up getting?" she asked.

Leaning against the cash register on the customer side of the counter, Paul sighed. "A new sports coat."

"Mellon loves those! Is it tweed?"

"Yes."

"Perfect. Mellon loves tweed." Mellon rocked tweed, in fact, particularly tweed jackets with elbow patches. He was a psychiatrist who leaned into the look.

"I get him tweed *every year*."

"Your life is hard."

"My life would be a lot easier if some silly child would buy my shop."

She made a face, happy to play the role of the obstinate teenager he had hired thirteen years ago.

"Leona," Paul said, "come for Christmas this year."

"Paul…"

He held up his hands. "I know, I know. Just think about it, okay? Mellon would love to have you over, and so would I."

He asked her every year, even though he and Mellon ran themselves ragged throwing a huge Christmas party for their families and many devoted friends. They didn't need Leona there, gunking up the social gears.

"You are sweet," she told him. "But you know I like being on my own. I'm very independent. Enigmatically aloof, even."

"Uh huh." Paul straightened up from the counter with a fond smile. "You're something, that's for sure."

Leona changed the subject to the day's sales and the other details he needed to know to close up later. She loved talking to Paul about even the most mundane aspects of running the shop and was actually sad to leave. But her shift had ended half an hour ago, and, more importantly, she had to get ready to meet up with Simon.

At home, she poured herself a glass of wine and meandered into her bedroom to change out of her black cigarette pants and tunic. She told herself not to be nervous about their date tonight. Dating wasn't her usual speed, but she'd enjoyed their dinner the night before, and she was sure she'd enjoy herself tonight, too. If she wanted something new from her life, she had to be willing to make changes.

After a certain amount of indecision, she pulled on a simple violet dress, figuring that it was classy without being too fancy for Thai food. She fussed with the apartment for a while, making sure it looked even more perfect than usual. Seven o'clock came and went. Pouring herself more wine, Leona thought that perhaps Simon would have to drive them to the restaurant after all. At seven-thirty, she was beginning to think she'd been stood up. More wine happened, followed by a dreadful reality show that she would've loved to watch and make fun of with Iris, if Iris hadn't moved away.

At eight, Leona decided to make risotto, still in her foxy dress and heels, just because she could. *Girl power*, said her third glass of wine. "Damn right," Leona told it. She splashed some wine into the risotto and stirred in fresh rosemary and chopped asparagus. Not very Christmassy, more of a spring dish, really, but so what?

Leona perched on the arm of her couch and ate a bowl of risotto. By nine, between the wine and the stupefying reality television, she was already starting to forget about Simon standing her up. So much for dating.

At the sudden clang of the doorbell, her heart clenched hard. She jogged down the stairs in her heels and flung the door open. Simon stood on the sidewalk, still in uniform, with his hat in his hands. The falling snow stuck to his heavy police coat.

"Leona."

Even in the dim light of a single streetlight, she could see the shadows under his eyes. "Are you all right? What happened?"

"Bad accident."

He didn't seem to know what else to say.

"Do you want some risotto?" she asked.

"Oh…sure. Thanks."

He followed her up the stairs into her apartment and the scents of wine and rosemary. She turned the television off and put on some music while Simon hung his hat and his police coat over one of her dainty dining room chairs. The reflective striping on his coat caught the light from her kitchen and flickered in the darkness.

She crossed into the kitchen to get him a bowl of risotto, but he caught her by the wrist and held her in place, staring at her violet dress. "You're not wearing black."

"I don't always."

Still gripping her wrist, he brought his free hand to her shoulder and drew his fingertips down the violet fabric, just before it met her skin. "I like it."

"Are you okay?"

His hand clenched tighter around her wrist, and he stared at her body with a pained, hungry look in his eyes. "No," he said finally, his voice soft. "Not yet."

"Tell me what happened."

He shook his head.

"Okay." She sighed. "Come here." She steered him toward the couch, sat him down, and fetched him a blanket, some risotto, and a glass of wine. Sitting down across from him in her accent chair, she crossed her legs and leaned back as if she wasn't at all worried by his haunted expression. As if nothing could touch them, now that they were here together.

It was what she would've done for Iris—what she *had* done for Iris, many times, when they were little kids. Every time Iris's mom flew into one of her rages, Iris would escape through the woods to Leona's house and knock on the screen door, her eyes huge in her small face. Since Leona's parents were never home, Leona would let Iris in herself, though she was barely tall enough to reach the door handle. She'd scrounge up some food for her friend, sit her down on the couch with a teddy bear, and tell her that everything would be okay. And it would be, even if Leona's only arsenal against the world was her own strength of will.

"This is really good." Simon gestured at the risotto. "Thank you."

He set his bowl on her coffee table and leaned forward, his muscular forearms braced on his knees. His pale blue gaze met hers. "You really are a nice person, Leona, you know that?"

She laughed awkwardly. "Are you trying to ruin my scary reputation?"

"Seriously," he insisted. "this is the second time you've been nice to me after I've been a dick."

"You haven't been a dick," she said, surprised. "You were just late. It's fine."

"Really?"

"Simon, I do realize that your job is *slightly* more important than mine."

"It's not like that."

"Please. It totally is, and it should be." She grinned. "I've had enough experience with the police to know that your work matters."

"Oh, God," he said.

Her grin widened. "Can I get you more risotto? Or anything else?" She started to stand, but he shook his head, staring down at her funky geometric carpet.

She was momentarily struck by the strangeness of having him in her apartment. Everything about him looked out of place, from his duty boots to his gun belt to his hair, only a fraction longer than a buzz cut. She ought to be annoyed at him for dirtying her carpet with his huge boots, but he looked so sad that she would have done anything to make him feel better.

She was losing her edge.

"So," she said, tentatively, "there was an accident?"

To her surprise, he answered her: "A car accident. A hit and run."

"A hit and run? *Here*?"

"That blind corner, over by Apple Mountain Farms."

"And someone was hurt? Do I know them?"

With a sigh, he slid his hands into his hair. "You

know her. Knew her. Nancy O'Shea."

Leona sucked in a breath. "Our chemistry teacher?"

"That's right, you were in that class with me. Yeah. Mrs. O'Shea. She was a great teacher."

Leona hadn't missed his use of the past tense. *Knew her. She was.* "What happened to her?"

"She was out for a jog and got hit by, I'm guessing, a truck." His tone was blunt, even cold, but his hands shook. "She was…crushed. Almost unrecognizable. She had no ID on her, so we had to bring her daughter over to identify her by her rings." He swallowed hard, his throat moving.

"Jesus." Leona had liked Mrs. O'Shea and her goofy, well-meaning efforts to make chemistry fun for a lot of cranky Vermonters. Leona had met her daughter, too, on the handful of occasions when they'd run into each other downtown. Even Leona, who knew nothing about families, especially loving families, had been able to tell the O'Sheas were close.

Without quite realizing what she was doing, she set her wine glass down on her coffee table and touched Simon's hand where it rested on his knee. Gradually, she wrapped her much-smaller fingers around his. "I'm so sorry, Simon." The words were inadequate, but what else was there?

"I'm not…" He sighed again. "I've been a cop for a long time, but it's such a small town… I'm still not used to seeing stuff like that. Gruesome stuff. She was… It was like when you see a deer on the side of the road, but much, much worse."

Leona nodded, horror prickling in her throat.

"Anyway…the Chief is assigning me to the case, but I don't know why. He knows I dropped the ball on the bombing investigation."

"That was *your* case?" Simon hadn't been on the force for *that* long. It didn't seem fair to give him what had to have been Grenton's biggest case in decades.

"I asked for it," Simon said. "Before the bombing actually happened. I asked to help investigate the bomb threats that the vet's office kept getting. I muscled my way onto the task force with the state police and the feds. I was so sure I could figure it out."

"I'm sure you did the best—"

"No, I didn't," he said sharply. "I didn't figure out anything. And then the front desk got blown up, and that girl, Kristy Woods, would've been killed, if she hadn't decided to take a piss."

Leona had seen the gruesome news reports about Kristy Woods' injuries. Shards of her own desk in her legs and abdomen. Infections. Her life had been spared only because she'd been standing halfway between her desk and the ladies' room.

"But she survived, even it was just dumb luck," Leona pointed out. "Anyway, I thought everybody knew it was that girl's ex. I read it in the paper, right before she left town, that he'd been stalking her for years."

"He did stalk her," Simon said. "But there was no evidence that he was involved with the threats, or the bombing. That's why the case is still unsolved. He was our only lead, and it went nowhere. The State's Attorney's Office says there's no chance of prosecuting him."

"Well…that's not your fault, is it? What were you supposed to do?"

Disentangling his hand from hers, he stood up and paced her living room. "Anything—I could've done *anything* to keep moving the case forward, to drum up information. If I couldn't *prevent* the bombing from happening, I should've at least been able to find a decent fucking lead afterward. That's my job, but I failed at it."

"Failed at it? Why, because you're not fucking psychic? That is so—"

"This is my *job*." He faced her, folding his arms across his chest.

Frustrated, she stood up and matched his gaze from across the room. "You can't control everything that happens in this town."

"I can try."

Amazed at his stubbornness, she shook her head. "I've never met a bigger control freak than you."

"That's rich, coming from you. Have you *seen* your apartment?"

"What about it?"

"It looks exactly like your shop. I've never seen a place with less dust. And you don't have a single personal thing in here. No photos, nothing."

"You have to have a family to have family photos." As soon as she said it, she regretted it. She had already shared too much with him—they had shared too much with one another.

"I'm—I'm sorry. That was uncalled for." He took a step toward her, then stopped himself, dropping his hands in confusion. "Believe it or not, I really wanted tonight to go well."

"I know." She'd been wrong to assume he'd ever thought of her as Christmas charity. She should have realized Simon didn't say or do anything he didn't mean.

Slowly, carefully, she crossed the room to him. He still wouldn't look at her. Stress stood out sharply on his elegant features, but instead of aging him, it made him look younger, reminding her of the beautiful boy he'd been in high school, with his straight nose, sensual mouth, the broad planes of his neck and shoulders. She would've loved to get her hands on him back then, but she'd always told herself he wasn't for her. He was too good. Proper. Traditional. The kind of man who wouldn't want anything to do with her, or what she liked.

She wasn't so sure about that anymore.

Last night, she could've sworn he'd wanted her to touch him. To take the initiative. And now, he was standing perfectly still, almost at attention, without meeting her eyes. She could sense his longing, his need.

She touched his stern, irresistible mouth, trailing a fingertip from his top lip to his bottom lip until his chest rose in a quick, stilted breath.

"You're right about me," she said. "I know what it's like to try to control everything around you. To make it perfect, the way you want it to be."

At his side, his hands twitched, as if he were going to reach for her, but once again, he restrained himself.

So interesting, she thought hazily. *That restraint.*

She cupped his face in her hands just like she'd wanted to last night, and scraped her palms across his five o'clock shadow to the curves of his jaw. His eyes finally met hers, blazing with desire.

"Simon," she said. Her head spun with the questions she should ask him. The parameters she should lay out for him.

She kissed him.

With a soft groan of relief, he wrapped his arms around her, his hard muscles digging into her sides. He gripped fistfuls of the back of her dress, tugging the hemline up around her hips. She couldn't stop herself from kissing him harder, exploring his mouth with her tongue, sucking his lip between her teeth. She wanted him like she hadn't wanted anyone in years.

He broke the kiss with an embarrassed exhale that was not quite a laugh, his breath hot on her lips. His hands still gripped her dress. "You—you know how to lead."

She couldn't deny it, and wouldn't. "You don't need to be the one in control with me. Let me lead, so you can relax. Just this once."

Chapter Four

AS ALWAYS WITH LEONA, SIMON was in uncharted waters. He'd never been kissed like this before—by a girl who didn't wait for him to move first and didn't apologize for doing what she liked. The experience was so new and so different, it was exhilarating. All he could think about was sliding his hands up her waist to her breasts, her collarbone, and higher, along her smooth throat—*fuck*, he thought, tightening his hold on her dress. Fuck.

She nipped his lip hard enough to hurt and smiled up at him through thick, dark lashes, her gray eyes almost black with lust. His racing mind could only register amazement. No one had ever looked at him like this, either: as if she'd already decided to eat him and was taking her time deciding where to start.

Her fingers found the buttons on his duty shirt. His heart pounding, Simon held still and let her undo them, one by one, with painful, exquisite slowness. She tugged the shirt off over his shoulders, dropped it to the floor, and caressed his stomach through his black undershirt, her smile widening. He shivered.

"How about those handcuffs?" Her purring voice was so sexy, it took him a moment to realize what she'd actually said.

"My handcuffs?" His first thought—depressingly—was about the ethical implications of using police equipment during sex. He really was a stick in the mud. His second thought—equally depressing in its own way—was about his ex, Ashley, who'd been really into the whole cop thing. Simon, on the other hand, was not. For him, it was his work, his life.

Then again, if Leona wanted it…

"Hang on," he muttered, undoing his gun belt. Normally he took it off as soon as he was off duty, but he'd been distracted. He pulled the handcuffs free and gave them to Leona to hold. Finally, he slid the belt off, unloaded his gun, and set it all down on her coffee table.

Still holding the cuffs, which looked huge in her delicate hand, Leona led him into her bedroom. All of his adolescent daydreams roared to life, more potent and visceral than ever before. Her bed dominated the room, with its black headboard and scarlet silk sheets.

Leona turned and kissed him again by the door, and he let her lead again, let her—

Click.

"What—?"

Absolutely not. He twisted his wrists. Metal dug into his skin.

"Did you just fucking cuff me?"

She grinned. "The safe word is 'knitting.'"

He fought the cuffs even though he knew for a fact there was no getting out of them without that key on his police belt. "What the *hell*, Leona?"

"I thought—" Her expression sobered. "If you want me to stop, I will. I'll take the cuffs off right now. Or any time it gets to be too intense, I'll stop. Just use safe word so I know you mean it for real, not as part of the game."

"The game," Simon echoed.

"Just the cuffs. I'm not going to hurt you," she said, with a rueful smile. "Unless you want me to, of course."

Hurt him? What was with this girl? He'd expected her to be adventurous, but he hadn't expected anything like this. When he'd acted out Ashley's cop fantasies with her, he'd called her a bad girl a few times and had pretended to cuff her once, perhaps a bit begrudgingly now that he thought about it. If she'd wanted to actually use his cuffs, she'd never said so.

He'd certainly never let anyone cuff *him* before.

Knitting, he thought. *Knitting.* He'd call all this off, go home, and try to forget about this whole day… including Leona Chaisty practically licking her lips at the sight of him in a T-shirt.

And then what? He'd go into work tomorrow to the unsolved bombing case and the O'Shea homicide investigation, and he'd go home tomorrow night to his empty apartment. His life would go on exactly the same, with only whiskey and fresh snow to punctuate the monotony.

"Just the cuffs?" he said.

"Right."

"Okay. All right." He swallowed hard. "What do you want me to do?"

She gave him a measured, appraising look. "Kneel."

With his hands behind his back, he had to go down carefully, one knee at a time. He felt unbearably self-conscious on Leona's immaculate oriental carpet, still in his tactical pants and black undershirt.

"Look at me."

His feelings scattered in a million directions. He dragged his gaze up to hers.

"You think I'm pretty, don't you?" Her voice was full of challenge, and so was her posture: one hand on her slim hip, the other toying with her long hair.

"Yes," he croaked.

"How pretty?" she demanded.

"Beautiful." He flushed. "You're the most beautiful woman I've ever seen." Other women had never compared to her, didn't have that fierceness she had.

"Then watch."

Yes. God, yes. Being caught in his own cuffs would be worth it, completely worth it, if he got to see her naked.

Gathering her hair over one shoulder, she turned around, treating him to an eye-level view of her ass and her long legs. Her graceful hands moved to the zipper on the back of her violet dress. She drew it down, revealing the back of her bra—black, just like he'd imagined. He couldn't help groaning, his cock swelling.

She glanced back, eyebrows arched, more like a mischievous dark fairy than ever. "You want to see more?"

"Yes."

"You'll have to beg."

"Please." His voice shook. "Please."

She purred. Slowly, she pulled the zipper the rest of the way down, to the top of her matching black underwear. She let the violet dress fall to the floor, puddling around her high heels, and faced him again. Her hair still lay across her shoulder, falling onto one pert breast and twining into the cup of her bra.

"Leona…" He couldn't take his eyes off her. "Uncuff me. I want to touch you."

Stepping out of her dress, she sashayed toward him in her skimpy panties. "I get to touch *you*." She ran a fingertip from his collar to his chest. "But you don't get to touch *me*. That's the game."

"Then touch yourself for me."

"What a dirty imagination you have, Simon." With a wicked smile, she traced her cherry-red fingernail along his cheek. "Where?"

Did that mean she was going to do it?

"Touch your mouth," he said through gritted teeth, praying she would.

She drew her hand away from him and stroked one fingertip across her lower lip, starting at one corner and sliding to the other. Her lip pouted out, and she did it again, back and forth, her eyes fluttering closed.

"Yeah," he groaned. "Suck on it."

Leona put two fingers into her mouth and sucked, tilting her head back to reveal her long, beautiful neck. Though she couldn't know what it would do to him, she slipped her fingers from her mouth and drew them down the delicate skin of her throat. The sight hit Simon like an explosion—so intense he thought he might come without the slightest touch. He shuddered, his breathing ragged, and reminded himself that it was too soon to tell her what he wanted to do to her. Despite the insanity of what they were already doing together, it was too much, too soon. Always.

It didn't matter. At the moment, there was something else he wanted just as much.

"Touch yourself. Your pussy." If he edged forward a few inches, he could kiss her there himself. But now that they were playing her little game, he didn't want it to end.

Her gorgeous eyes met his. She held his gaze as she slid her palm from the cup of her bra down her stomach to her panties.

"Oh, God." His heart was pounding, and his throat was so dry now that it ached. "Yes. Touch yourself for me."

She slid her hand underneath the silky fabric.

"Show me how you like it." He needed to sear the image into his brain, so he could hold onto it forever.

Vulnerability showed on her face for the first time, in the creasing of her eyebrows, the tense flutter of her eyelashes against her cheeks. "Simon…"

"Take them off. Please." He tried to swallow, but couldn't. "I need to see how wet you are when you come."

With her free hand, she pulled her panties past her hips and let them fall to the floor. He stared, mesmerized, as she slipped a finger inside herself and pressed against her palm.

"I want you so bad." The words tumbled from his mouth. "I've been hard for you for days."

"Mmm, yes." Her cheeks and the tops of her breasts were flushed. He wished he could run his hands across her skin. But if he could have touched her, none of this little show would have taken place. He wouldn't be watching the most erotic thing he'd ever seen.

Her whole body stiffened, and she gave a little shudder, then again, and again, as the orgasm ran through her body. He couldn't have looked away even if the living room had spontaneously combusted behind him. Just when he thought she couldn't get any sexier, she went and did it.

A slow, delicious smile spread across her face, and *that*, he thought, was the best part.

She blinked. As her eyes cleared, the smile only grew broader. She wasn't self-conscious at all, standing in front of him in her bra and her high heels.

"You look so sexy like that. At my mercy." She looked him up and down. "Too bad that position will make it harder for me to fuck you."

Simon's already aching cock jumped. Without another word, she walked past him into the living room, her heels ticking on the hardwood. A few seconds later, he sensed her crouch behind him. The cuffs unlocked with a *click*. Wincing, he brought his arms together in front of his chest, stretching his shoulders and massaging his wrists.

"Let's take this off," she murmured from behind him, sliding her hands underneath his T-shirt. She pulled the shirt off over his head and reached around his waist to undo his fly. Simon brushed her hands away and did it himself, standing and shucking off his shoes and clothes.

He turned toward her, intending to pull her in for a kiss and take back some control over this situation. But as soon as he looked at her beautiful body again, insecurity paralyzed him. He didn't know how to please her. Even with his exes, he'd been nothing to write home about, and this was on a totally different level. This was—*everything*.

If Leona picked up on his uncertainty, she didn't show it. She sidled up to him and rested a hand on his chest. In her free hand, she held a condom.

"You are *incredibly* good-looking." Her gaze swept over his body. "I should've taken your clothes off before I cuffed you."

"Next time," Simon said, with an edge to his voice. He had no idea why he'd said it. He could hardly think, so consumed with lust.

"Next time, I won't go as easy on you." Leona put her hands on his biceps and pushed him toward her bed.

She sat him down and climbed onto his lap, unwrapping the condom and sliding it onto him before he could offer to do it himself. "I've got you," she whispered in his ear, as she eased him onto his back. "I want you to be selfish. You can't hurt me. You don't need to worry about my pleasure. Just let go."

He wanted to argue with her, to fight the hypnotic quality of her voice. Her pleasure was always more important than his. He'd do anything to see her come again.

She took him in hand and slid him inside her. His breath tore out of him, followed by strangled curses. All arguments were forgotten as she shifted her hips.

He gripped her waist to get the rhythm right. This was the first time he'd truly touched her tonight. He wanted so much more, wanted to touch and kiss and lick her entire body, wanted to make her come, crying his name, while he was deep inside her.

But he couldn't last after what she'd put him through. All he could do was what she'd told him to do: let go. The tension spiraled inside him, building and building, until finally it shattered, crystal-sharp and so intense that it hurt.

Afterward, he struggled to return to Earth, still gasping for breath.

What the fuck had just happened?

He'd showed up here hours late, told her about his awful day, and somehow ended up handcuffed on her floor, watching her strip. He'd been so…so passive. So vulnerable with her.

He met Leona's smiling eyes and instantly wished he were hard again so they could have a second round. What was wrong with him? She was completely deranged, and she'd taken all kinds of liberties he hadn't given her permission to take.

Except she'd given him that safe word. She would've stopped if he'd used it. He just…hadn't.

Climbing off of him, Leona caught the condom in her hand and tossed it into a trashcan by her dresser. She kicked her shoes off and sat back down on the bed next to him. "Well, that was fun. Thanks."

"'Thanks'?" He pushed himself up to a sitting position on her silky red sheets. "I don't know what you're thanking me for. I didn't *do* anything."

She arched an eyebrow. "You gave me orders practically the entire time."

Orders? No. If anything, every word he'd said had been a plea. To display herself for him. To touch herself for him. As if he mattered. As if she found him attractive, interesting, worthwhile in any way. He would've begged her for that again, but he couldn't, because it was over and time for him to leave. He hadn't hooked up with a girl in years—since college, at least—but she probably hooked up with different guys all the time. *Lots* of guys, just like she'd said.

His whole body burned with embarrassment, thinking back on what he had asked for, how inadequate he had been, how much he had wanted. He wished he felt just as sanguine as she clearly did.

Chapter Five

SIMON WAS FROWNING DOWN AT her scarlet sheets. "I should get going. I've got to go in early tomorrow."

"Okay." Leona shrugged, though she was surprised that he wanted to leave already. She supposed she didn't know what standard operating procedure was for hooking up with someone in your own house. It might be normal to leave right away, especially if you had to work the next day.

"Do you want anything before you go?" she asked. "Or…do you want to talk for a minute?"

It was still her responsibility to do after-care, wasn't it? It had to be. Even though they'd kept things pretty vanilla, she wanted to make sure he felt all right. She was sure he'd enjoyed himself once he'd warmed up to the idea of the cuffs. She hadn't imagined his lust-glazed expression, or the way his beautiful body had seized up when he'd come. But he'd seemed disconcerted at first.

He pulled on his black work pants and T-shirt, his brow furrowed. Leona studied him, curious—then concerned by the depths of his frown. Maybe he hadn't enjoyed himself after all?

"Simon?"

He ran a hand through his hair and shook himself a little. "I have to go." His tone was brusque. His cop voice. As if he couldn't wait to get away from her.

She stood, turning toward the wall, and pulled her dress back over her head. One of her long silver earrings tangled in her hair. She took a second to untangle it, wishing she knew what to say. There was a good reason why she'd stuck to private clubs and play parties her whole life. She knew what people expected from her there.

Sensing his eyes on her, she reluctantly glanced up. He was staring at her hand—her earring? His expression was intense, almost pained, and so fixated on her fingertips that it was almost as though he'd forgotten where he was.

Earlier, watching him from under her eyelashes while she'd drawn her fingers down her throat, she thought she'd seen this same expression. She supposed he was always a focused man, but this had been more than that. A bit like…

No. Not a chance—she must have been imagining it. She'd been in the lifestyle too long, that was all. That much was obvious.

She freed the earring from her hair. Their eyes met, and Simon's cheeks shaded even darker. He tore his gaze away from her.

"See you later." He walked out of her bedroom. She didn't respond, didn't follow him, just sat down on the edge of her bed and listened to him scoop up his gun belt off of her coffee table. The door to her apartment slammed shut.

Since Leona had the next day off, she decided to do her once-annual day of Christmas shopping. Buying presents was the only part of Christmas she actually liked, and today she was especially glad to be out, distracting herself from the lingering awkwardness of last night.

Soon enough, she found the perfect Christmas present for Paul and Mellon: a swanky granite cheese board with matching swanky knife. On the off chance that Iris actually sent Leona her new address, Leona bought her a hat, scarf, and gloves in matching teal. Wherever Iris was, it had to get chilly sometimes, and Iris wasn't the type to remember to bring something warm.

On her way back home, Leona pulled into the liquor store parking lot, telling herself she might as well finish the rest of her Christmas preparations today. Though she didn't put up any traditional decorations, she did dig a fiber optic palm tree out of her closet every year, the better to drink margaritas and watch beach-themed movies. Iris had always called it Leona's Cabana Christmas. She used to stop by in the middle of the day for a margarita and a brief respite from her family. This year, it would just be Leona, Cuervo, and *Jaws 2*.

As Leona paid for her tequila, her thoughts turned inexorably back to Simon. It was mid-afternoon; he was probably still at work, even if he had gone in early. She told herself that was fine; she'd see him around eventually.

She hesitated halfway to Lulu, an uncharacteristic sense of regret nagging at her.

A few times, she'd hooked up with guys who were desperate to get with her…until they came. She supposed they were ashamed of whatever they'd done—or, more likely, whatever she'd done to them.

She hadn't expected that from Simon. She didn't know why. No good reason.

Still… The way he'd held still so she could undress him, the way he'd yielded to her kiss, the pure sex in his voice when he'd said: *What do you want me to do?* She'd assumed he was into it, that he was enjoying himself. But she should know by now that it was wrong and just plain stupid to make assumptions when it came to kink, even kink as mild and commonplace as using a pair of handcuffs. She might have scared him, hurt him, out of her own selfish desire for him.

Leona hiked across the strip of snow bordering the liquor store parking lot and walked up Simon's driveway to his front door. Shifting her bags to one hand, she rang his doorbell. When he didn't answer, she rang it again. Nothing. He had to be at work.

After a few moments of indecision, she returned to Lulu and drove home. She walked around the ice cream shop to her front door—just as Simon stepped down from her stoop.

He was wearing jeans and a parka, with his wool hat pulled down over his forehead, but he might as well have been kneeling on her floor in his undershirt again, with the muscles in his neck and shoulders straining against the handcuffs. She couldn't remember the last time someone had affected her so much—stealing her breath even a day later.

"I was just ringing your doorbell," he said. "I don't have your number."

"There's a good reason for that," she replied, affecting calm. "I live in the Stone Age and don't have a phone."

"What? Really?"

"Well, I have a landline, but obviously nobody uses

it, because nobody uses landlines anymore."

"Except you."

"Right." She smiled cautiously. "What brings you here? Want to come up?"

"No," he said, frowning at the sidewalk. "I don't trust myself in your apartment."

Ouch. She had scared him, then. That was the last thing she'd meant to do. She had wanted to help him relax—even, perhaps, to feel safe, after what he'd been through at work that night.

She had once taken a lot of pride in being a good Domme. More importantly, she hated the idea of hurting Simon.

"There's a back porch behind the ice cream shop," she said. "It's somewhat public, if you'd rather talk there."

He gave a curt nod, and she set off down the brick pathway leading behind her building. The ice cream shop's back porch overlooked a small garden, dormant for the winter, and the parking lot where Lulu lived. Since it was the off-season, the porch was empty except for a wooden swing. She perched on the edge, letting herself drift back and forth.

Simon climbed the steps onto the porch. She patted the seat beside her and he joined her, his expression still shuttered.

"I'm really sorry I scared you last night," she said. "I honestly thought it might help you feel better."

He winced. "So you were being nice? That's what every guy wants to hear."

"I don't mean—it wasn't a pity fuck, if that's what you're thinking. I obviously really wanted to sleep with you." She'd wanted it far too much. "As far as topping you was concerned…I thought if you didn't have to do too much, you'd be able to turn your brain off for once."

He leaned back on the swing and stared up at the snow glittering on the porch's trellised roof.

"What's…" He cleared his throat. "When you say topping me—"

"Dominating you," she said softly. "The 'D' in BDSM. Domination and submission."

His eyebrows creased together slightly, his frown intensifying, but he didn't look away from the glittering trellis. She studied him, her heart sinking. She'd thought he might be inexperienced, but apparently he had no kink experience at all. What had she done? Why had she thought any of this was a good idea?

She swept a hand through her hair with a tight sigh. The thing was, she had picked up on *something*. She'd interpreted his odd little vibe as submissiveness, but she could've been wrong. He'd given her orders the entire time he'd been cuffed. At the Italian restaurant, she'd teased him—just to get a rise out of him—about being a big, macho cop who liked to give orders, and his reaction had been so…scrambled. He'd looked offended, confused, and also…flushed. His eyes dark.

He could be a Dom, or a sub, or someone who just genuinely didn't know. She wasn't sure how someone could get to their late twenties without exploring those kind of urges, but she supposed anything was possible.

Simon cleared his throat, and Leona looked at him, still sick with concern.

"So," he said. "You're a Dominatrix?"

If she said yes, would that end this—whatever it was they were doing together?

"I like all aspects of BDSM," she said finally. "I've done plenty of both Domination and submission."

She'd subbed plenty of times, especially when she was first starting out. And she did like it, sometimes. She would do it for him.

He slouched forward, his elbows on his knees. "Right," he said bitterly. "You've been with lots of guys."

"I'm not going to apologize for having a sexual past," Leona shot back. "If I was a man, you wouldn't think twice about it."

"If you were a man, I wouldn't want to sleep with you."

"And the fact that you want me makes it okay for you to judge me? I don't think so."

With a harsh exhale, he put his face in his hands. "No. Of course not. I'm just—I've never done anything like this before, and you have. It's weird for me."

"If you don't like it," she said slowly, without quite realizing what she was saying, "we could do something else. If you still wanted to." Was she truly offering him vanilla sex? What did that even involve? Missionary all the time?

Glancing at him again, she intended to take it back. But as soon as she met his eyes, she realized she didn't want to. She'd rather have boring vanilla sex with Simon than go back to the scene. The realization made her feel weird, nervous, as if her skin were too tight.

"I liked it," he said suddenly. "That's the thing."

Her body hummed. "You liked it? Was there something specific...?"

"All of it." He swallowed. "I loved watching you. You are unbelievably sexy. And...I liked the cuffs."

"You did?" Her heart raced. Had she been right all along? "But—liking the cuffs...that's a bad thing to you?"

He nodded, his expression grim.

"There's nothing shameful about submitting, Simon," she said. "Though, for the record, you were not very submissive with me last night. You were fighting me the entire time. And giving me orders."

He cast her a begrudging smile. Her heart giving a painful squeeze, Leona smiled back.

"If you want, you can tie me up next time." He ought to explore both sides, see which felt right.

"Leona…" He wrapped one of his large, callused hands around a slat in the back of the swing. His mouth opened and closed, a muscle in his jaw twitching. He shook his head. "I can't tie you up."

"Why not?" Was this some kind of hang up—good guys don't tie girls up?

Or was it something else? He was gripping the slat in the swing so hard his knuckles were white, his expression almost as intense as it had been last night, with his brow furrowed and his lips slightly parted.

Slowly, she brought her hand to the side of her neck, pretending to adjust one of her teardrop earrings the same way she'd adjusted her earring the night before. His gaze snapped to her hand. Nervous excitement fluttered low in her belly. She had to be imagining this, all of it—but there was the slightest possibility that she wasn't, and that had her completely captivated.

Unable to resist, she touched a fingertip to the side of her neck, just under her ear, and drew it slowly downward, as casually as she could. But there was nothing casual about Simon's expression. Fascinated, she slid her fingertip sideways across her throat. His gaze tracked the movement. She added her thumb, so that her hand loosely encircled her neck. Even through his jeans, she could see Simon getting hard. Her pulse quickened.

Surely not. Surely, even if he was kinky, even if he was Dominant, he couldn't be into something like this.

He jerked to his feet so abruptly that the entire swing shuddered on its chains.

"Wait," she said. "Please, let's talk about it—"

But he'd already jogged down the steps, down the pathway, and out of sight. Once again, she let him go.

Chapter Six

THE NEXT MORNING, AT THE beginning of his shift, he drove toward Mrs. O'Shea's house for his meeting with her daughter.

He felt jumpy, restless, and kept trying to scan through his list of interview topics, hoping it would help him stay focused. Keep his mind off Leona. But, as important as this interview was, he kept dwelling on Leona's heavy-lidded, curious eyes when she'd asked him why he couldn't tie her up. She'd run her fingertip down her throat, watching him. Reading his every thought.

She was so clever, so fearless. She'd zeroed in on something he could never have said aloud, something he could barely stand to admit to himself. Small wonder she terrified him. And now…

He loosened his grip on his steering wheel, all too aware of how big his hands were, how breakable the world around him was, even his old cruiser. He sipped his lukewarm coffee and told himself to stop shaking. In a way, nothing had changed. He'd known from the beginning that she was out of his league. That they could never be what he wanted.

The fact that he was a freak, and that she had figured him out so quickly, was just the last nail in the coffin.

His GPS binged at him. The next turn was Mrs.

O'Shea's house. He had to concentrate, push aside all his fucked up longing for Leona. He owed it to his former teacher, and to his town.

Simon pulled into a rutted dirt driveway that led him down into a shadowed grove. A flagstone path led him through the grove to the front porch, where Mrs. O'Shea's daughter, Penelope, stood alone, gripping the chipped porch railing and staring into the distance. She had pulled her curly red hair back into a severe bun. It made her look older, her strong features harsher.

"Miss O'Shea? This still a good time to talk?"

She glanced at him, her eyebrows tightening. "Officer Labelle. Yes, of course." Tendrils of hair escaped from her bun. She opened the front door, and they went into a dark kitchen. A few empty boxes and bags lay untouched in the center of the floor.

"I can't bear to start packing it up," she said quietly.

"I understand," he said. "I'm very sorry for your loss. She seemed like a very special woman."

"Yes, she was," Penelope O'Shea said, sitting down at the kitchen table and gesturing for him to join her. Apart from the darkness, the place was cheerful and homey, with country linens and wood cabinets and lots of little knickknacks scattered around. Wooden farm animals and such. It suited the Mrs. O'Shea in his memories and made her absence that much more striking.

Simon had done many interviews over the years, but not many as emotionally fraught as this. He started slowly, for her sake, asking open-ended questions about Nancy O'Shea's life, her interests, her last few weeks. Eventually, he turned to the day of the accident.

"Did she always jog along that road? She didn't consider it dangerous?"

"She never believed that bad things could happen, to her or to anyone," Penelope replied, scrubbing her face with her hand. "She's—she *was* such an optimist. I never understood it, myself. She used to tease me about being a pessimist, and I'd say, 'I'm a pragmatist, that's all.'"

He smiled ruefully. He'd had plenty of conversations like that himself.

A few silent seconds passed. Simon steeled himself to ask a pragmatist's question.

"You understand, Miss O'Shea, that I have to ask you…"

She glanced at him sharply, then stood up and turned slightly away, hugging her arms to her chest.

"Was there anyone who might've wanted to hurt your mother? For any reason?"

"I know you have to ask," she said softly, her voice a little thick. "And, truly, I don't know. I can't think of a single person who disliked her. How could anyone not have liked her?" She sucked in a breath. "And before you suggest otherwise—my father is a good man, and they've been on great terms since the divorce. There's no way—" She shook her head. "Just no way."

"I understand." He got to his feet. He'd have more questions for her later, but for now, he was unwilling to trespass any longer upon her grief. "Thank you very much for your time, miss. If you think of anything else, please let me know." He started toward the door.

"Are you going to solve this?" she asked suddenly. "Whether it was an accident or… It's still a—a crime either way, right?"

"It's a very serious crime, yes." At minimum, the driver had left the scene of a fatal accident. If they'd been driving negligently or recklessly, the State's Attorney could charge them with involuntary manslaughter.

"Are you going to solve it?" she asked again. "Because the bombing—the vet's office—"

He flinched, suddenly understanding the meaning behind her question. She didn't just mean the department—she meant *him*, specifically.

"We're going to do everything we can, miss," he said. "I promise." God help him, he would not let Mrs. O'Shea's death go unsolved. He wouldn't be able to live with himself if he did.

He excused himself and left Penelope standing alone in the darkness, gazing out of her mother's kitchen window. Small crystalline snowflakes had started to fall during his interview, and they crisscrossed the roads in glittering white strands as he drove back to the station, still turning the interview over in his mind. Her question ate at him—but so did her swollen eyes, the quiet anguish in her expression. Sometimes it was worse to see someone so proud end up so broken. Like they had further to fall, and would break harder, more completely.

Back at the station, Bryan Keene and Kyle O'Malley were standing in the main office, sipping coffee and shooting the shit. O'Malley, a former Army medic with a newborn son, looked half-asleep as usual. Keene, meanwhile, was eternally his huge, brash, loud self. He'd been a senior at Simon's tiny high school while Simon was a freshman and had ended up at Grenton PD after a stint in the Marines. Simon, who had joined the department after getting a bachelor's degree in criminal justice, was the only one besides Jack, the rookie, who wasn't military.

With a nod hello at his coworkers, Simon crossed through the cluttered main room toward his own small office at the back of the station. He sat down at his desk with his thoughts still a jumble of amorphous concerns and his body heavy and sluggish with sadness—both borrowed and his own.

"Hey." Keene sauntered in uninvited and squeezed into one of the chairs opposite Simon's desk. "How'd it go with Mrs. O'Shea's daughter?"

Simon shrugged. "Standard. Not much info. Doesn't think anyone would've done it on purpose."

Keene's eyebrows rose. "Do *you* think that?"

"Dunno." He hoped not, but the darkest, most pragmatic part of him told him he could not rule it out. "No cameras on that stretch of road, no witnesses to the accident. Just got to wait to hear from the collision reconstruction expert and the forensics lab."

"How much longer for that?"

"Weeks, probably. Months."

Keene grunted. "Slow fuckers."

"Guess it's complicated," Simon said, with a slight, sad smile, running a hand through his hair.

"Nah," Keene said. "They just don't care as much as you do."

Simon glanced at Keene in surprise.

"It's not a bad thing." Keene sipped his coffee. "Why else do you think the Chief assigned you to the case?"

"Dunno." He just knew the Chief shouldn't have. Penelope's question was proof enough of that.

Keene shook his head, exhaling. "Ray Waller's doing good, the pastor says," he said. "He's been sober the last couple days."

Simon just nodded. It was hard to muster much enthusiasm, when they both knew how quickly Ray would fall off the wagon again.

"You doing any better?" Keene asked.

"I'm fine."

"Yeah, you look fucking great."

"What's that supposed to mean?"

"I mean you're wasting the fuck away. Even you need to eat and sleep occasionally, Labelle. I meant what I said about penance. Sometimes cases just don't get solved."

"I eat," Simon said, though he couldn't actually remember, off the top of his head, when his last meal had been.

"If you say so." Keene sighed. "Talk to me sometime, buddy. All right?" He peeled himself out of the chair and left.

Simon stayed late, flipping through documents long after he'd stopped seeing them. When he finally went home, he sat down at his own dark kitchen table and drank a beer, worn out and heartsick. He wished he had someone to come home to, someone he could talk to—truly talk to. He liked Keene and the rest of the guys at the station, but they just didn't think about things the way he did. Keene could accept that sometimes a case just didn't get solved, but Simon couldn't. It ate at him that he'd fucked up the bomb threats investigation, that he could've done better, could've stopped somebody from getting hurt.

Leona was right about him—he was a control freak.

He slumped in his chair, thinking about their charged argument in her apartment, their thrilling, overwhelming hookup, their painful conversation on the porch swing.

His doorbell rang, and he jumped about half a foot.

Leona stood outside in the pale glow of the Christmas lights, holding a six-pack. He stared at her in shock.

"I was hoping we could talk," she said. "Just talk, to be clear. No sex, or miscellaneous sexy things." She lifted the six-pack. "I brought beer, if that helps? I realize it's a terrible bribe, since it was literally the easiest thing I could get you. Sort of like if you brought me ice cream. Although, honestly, anytime you want to bring me ice cream, you should go for it. I always—"

He interrupted her, unintentionally, by laughing, pinching the bridge of his nose. It was the first time he'd laughed all day. He passed his hand across his face and took a breath. "I didn't think you'd…" He shook his head, his heart racing. "Come in. Please."

With a smile, she walked inside and set the six-pack on his kitchen table. Simon hung up her coat, then opened a beer for her and a new one for himself. Leona plunked down on his couch, holding her beer next to her crossed legs. Dressed in jeans and a plain black top, with her long hair falling loosely around her shoulders, she looked girl-next-door for once. Which she was, sort of.

"So…I'm really sorry about what happened," she said. "It's been a couple years for me, and I'm rusty. I should've realized that I was moving too fast." She tapped her fingers on her knee, while Simon had unhappy visions of Leona handcuffing other men. "I should've talked to you, done a better job of sussing out your experience level, before we did anything. But I didn't, and I'm sorry about that. And now…I guess I feel like I've opened up a can of worms for you. And I don't want you to feel like you have to deal with it on your own. So…that's why I'm here."

"Can of worms," he echoed, pressing his sweating

palms into his knees. Of course she hadn't just figured it out. She wanted to talk about it, too, and dredge it up into the open—the last place where it belonged.

"It seems to me that talking about Domination and submission has got you thinking about something that you want," she said. "Something that you fantasize about, but are afraid of."

"I can't…I can't." Just thinking about it made his skin crawl.

"Simon…you're not going to shock me. Do you want me to tell you some of the stuff I've done?"

"No." But he did. He wanted to know absolutely everything.

"All right," she said. "If you aren't going to tell me, then I'll guess."

Filled with dread, he stared at her. She gazed calmly back at him.

"You're secretly kinky. Very kinky. And you have a fetish. Something to do with the throat or neck. A choking fetish?"

He wanted to yell at her. He wanted to tell her that that was the sickest thing he'd ever heard, that she was crazy for saying it, that he had no idea what she was talking about.

"It's *okay*," she insisted. "It's just a fetish. There's—"

"Just a fetish!" He lunged to his feet and paced his apartment. "I'm a fucking cop—I can't go around choking women!"

"I never said that you should. But if you wanted to try something with me—"

"No. Never." He shuddered.

"Simon, come here."

Her soft command made him stop pacing. But he still couldn't bring himself to go to her.

After a moment, she came to him, taking his elbows in her hands and steering him gently toward her until they were facing each other, just a few inches apart. "You've never done it before, right?"

He started to pull away. She tightened her grip on him.

"My first girlfriend," he said reluctantly. "I put my hand on her neck, and she panicked. That was the only time."

The memory still hurt. He hadn't even realized what he was doing. He'd always had these fantasies about… leather and ropes and God knew what else. Weird shit. But he'd never intended to act on any of it, and certainly not with shy, skittish Mallory. They had just been making out behind the high school; it had been perfectly innocuous, except that he couldn't stop looking at her throat. That smooth, delicate skin had just been so beautiful…so vulnerable. Without thinking, he'd wrapped his hand—already big for his age—around her neck, enfolding it almost completely in his fingers.

Mallory had jerked away from him, her eyes huge and scared. Later, she'd asked him if he was a freak. Instead of telling her the truth, he'd called her crazy and broken up with her on the spot.

"So, that time," Leona said carefully, "when you touched her neck, did you squeeze?"

"No! Of course I didn't. I wouldn't have. I would never."

"Okay. I know." She rubbed his arms, as if he were going to catch a chill. "So, when you fantasize about this, what exactly happens with your fantasy woman that turns you on? Is it the way she struggles for air?"

She asked the question so earnestly that for once he actually thought about it, going back through the shameful fantasies that broke through his barriers right when he was about to come.

"She can always breathe fine," he said. "It's just my hand there. The wrongness of that. Because I could hurt her, but I don't. Because I wouldn't."

Leona's mouth quirked up. "I thought so."

He flinched. "It's not—it's still fucking sick. Even if I'm not choking someone 'til she passes out."

"It's completely different from that," she said. "Look, breath play—cutting off air supply—is really dangerous, right?"

Breath play. She made it sound so nice, almost ethereal.

"But what *you* want—it's still a little dangerous, but I think you could find ways to do it relatively safely—"

"No—no."

"Just listen, Simon." She laid one hand across his throat, her fingers cool against his skin, her thumb gracing the underside of his jaw. "Is this enough for you? If you did it to me."

The thought alone made his cock swell. Why was he like this?

"It would be enough," he managed. "But I still won't—"

"I wouldn't do it during sex itself, in case you lost control and accidentally squeezed," she continued. "But during foreplay, you could do it to me, or I could do it to myself, if that works for you."

She brought her same hand to her own throat, cupped her jaw, tilted her face upward. Simon had a sudden, vivid fantasy of sliding his thumb between her teeth. His heartbeat roared in his ears, and his already aching, swollen cock strained against his work pants.

Dropping her hand, she took a step back.

He shook himself, trying to get a grip. No sex tonight. He knew that.

"I bet you'd like it if I wore a collar," she mused. "Because I could wear that the entire time."

"A collar?" His head was still fuzzy with lust. "Like a dog collar?"

"Sort of." She smiled. "The good thing about a collar is that it's in a fixed position. You can play with it, but you probably can't accidentally strangle somebody with it."

"Oh, good," he said bitterly, his erection flagging. "Leona—why doesn't this scare you? Why don't you think I'm a monster?"

"You can't help how your brain is wired." With a shrug, she fetched her beer from his coffee table. "Anyway, as far as I can tell, this is not about hurting people, if that's what you're afraid of. It's about Dominance—the power you have over your partner, and your own self-restraint. It's just another way of saying *you're mine*."

You're mine. That was exactly what he wanted to say to her. And yet, with Leona the sometimes-Dominatrix… "That doesn't bother you?"

Her smile turned wicked. "It gives me a lot of power over you, too, you know. All I have to do is this…" She brought her fingertip to the smooth curve of her throat and drew it downward until she reached the hollow of her collarbone. He swallowed a groan.

"Very sexy," she purred, watching him.

He turned away, and this time, she let him go. He ran his hands through his hair, breathing hard. Could there really be a safe way to act out his desires with her? He already wanted her so badly. If she was truly willing to do this for him, or better yet if she was into it—

But it was still *wrong*, wasn't it? It was creepy and

domineering and weird, and there was no way it was safe. At least, not safe enough.

"I don't know," he said. "It's just so…"

"It's a lot to think about. You need some time to mull it over." She set down her beer and picked up her handbag. "It's getting late. I should go. But I'll check in on you—"

"Can we go out again? Dinner or something? We never did go to that Thai place."

She drew her arms together. "Oh. Sure. That would be nice."

Her tone was guarded, cautious. He didn't know why he'd asked. She'd said she was interested in trying out a few dates, but it seemed pretty clear that she wanted him for sex. He probably should've been happy about that, but he wasn't.

Too late to back out now. "How about Friday?"

"Perfect." Her expression softened, and he felt a little better. "See you then."

Chapter Seven

FOR THE NEXT TWO DAYS, Leona put Simon out of her mind. Mostly. They didn't run into each other, and the hordes of holiday shoppers leaving smudgy fingerprints on Leona's favorite vases distracted her enough for the time to go by fast.

On Friday night at six, when her shift ended, she realized she was nervous. Or that odd, ticklish feeling was excitement? Simon just kept getting more fascinating. There was so much more to him than she had thought at first. When she'd run her fingertip down her throat, his gaze had practically branded her.

Back at home, she changed into a slinky black top, tight jeans, and heels. A few minutes later, she pulled into Simon's driveway. He was waiting on his porch, wearing a dark brown barn coat over a collared shirt. He had his cop face on, but when she leaned across the car to pop the passenger side door open, he gave her a guarded smile.

"Hello, darling," she said, as he slid into the car next to her, bringing the cool, clean scent of his shaving cream. She wanted to cup his freshly shaved face in her hands and kiss him, but she held back.

"How was your day?" she asked.

He shrugged. "All right. How was work?"

"Ridiculously busy, but good." *Look at us, acting like a couple*, she thought, as she nudged Lulu's sizeable nose into the street. It was certainly far more foreign to her than discussing a fetish. It should have bothered her. But as she told him a few highlights from her chaotic day, she found herself secretly delighted to see his tense shoulders relaxing, his face opening up. She especially loved to make him laugh. His laugh always started out so reluctant, even begrudging, but quickly turned rich and resonant.

Spotting the Thai place, Leona pulled into the lot, excited about the possibility of pad see ew.

"Can I ask you something before we go inside?" His eyes turned serious again, even sad.

Her skin prickled. "Sure."

"Do you have a—a fetish, or anything?"

She shook her head, relieved. "Nope. I mean, I like to tie guys up and make them tell me how pretty I am, but that's not really a fetish as much as me having a huge ego." She was joking. Mostly. She did like to be admired—who didn't?—but she didn't need it to get off.

Simon still looked completely serious. She was about to clarify that it was a joke when he said: "You don't need to tie me up to get me to tell you that. Unless you want to, I guess."

"Aren't you sweet," she said, with a confused mix of joy and embarrassment.

"I mean it." Leaning across the center console, he tucked a strand of her hair behind her ear. His fingertips trailed down the side of her neck. His eyebrows creased. A flush crept slowly up his cheekbones.

Was he thinking about it—was he going to try it?

With a little sigh, she tilted her head back, exposing

her throat but still letting him lead. His hand settled alongside her neck. She wondered if he could see her heartbeat, ticking faster and faster underneath her skin.

He stroked her jaw lightly with his thumb, back and forth. It would be so easy for him to slide his thumb down onto her throat, slip his fingers into her hair, let his big hand engulf her. Strange how badly she wanted him to.

He brought his mouth to hers and kissed her, very gently, deepening the kiss slowly, with lazy strokes of his tongue. Her head spinning with desire, she sank back into the seat.

"You are beautiful," he murmured, pulling her lower lip between his teeth. "You are perfect, Leona Chaisty."

His other hand came to her throat, but after the slightest touch, he slid his fingers into her hair and pulled her in for another kiss. His taste, his touch, his words drove her wild. She wanted to fuck him right here, in the car, in a public parking lot.

He drew back, releasing a tight breath. "Christ, you're trouble."

She laughed, a little giddy. "To be fair, you started it." She paused. "I suppose a cop can't get caught fucking in public?"

"Uh, no, definitely not."

"Operative words being 'get caught'?" she suggested.

At that, he grinned back. "Impossible woman."

Inside, they were seated at a booth in the middle of the restaurant, where they ordered drinks. As the waiter walked away, Leona slipped off one of her heels and drew the top of her foot along Simon's leg. He tried to give her a stern look, but his mouth kept crooking up at one corner.

The waiter came back with their drinks, and they

both ordered extravagant noodle dishes. Afterward, Leona glanced around, admiring the restaurant's cheerful, elephant-themed decorations.

The hostess walked into Leona's line of sight, cutting off her view of a gold elephant on the far wall. Two women followed the hostess to a table in the center of the crowded restaurant. The taller woman had shimmery ash-brown hair. Even from across the room, Leona could see her wide, expressive smile, so much like Leona's own.

Leona's whole body went cold. No way it was her. She lived in Massachusetts now. There was no reason for her to be in Vermont.

Leona shivered so violently she knocked over her water glass. Simon caught it before it could fall to the table. Water sloshed across the tablecloth.

How could she be here? Her night with Simon had been going so well. This was like some kind of cruel prank.

"You all right?" Simon asked. "What's up?"

Leona balled her hands into fists in her lap. "It's nothing."

"Do you know that woman?" Of course Simon, cop that he was, had noticed.

"Never seen her before," she lied. She was still shaking, which just made her angrier. She shouldn't *care*. Not after all this time.

"She looks a lot like you."

"No, she doesn't." Leona had started dyeing her hair black at fourteen, and still did, so that she *wouldn't* look like the willowy, gray-eyed woman a few tables away. The woman who meant nothing to Leona, because Leona meant nothing to her.

The waiter was back, holding steaming plates of

noodles. Too late to escape.

"Leona…tell me what's going on," Simon said, after the waiter left.

Reluctantly, she met his gaze. His light eyes were concerned, but his mouth was set in a grim, schooled line, as if he were waiting to find out how many heads he had to bash together. She felt a sudden rush of affection for him.

"That's my mother," Leona admitted.

"I'm guessing you guys aren't close."

"You could say that."

"I heard about the mall," Simon said quietly. "That they left you at a mall for an entire day, when you were a kid."

She stared at the condensation on the side of her beer. "It was two days."

"How did they leave you at a mall for *two days*?"

"They used to drop me off at one sometimes, while they went to the casino in upstate New York. It was on the way. But I guess they forgot about me and went home. It wasn't…totally uncommon." She didn't look at him as she said it. Even after all these years, she still felt a little bit ashamed of being so irrevocably unwanted.

"That is so fucked up."

"Actually, at first, it was kind of cool. Being locked in the mall overnight, you know. But then the next day, the mall cop caught me stealing a pretzel, and I ended up spending the rest of the day at the local police station. Until my folks finally showed up." She laughed. "Told you I had some experience with the police."

"Jesus Christ," he muttered. "That is insane."

Simon scowled across the restaurant at Leona's mother, who was laughing at something her friend had said. Leona was sure he thought her mother looked perfectly nice and normal. Everyone always did, including Leona's own friends. The same friends who had nicknamed Leona Maleficent.

"How could she do that to you?" Simon asked, turning back to Leona. "What's wrong with her?"

She sighed. "There's nothing wrong with her. Or my father. It's not like they're evil. They were young. They didn't want a kid. They just wanted to be able to do whatever they felt like, whenever they felt like it."

That had always been the worst part. They didn't actually *dislike* her. They'd never screamed at her or beat her. They had just never cared if she were there or not.

"Could be worse," she said. "I could've had Iris's mom. Complete psycho."

He shook his head. "You can't just abandon your kid at a mall. That is not okay."

She freed a piece of broccoli from a tangle of noodles, but couldn't stomach actually eating it. She set her fork back down. "It wasn't being left at the mall that made things so hard for me, growing up. It was the little stuff. Never having any food in the house. Washing my shirts in the sink because the washing machine was always broken. Walking everywhere because no one ever remembered to pick me up. It was never malicious. It was just, 'oh, Leona, you're here?'"

As soon as she'd turned eighteen, she'd moved out. Paul had co-signed a lease for her so she could get her own apartment. It was, without a doubt, the nicest thing anyone had ever done for her.

She'd wondered if they'd notice her absence, or maybe even miss her. But they didn't. A few times, she'd seen them walking around downtown with friends, and they'd waved at her as if she were someone they used to play cards with. *Oh, Leona, you're here?*

"We should get out of here before I end up saying something to that goddamn woman."

Leona looked up at Simon in surprise. He still had his cop face on, but she could see his fury in the narrowing of his eyes. She couldn't remember the last time that she'd actually told someone about her family. She hadn't expected anger. At most, she'd expected to be pitied.

"I'll get the check," he said, "if you want to go out to the car."

"It's all right." As soon as she said it, she regretted it. She desperately wanted to go out to Lulu. Anywhere but here, watching her mother not see her.

"It's not all right," he snapped. "Go outside."

Numb and shaky, she picked up her purse. She should thank him. She wanted to, but the words froze in her throat. She couldn't stop herself from looking over one last time. It was like looking in a mirror, but aged by about twenty years.

Her mother happened to look up. Mild recognition flashed across her face. She smiled Leona's smile and fluttered her fingertips in a vague, polite wave, as if she couldn't quite remember Leona's name.

Leona did not wave back. She was trapped in a nightmare she couldn't wake up from.

Her mother's friend glanced over and waved awkwardly, too. Leona didn't recognize her, but it didn't matter: they were all the same. Her parents' friends had always been puzzled by the pale, gangly child who'd lingered around the edges of their parties. The women had ruffled her hair while the men had told her to smile, but she'd never minded, because she'd liked the attention.

Pathetic. She drew a trembling breath and thought of Lulu. All she had to do was walk outside. Then she could be with Lulu, and Simon, and she could go back to her beloved apartment. She could exorcise this night from her mind forever.

Chapter Eight

SIMON WAVED THE WAITER OVER and barked at him to bring the check and wrap up Leona's untouched dinner. He tried to wait calmly for the waiter to come back, but as long as that woman was still in the restaurant, laughing with her friend, Simon couldn't be calm.

He stalked over to their table. Leona's mother glanced up at him with a puzzled, polite smile. "Can I help you?"

"What the hell is your problem?" he demanded. "You run into your daughter after, what, five, ten years, and you can't even be bothered to say hello to her?"

"I'm sorry, who are you? One of my daughter's playthings?" She gave him a sly, assessing look, while her friend tittered.

He knew better than to rise to bait, even if it hurt. It figured Leona's mother would be just as cutting as she was, without any of her kindness.

He folded his arms across his chest. "I asked you a question."

"Well, in that case, let me explain: my daughter made it clear to me years ago that she doesn't want a relationship."

"No. *You* made that clear to *her*, when you left her at

a mall for two fucking days."

Leona's mother rolled her eyes. Her friend tittered again. Simon wanted to split their table in half with his fist.

"Forget it," he snapped. "You obviously don't deserve her."

Why had he bothered? He should have trusted Leona's judgment. Should've known that if there were anything worth saving there, Leona would've saved it.

He turned to leave, but then she laughed. Her laugh was a perversion of Leona's—so much crueler, and roughened by years of cigarettes or joints. He could just detect the faintest smell of pot underneath her perfume, and it killed him to think this woman had been getting high and laughing with her asshole friends when she could have been looking after Leona.

Simon turned back to face them. His voice low, he leaned on the table to stare her in the eye. "Listen to me, Mrs. Chaisty. If you want to be part of Leona's life, you have to treat her like a human being. Until then, you stay the fuck away from her."

She glanced at her friend. "Can you believe this, Molly? I'm being lectured by—"

"I don't think you understand me," he growled. "If you ever see Leona in a restaurant again, or anywhere else, you turn the fuck around and leave." He straightened up, pulled out his wallet, and flipped it open to show her his badge.

She blanched, but she cast him a defiant look. "You can't just—"

"Really?" he interrupted, sliding his wallet back into his jeans. "How clean are you living?"

She cleared her throat primly and stared at the tablecloth, while her friend looked anywhere but at Simon.

"Right." He gave an irritated sigh. Prescriptions, if he had to guess, in addition to the pot. That would certainly help you forget your kid at the mall for days. Especially if you were already an asshole.

Without another word, he went back to his table, snatched up the take-out bag and his credit card, and left, letting the door slam behind him. He was still simmering with rage as he walked down the steps, but as soon as he saw Lulu, idling in the parking lot, the rage mixed together with something even deeper. Leona had her arms draped over Lulu's steering wheel, her chin resting on her wrist, as if she were cuddling a teddy bear. A teddy bear with a V-8.

How could this night have gone so badly? All he wanted was to pull her into his arms.

He got into the car. "Hey."

"Hi. Thanks, by the way."

"Of course."

Leona threw the car into reverse and pulled out into the street. They drove back in silence, apart from the quiet burbling of the radio. They were almost at Simon's house when she spoke.

"Come to my place. Please."

He could tell she was in a dangerous mood, and he had honestly no idea what he was getting into if he agreed, but—

"Okay."

She released a breath. They parked behind her building, and he followed her inside, his pulse racing.

Upstairs, in her lavender dining room, Leona turned to him. "Simon…thanks. Seriously. Thanks for listening, and for letting me leave. And getting the check, obviously."

"I wish there was something else I could do."

She stepped in close, reminding him that the kiss in the car had been nowhere near enough. He'd been obsessing about her for days. Her striptease. Her dirty talk.

"There is something you can do. If you're ready."

"What?" His chest tightened. Did she want to cuff him again? Did he mind if she did?

"I want this." She took his hand. His breath caught.

She brought his hand to her throat and pressed it against her soft skin. Her eyes fluttered shut, and she sighed as if she'd been aching for this just as much as he had.

Earlier, he'd been unable to resist running his fingertips across her pretty neck. He'd toed the line just like he always did, touching her no more than any man would touch a woman he was about to kiss. It had still been different, because she *knew*. But now…

Now his knees were actually shaking. He couldn't remember ever being this nervous about anything, even the police exam. He was so nervous he wasn't even turned on; it was more like being hyper-aware, with every inch of his skin zinging with electricity. They couldn't do this. It was wrong, it was sick, it was—

"Tell me I'm yours," she murmured, her eyes still closed, her graceful hands pressing his fingers more firmly against her skin.

"You're mine," he whispered, his voice trembling. He stroked her throat with his thumb, and she sank into his touch.

He added his other hand, and she dropped her arms to her side to make space for him.

A low heat grew inside him, burning away some of his fear. "You're mine. My woman."

"Yes," she breathed. "Yes."

His heart thudding, he pressed his thumbs to the underside of her jaw. When she didn't flinch away, he guided her face upward. "I can make you do anything I want."

"Anything."

He brought his mouth down to hers and kissed her. Still toeing that line, but God, he loved the curve of her lips, her scent, her taste.

"Simon," she groaned against his mouth, "I want you to hurt me."

He snatched his hands away from her throat, his body turning to ice. "What?"

"Not like that," she said. "I'll show you."

"I can't hurt—"

"Please." Her eyes were solemn. "When I sub, I like—I like pain. It's not dangerous. Although…I understand if you don't want to."

Simon stared at her, speechless. She liked pain. She liked to be Dominant. She liked it when he—when he put his hands on her. How could he ever be enough for her?

He couldn't, of course. Looking at her now, he realized it didn't matter. As long as she wanted him around, he'd do his best to make her happy.

"Show me."

She studied him for a moment, then nodded and led him into her opulent bedroom. She ducked inside her closet and returned holding a black, leather-wrapped riding crop.

Simon took it with numb hands. It was sturdier than he would have liked.

She pulled her top off over her head and let it drop to the floor. Her heels were next, followed by her jeans, her bra, and her panties.

"You don't have to do it hard. Just flick your wrist. Anywhere on the shoulder blades or ass is fine. Just not on the spine or other bones." Her eyes met his. "My safe word is 'mercy.'"

Before he could do more than nod, she turned away and knelt on the floor in front of her bed. Gathering up her long hair, she drew it over one shoulder, exposing her pale back to him. She sat down on her heels and stacked her forearms on the edge of the mattress, bowing her head very slightly. The position accentuated the subtle hourglass of her waist and hips, the curves of her ass. He'd never seen anything so beautiful in his life.

So…now he had to hit her. That was what she wanted.

His palms were sweating. What would the guys at the station think, if they knew what he was doing?

It didn't matter. She needed this, and in the depths of his subconscious, he understood that need. He could do this for her.

Tightening his grip on the crop, he stepped forward. Should he speak? He didn't know what to say, but he wanted to let her know it was coming. Touching the crop's spatulate leather tip to her skin, he drew it down the ridges of her spine. She shivered.

Taking a deep breath, Simon brought the crop up and flicked his wrist toward her right shoulder blade, just like she'd said. The crop swished through the air and hit her skin with a sharp *whap*. She flinched, her breath catching in a gasp. Almost immediately, the gasp dissolved into a low moan. It was the sexiest thing he'd ever heard, and he was suddenly incredibly turned on.

Leona, what are you doing to me?

He hit her again, and she moaned again. He licked his lips, steeled himself, and brought the crop down a third time. "You're mine," he told her. This time, her moan grew even more tortured.

"I'm yours," she panted. "All yours."

"If I told you to suck my cock right now, you'd do it."

"I'd have to, or you'd punish me."

"I'd beat you," he growled, "until you begged to suck me off."

Where the fuck had that come from? He could never have imagined something so awful coming out of his mouth. Instead of looking horrified, Leona shivered, her face pressed into the side of the mattress, her eyes tightly closed. "I'd beg you…I'd beg for your cock."

Three pink blotches marred her perfect back. He didn't want to risk leaving a bruise, but he could tell it was too soon to stop. From the way she was reacting, he had to be doing something right.

"Get up." The words came out as a hoarse command. "Lean across the bed."

She was high on him, on his harsh voice and the sting of the crop in his hands. He was a natural Dominant—so controlled in his ruthlessness, his harsh orders utterly perfect.

She stood and draped her upper body across the mattress, just as he'd told her to do. Her legs were trembling, very slightly. She loved dirty talk of all kinds, and she liked pain, but obeying someone else, ceding her body, the actual process of submission…that was always so difficult for her.

She trusted Simon, in and outside of bed, and that counted for a lot. She *wanted* to sub for him, lose herself in the pain, let him explore his urges.

She was going to obey, no matter how difficult it was.

The crop came down again, this time on her ass. A renewed surge of mingled pain and pleasure shot through her.

"Simon," she gasped, breathless. "You're incredible."

The crop slapped her on the ass once more. "Beg me for it, then."

"Fuck me. Please."

Whap.

"Spread your legs," he ordered her. Tendrils of fear curled inside her. *I trust him*, she reminded herself. *I want this.*

She edged her legs apart. Leaning over her, he kissed her upper back, where her skin was most raw. His big hand cupped her sex, and she froze, waiting to see what he would do. Slowly, deliberately, he stroked her, big circles at first, until slowly she started to relax, to let him take this intimacy. He narrowed his focus to her clit until she was squirming and panting on the bed.

He slid two fingers inside her, fucking her with his hand while he kissed her shoulders and back. "You're so wet," he rasped, his breath warming her shoulder.

"Just for you." Why did she crave his possessiveness?

With his free hand, he swept her hair away from her neck. Her tortured nerves caught fire with anticipation. "Yes," she moaned, "yes, *yes*."

His hand encircled her throat, bringing her higher than ever. She'd never been into choking before, but now nothing was more erotic. She shook with desire for him.

"Fuck me," she begged, and this time, she meant it.

His weight lifted off the bed. Her mind hazy, Leona watched him stripping off his shirt and jeans. He had a beautiful body—all lean, well-defined muscle, with athletic shoulders and a flat, ridged stomach.

"Condoms?" His cheeks were flushed, his eyes blazing with desire, and he was clenching and unclenching his big hands.

"Nightstand." Leona started to push herself up, but he shook his head.

"You stay put."

He found the condoms and rolled one on. Climbing back onto the bed, he lay down on his side behind her and dragged a callused palm up the curve of her waist. He reached her breasts and squeezed, while his lips pressed against the back of her neck, each kiss purposeful and proprietary, as if he were staking out a territory on her body. She wished it were safe for him to put his hands on her throat again. *Collar*, she reminded herself, as she opened her neck up to his kisses. *Next time.*

"Tell me you want me." His breath was hot in her ear.

"More than anyone."

"Good." He pushed inside her. She twisted her hips to bring him all the way in, until he filled her completely, stretching her open. God, he was big, and thick. She sagged against the hard planes of his body, letting him take her over.

His fingers found her clit again, igniting her skin. He nipped her ear, and that alone almost did her in.

"I want you to scream my name when you come," he murmured. "I want you to scream so loud you wake up the whole fucking town."

"No problem," she gasped.

He chuckled, but balanced his laugh with a harder

thrust, more pressure on her clit. She was so close, her whole body was tightening, releasing, tightening—and all she could think about was how well he fit inside her, how skillful his hands were. His *hands*—his hands were—

"Simon—" she cried, shaking, "oh, Simon, yes, yes—"

The words dissolved into a scream as she climaxed, her inner muscles clenching around him. While she struggled to regain her breath, he kissed her face and hair, ran his hand up her thigh and the curve of her hip. "Jesus, Leona." His voice was thick and rough.

"More," she pleaded. "Fuck me hard."

With a growl, he guided her downward onto her stomach, trapping her between his body and the silky sheets. Kissing her cheek and temples, he fucked her slowly at first, but then harder and faster, his breathing growing more strained. She watched him over her shoulder while he propped himself up on his forearms, the muscles in his arms and shoulders bulging. His cheekbones and throat flushed deep red. "So beautiful…" he groaned, into her hair. "Leona…you're so beautiful."

She had to wonder if he knew he was saying it. The words were tantalizing, as sharp and painful in their own way as the crop.

His body tensing, he groaned again, this time wordless, low, and harsh. His expression was pained, the muscles in his jaw clenching. She had another one of those bewildered moments where she couldn't believe she was seeing him like this. He was so wholesome, so classically good-looking; watching him fall apart made her feel even more depraved than usual.

She wished she had seduced him years ago.

The tension left his body in slow pulses. Afterward,

he kissed her shoulder blades, letting his lips linger on her stinging skin.

The gentle gesture should have been soothing—it *was* soothing, it truly was, but as her pleasure faded, she felt out of sorts, the way she always did after she subbed.

She had asked for this, she reminded herself. She'd chosen it. Still…she felt a little off, as if she had put on someone else's clothes. They fit—she *could* wear them. But they weren't hers.

Simon pushed himself off her and got to his feet. Leona rolled onto her side, still admiring him. He had the body of a man who couldn't relax: tight bundles of muscle, coiled around bone.

He came back to the bed and sat down on the edge of the mattress, resting his hands on his knees. "Wow," he said, half to himself. "That was…wow."

She propped herself up on one arm and resisted the urge to draw her free hand along the lines of his gorgeous obliques. "Did it feel a little more natural this time?"

"Natural?" He glanced over his shoulder at her, his brow creasing. "I don't know about natural. It was… different."

He wasn't shutting down or running off, which was a good sign. He probably needed more time to get accustomed to acting on his Dominant urges, especially if he'd been suppressing them for a long time. She'd never had that problem, but she used to know people who did.

"And for you…" His eyes concerned, he brushed a strand of her hair from her face. "It was all right?"

"It was amazing."

"You tensed up, at one point," he said carefully. "After

I told you to stand up, you seemed…anxious."

So that was why he'd slowed things down. She knew how observant he was, but still, she was… What was the word? Touched. She was touched that he'd been paying such close attention to her.

"I was fine," she assured him. "But thanks for asking. You are sweet."

"'Sweet,'" he said, with a wry smile. "Great. Really sexy."

"It is sexy." She slid off the bed and fetched her robe. It was impossibly short and made of black silk; it always made her feel better. She slipped it on over her bare skin, then pulled her hair up into a bun on the top of her head and stuck it in place with a silver hairpin. "You know, I'm finally hungry. How would you feel about a snack?"

Simon's gaze fixed on the hem of her robe, which just skimmed her hips. Shaking himself a little, he stood up and reached for his jeans. "Sure, I could eat."

She wandered into her kitchen, barefoot. Wearing his jeans and undershirt, Simon followed a few steps behind. She poked around her kitchen cupboards, looking for ingredients. "Do you like crepes?"

"Never had them."

"First time for everything."

"No kidding," he said dryly.

Chapter Nine

SIMON'S HEAD WAS STILL SPINNING from what they'd done. He felt weird and shaky, but also… good. Really good. More alive than he'd felt in years. Touching her throat during sex had gone all right. Not as scary as he'd expected it to be. And the way she'd screamed his name had been a high school fantasy come to life—except that it had been more raw and emotional than anything he'd ever been able to dream up.

He hoped this hadn't been just another fuck to her.

Nervous, Simon glanced across the kitchen. The absurdly tiny robe brushed the underside of her ass as she reached up into a cabinet and pulled down a container of flour. How many guys had seen her in this robe? Fucked her in it?

He shouldn't be jealous, he knew that. She'd been right to call him out on that a few days ago, but he still wanted her all to himself.

"How did you get into this kind of stuff?" The question popped out of his mouth by accident. He shouldn't have asked. It was none of his business.

Leona, though, didn't look offended. Her expression thoughtful, she pulled a mixing bowl out of a cupboard and cracked a couple of eggs into it. "Do you remember David Bourdon? He was in high school with us."

This was the last thing he'd expected to hear. David Bourdon's arrogant, square-jawed face leapt up from Simon's memory. "He was a jock. Football team. A junior when we were freshman." He hesitated, an unpleasant squirm of jealousy in his stomach. "Did you guys date? I never heard about it."

"We didn't date."

"Then what?"

"Well…" She added some milk to her bowl of eggs and whisked it all together, her movements easy and practiced. "I used to give David a hard time, you know. All the time. Tease him, sort of rough him up, that kind of thing, even though he was way more popular than me, and older than me, too. I was trying to flirt with him, I think, but really awkwardly."

This didn't surprise Simon too much, though he doubted she'd been awkward as much as a force of nature. He remembered all too well how dangerous Leona had been at fourteen. David Bourdon had never stood a chance.

"Anyway, I think he saw something in me. He invited me over one weekend, while his folks were out playing golf or something." She shrugged. "We saw each other almost every Sunday for over a year."

Simon tried to swallow his surprise. "You mean for sex? And he was…into this kind of stuff?"

Still not quite looking at him, she added flour and sugar to the eggs and milk. A strand of black hair escaped from her bun and fell alongside her face. He wanted to touch it.

"I'm only telling you this," she said, "because he moved to North Carolina years ago. Otherwise, I wouldn't."

"All right," he said cautiously.

"Dave was a sub. He was in the closet—extremely in the closet—but he knew how he was. He liked to be punished. Hog-tied, beaten, that kind of thing."

"Jesus." Simon's face grew hot. A big jock like Bourdon, a sub. And Leona… "So, back when I was trying to cop a feel in the movie theater, you were tying up an MVP football player and beating him with a—I don't even know."

"A cane, usually," she said softly.

"A *cane*," Simon echoed, incredulous. "Doesn't that fucking *hurt*? I'm sorry," he said at once, "I don't mean to sound…" Like a judgmental prick. Too late.

"It definitely hurts. But in a good way. There are… techniques. In how you do it, and in how the sub accepts the pain."

"That's a lot of self-control for a fourteen year old. To use the right technique."

"It wasn't that hard for me. It was fun. I was good at it, the way other people are good at sports."

He thought of her standing on the very top step of the stepladder in her shop, utterly at ease. She'd always been poised and graceful, and she was a lot stronger than she looked. He could picture her tying up Bourdon and beating the hell out of him without breaking a sweat.

"So what happened?" he asked, flushing. "If you guys were so compatible."

"He met a girl he wanted to date." Leona turned away from her mixing bowl and rifled through her cabinets. "You know, actual dating? He wasn't out to her, though. He wanted to keep seeing me on the side, but I said no. Didn't want to help him cheat on her."

Simon struggled with a flash of anger. "That was

decent of you," he managed, because it was. Decent of her, terrible of Bourdon.

She just shrugged again. "I tried to convince him to come out of the closet to his new girl, but he said she wouldn't date him if she knew. Anyway, that was when I decided to wait until I could do this properly. When I was eighteen, I joined some BDSM groups and started going to parties and private clubs. That way, it would all be above-board. Open, honest, you know."

Something about this response struck him as strange. It was mature of her to make that decision as a teenager, but he knew her well enough to know that she'd always been mature for her age.

Maybe it was that her life sounded so…lonely. A secret relationship with a man who dumped her for another girl—a girl he couldn't even be honest with. And then BDSM groups, whatever those were, where she could meet people for sex.

"Is that how you met guys you could actually date?" Simon asked. "You know, not assholes who made you keep it a secret?"

Leona turned toward him, her eyebrows rising.

"Dave wasn't an asshole," she said, but she glanced down as she said it. "He was…unhappy. He hated himself."

Simon took a step toward her. Leona was tall, but with both of them barefoot, he had a good four inches or so on her. She seemed somehow more vulnerable without her usual heels on. And she was hiding something, he knew it, even though he didn't know what that could be.

"You didn't answer my question."

"I haven't…"

"You haven't what?"

"I've never—I've never dated anyone. Ever." She didn't blush. Her tone was matter-of-fact. But she still wouldn't look at him. "The closest I've ever come to it was when I used to see Liam."

"Liam?"

Leona turned back to her batter, and Simon let her go, as much as he didn't want to. "He was an older man from upstate New York. A sub. I met him at a party."

Another sub, Simon thought, with a confused stab of emotions. She'd told him she liked variety, but both of her long-term sexual partners had been submissive.

"We saw each other once or twice a week for a year and a half, just for sex," she was saying. "He always wanted to give me gifts, take me out to dinner, but I always said no."

"Why?"

She poured a ladleful of batter onto a frying pan and spread it out across the pan, while the batter sizzled and hissed. "I don't know."

"You must have some idea." Simon moved closer to her again. He didn't know how much longer he could last without touching her.

"I really don't." She sounded resigned. "I didn't mind the age difference. He was funny, nice… If anything, he was *too* nice."

"Oh." He sighed. "Yeah, I get that."

She glanced over her shoulder at him, her gray eyes curious. "You do?"

"Yeah, my ex, Jen, was like that. I was always hurting her feelings, no matter how hard I tried not to."

"That doesn't sound like you."

Simon leaned against the counter next to her. "It was never intentional. I was always running late, or not getting her the right thing for her birthday, or saying the wrong thing."

For the two years that he and Jen were dating, all he did was disappoint her and make her sad. He finally broke up with her because he couldn't stand feeling like such a failure. Years later, he was still ashamed of how he had treated her.

"That doesn't sound like you, either."

Surprised, Simon glanced at Leona, who was scraping the crepe up off her pan and adding new batter.

"Do I know her?" she asked. "Your ex."

"Maybe. She was a year below us in high school. Jennifer Sanders."

Leona laughed. "No wonder! She always seemed like a princess." She cast him a teasing smile. "Blondes, huh? What're you doing with me?"

"She was the exception. I usually go for brunettes." More accurately, he usually went for Leona.

"All right, who else? You said there were three."

"You can't seriously want to talk about this." And he didn't want to tell her about his series of failures.

"You asked me about my history," she pointed out, as she flipped the new crepe.

"Mine's a lot less interesting." *Interesting* wasn't a strong enough word to describe Leona's past.

She gestured playfully with her crepe spatula for him to talk. Just to annoy her, he caught her wrist. Her eyes sparkled with challenge, but she didn't pull away. She let him slide his thumb along the delicate skin below her palm.

"First was Mallory, in high school," he said. "You were in math class with us, if you remember." Mallory had hated Leona. Simon had a feeling she'd noticed the way he looked at her.

"Math Class Mallory. Okay. And after her?"

"That was Jen. I met her in college, but it took us a while to get serious. I was twenty-three when we started dating, I think."

"Princess Jennifer. Got it." Leona grinned.

Simon let that one go. "About a year after I broke up with Jen, I started dating Ashley Stefano." Whatever you could say about the other two, Ashley was rock-solid proof that Simon was inept at relationships. She was clever, funny, pretty, everything a man could ask for. "I liked Ashley."

Leona tugged her wrist out of his grip and loosened the crepe from its pan. It was darker than the others, since he'd kept her from taking it off the heat. It still looked delicious, if not quite as delicious as Leona herself. The neckline of her robe had fallen open, revealing her collarbone and one white shoulder.

"So, what happened?" she asked. "Why did you guys break up, if you liked her so much?"

Could she possibly be jealous?

Not a chance. This was Leona.

He shrugged. "Honestly? The sex was terrible." He had never said that part out loud before. Even when he'd eventually broken up with her, he'd given Ashley a line about not being ready for commitment. She must have known, though. It had been terrible for her, too.

"You never did anything kinky with her?"

"No."

Sometime after the failed experiment with acting out Ashley's cop fantasies, Ashley had asked him if there was anything he wanted to do in bed. He'd shrugged it off. Those unnerving urges he'd had over the years, he'd kept to himself. How could he have told her the truth? It would've been like Mallory all over again.

He'd always figured he'd never be able to be honest

with anyone. He could hardly stand to be honest with himself.

But…Leona knew the truth. She wasn't afraid of him. Wasn't disgusted by him. It had gone okay, or even better than okay.

It made him wonder what else they could do together. What else she'd done before. What she liked. Everything about her.

Leona hadn't thought about Liam in a long time. She'd been only twenty-two, some thirteen years younger than him, when they'd first started hooking up. He was sexy, though, and kind. Too kind, like she'd told Simon. Unlike Simon's ex, Liam didn't constantly have hurt feelings. The problem with Liam was that he'd submitted to her in every way, not just in bed. She could've crushed him under the strength of her will without even realizing what she was doing.

"So, because you don't date…" Simon said slowly from behind her. "That's why you got so uncomfortable when I asked you out?"

"Did I? And here I thought I was playing it cool." She smiled over her shoulder at him, but he didn't smile back. He stepped toward her, practically pinning her to the oven. His hands found her waist, and his body brushed against her back.

"Why did you say yes?" His voice was tight, his breath warm on her ear.

"How can you even ask that?"

His lips brushed her cheekbone. At this rate, she was going to burn a second crepe.

"Tell me."

"Well, first of all, I haven't done any of that stuff in two years. Two *long* fucking years, Simon."

"I'm glad I could break your dry spell." Simon pulled the hairpin from her bun. He caught her hair before it could fall and wound it around his hand, tugging it to one side, not too gently. Pleasure frissoned through her. "Is that the only reason? Because it's been a while?"

"You know it isn't." The words tumbled out almost by accident, as if Simon had freed them from her chest the same way he'd freed her hair from its pin.

Keep it together, Leona. She reached across the stove to turn off the burner and left her hand on the knob, bracing herself above the stove's simmering warmth, soaking herself in the crepe's sweet, vanilla smell. She was probably still out of sorts from subbing. Or from seeing her mother.

Or it could just be from *Simon*. He'd gotten under her skin somehow. He was cranky and stern and sweet and caring, all at once. He was…

A challenge.

She flinched as if the thought had burned her.

"Leona…" Simon breathed her name into her ear. "Tell me about what you did with those guys. David Bourdon, and that other guy. Liam."

"Why?"

"Because I want you to do it to me."

Warmth flooded her belly, and her breath pressed out of her in a little gasp. The thought of Simon with his arms tied behind him, his muscles flexing, sweat standing out on his skin. No—she couldn't. Last time, he'd been upset with her.

Besides, between his fetish and the way he'd topped her tonight, he had to be a closet Dom, despite what she had thought at first.

"You're not a sub, Simon." Her voice shook.

With a sigh, he released her hair. It fell across her shoulders, dragging her silk robe across the still-tender skin of her back.

"I don't know what I am." One of his hands still gripped her waist. His fingers tightened as he spoke. "I've never *done* anything like this before. I want to...I want to learn about it. Try it out. With you."

"Simon...I'm not your sex ed teacher."

"No, that was Mr. Harris." She could hear his smile. "You were in that class with me. Now I know why you always looked so bored."

"I was just trying not to stare at Mr. Harris' ear hair." She giggled helplessly. "How can one person have *so much* of it?"

"Good question," he agreed. "So thick and black, too."

"Very distressing," she said. "They must have made him our teacher on purpose, to turn us off sex. Abstinence-only ear hair."

"Thank God it didn't work," he said. "But then again, nothing would've turned me off sex while you were in the room."

She stiffened. "You mean back then? You had a thing for me in high school?"

"I've always had a thing for you," he murmured, kissing her jaw and cheek.

"I had no idea," she said, torn between flattery and a nagging sense of discomfort.

"Tell me what you did with those guys." His voice pitched low and husky. Fencing her in with his arms, he pressed his body against her back. He was hard again. The realization made her light-headed.

"I've already told you about David. And I'm not

going to cane you, Simon. You wouldn't like it."

"Fine." His mouth moved to her neck, his kisses the softest touches of his lips to her skin. "What did you do with Liam?"

His sexy, masculine scent stole through the crepe's vanilla. With his body pressed against her like this, his erection insistent against her ass, she was losing her resolve.

Leona tried to steady her breathing. "Liam was into body worship. He liked to—to kiss my feet while I read the paper. That kind of thing."

Simon made a considering, thoughtful sound deep in his throat. "I can do that." The words came out careful, deliberate, and Leona, suddenly frustrated, turned to face him, even though he'd pressed her so tightly against the stove there was hardly room to move.

Looking up at him, she saw the intensity in his pale blue eyes. His skin and sensual mouth were flushed with lust. She licked her lips, trying to find her ability to speak. "You're serious."

"I'm serious." His gaze dropped to her lips, then to the neckline of her robe. "Let me worship you."

"I don't want it to be like… The first time, you didn't like it."

"I did like it," he said softly. "I was just…a little overwhelmed."

She gave a rueful laugh, almost an exhale. "I'm sorry."

"Don't be." He brought his hand to her face and stroked her cheek with his thumb. "Leona…"

She couldn't resist him anymore—not with the way he was looking at her now, or the way he'd just breathed her name.

"Okay," she said. "Come with me."

Simon stepped back, dropping his hands to his sides,

and she didn't look at him again as she walked to her kitchen table. She turned a chair around to face away from the table and sat down with her legs apart.

His gaze snapped to where the short robe just covered her sex, and he prowled toward her.

"Kneel." Usually, topping someone made her feel calm, even a little aloof, like a director, guiding her sub through his pain or his punishment until he found what he was looking for. With Simon, it was different. Everything was different.

Simon got down on his knees in front of her, and her heart skipped a beat.

"Take off your shirt."

He glanced up at her face. He'd pushed her for this, but now his eyes were nervous. His hands moved to the hem of his shirt. Slowly, he pulled it over his head and dropped it onto the floor behind him, the muscles in his arms and shoulders flexing. The *body* on this man, she thought, for the hundredth time.

"Good," she told him. His expression calmed a little. She took a moment to study him while she debated how much she should instruct him. Liam had been perfectly happy to kiss and lick her skin for ages while she'd totally ignored him, but she didn't think that was what Simon wanted. He liked being the focus of her attention as much as she liked being the focus of his.

Decisively, Leona lifted her foot and set it down on his hard, sculpted shoulder.

"Kiss my ankle. Do it right." Never mind the fact that with that mouth, he could do no wrong.

With one hand on the outside of her leg to steady her, he brushed his lips across her anklebone. His lips parting, he sucked at the nub of the bone, then moved lower to kiss and lick her instep.

"You're lucky you get to touch me like this." She shaded her tone darker, hoping to cue him into the dirty talk part of the game.

"I know."

The gravity in his voice made her impossibly wet. She'd always appreciated subs who were good actors. They helped her believe she wasn't peripheral to the scene, as if she couldn't be easily replaced by any other half-competent Domme.

But Simon...was Simon acting?

He drew his tongue along the top of her foot to her toes, painted bright red. As he turned his head, the muscles in his neck bulged. She wanted to trace her fingernail down his neck to his chest, his flat stomach. *Later*, she told herself. For now, they were playing a different game.

"Tell me how lucky you are," she said.

"I'd be even luckier if you opened your robe."

"Insolent pet," she chided him, but she couldn't help smiling. She untied her belt and let the silk slip open.

Simon groaned as his gaze slid over her body.

"Keep kissing me," she ordered him, though she loved the way he was looking at her. "Higher."

His eyes closing, he took a deep, shuddering breath. He pressed his lips to her calf. Inching forward on his knees, he trailed kisses up her leg. His erection had to be hurting him by now, straining against denim. Leona came up with her next order.

"Unzip your jeans."

His eyes opening, he cast her a puzzled, apprehensive look. But one large hand went to his fly, undid the button, drew the zipper down. His jeans gapped away from his abs.

"Pull them down." She pressed her heel into his

shoulder, not hard enough to hurt, just hard enough to remind him that she was there. "Your boxers, too."

Still up on his knees, he lowered his jeans and boxers below his hips, freeing his cock. An appreciative purr escaped Leona's mouth, though she knew she should stay in character. He was just so beautiful, kneeling in front of her like this, fully erect, with his chest and stomach bare.

"Take your cock in your hand, but don't stroke it." His flush darkened—a blush, Leona realized fondly. He was embarrassed to touch himself in front of her, even though she'd done the same for him, at his request.

Slowly, his thumb and forefinger slid around the base of his cock. He brought his hand upward and wrapped the rest of his fingers around his length, taking a shallow breath in through his nose. She could sense how badly he wanted to stroke himself, but he inched forward on his knees again and brought his mouth to her inner thigh. She let her foot slide off his shoulder and down his back. Normally, she'd be in heels, the better to prick her sub with her stilettos. Under the sole of her foot, his warm skin was strangely intimate.

"You smell incredible," Simon murmured, kissing his way up her thigh. His shoulders trembling, he kissed the inside of her hip.

"Keep talking." The point of this particular game was to prolong it. Leona leaned back in the chair, pretending to be unaffected by him. "Don't stroke."

"I want—I want to eat you out."

"I told you to keep talking."

"Fine," he said peevishly. Leona smiled. Typical Simon. Even more typical, he disobeyed her and kissed her right on the clit, making her squirm.

"If you want me to talk, I'll talk," he said, kissing her

there again. "You have…the prettiest smile I've ever seen." Simon punctuated the words with a teasing lick. "Your eyes are, like…pure gray, like rain clouds." He licked her more firmly. She groaned in spite of herself, and so did he.

"Simon…" Rain clouds? He didn't need to be so elaborate with her. She knew it was just a game.

"You taste even better than you smell," Simon said. "The way you screamed my name tonight, when you came…I've fantasized about that since high school, and it was still better than anything I ever could've imagined." He stroked her with his tongue, sucked her gently into his mouth, stroked her again. Pleasure spiked through her. Dimly, she thought: *high school?*

He slid a finger inside her. She gasped, her back arching.

"I want you so much," he muttered. "I could fuck you all night and it still wouldn't be enough." His kisses grew more focused and deliberate, somehow responding to all of her smallest, unconscious movements, the better to tease the pleasure out of her. She was already climbing recklessly toward orgasm, despite her intentions to prolong the game. She should've realized he'd be amazing at oral, since he'd been so good with his hands earlier that night. Those patient, possessive hands. His ex-girlfriends had been lucky women.

"Is this good for you?" he asked. His hesitance just made her wetter. Did he not know how incredible he was at this? Surely one of his exes had told him?

"It's—ohh." He kissed her again, and all her bones turned to liquid. *That mouth,* she thought, sinking back against the chair, her head spinning. "You're—the best, ever."

He froze, his shoulders tensing. "I'm…oh. Fuck."

She started to sit up, worried she had offended him. He might not like being compared to other men, even if he came out on top. Before she could speak, he kissed her again, getting into a rhythm that made her want to scream.

"Stroke yourself now," she panted, desperate to see him getting close, too, since she was so close. From this angle, she couldn't see his cock, just the flexing of his shoulder and bicep as his hand moved.

Simon moaned into her skin, ragged, deliciously vulnerable. She was slouched back in the chair with her leg still draped over his shoulder, one hand in his hair and the other hanging by her side. She had a vague sense that she should give him a few more orders, slow down the game, tease him the way she suspected he wanted to be teased; but she couldn't. The tension inside her was building exponentially, and she kept panting and making little sounds that a self-controlled Domme would not make. The orgasm took hold of her, shaking her whole body and pulling a scream from her throat.

Bit by bit, it released her. She began regaining control over her body, but her mind was still dazed, and she was still gasping, "Oh, Simon, oh, Simon…"

His hand gripping her hip, he pressed his forehead into her thigh. His jaw clenched while sweat beaded along his temple. The sight of him was even more dazzling than the orgasm.

Wrapping his arm around her waist as if he needed her to steady him, he groaned, deep and guttural, into her inner thigh. A spasm ran through his shoulders as he thrust harder into his hand, once, twice more. He was magnificent.

His spasms faded, leaving him gasping for breath

between her legs, his head still pillowed on her lap. He didn't pull away, and she didn't want him to.

She smoothed his hair, swept the sweat away from his temple. She'd told him he was lucky to touch her, but she knew she was the lucky one.

Chapter Ten

SIMON COULDN'T TEAR HIMSELF AWAY from Leona's silky skin, scented like ginger and sex. He could die a happy man like this, with her legs twined around his body and her waist tucked in the crook of his arm.

With a sigh, he lifted his head from her lap, but he didn't release her. He wanted to start kissing her again. Worshipping her. She had been so cold and collected at first, his forbidding fairy queen, only to unravel under his touch.

He kissed the top of her thigh, trying to come up with a name for the emotions sifting through him.

She stirred at his kiss, sighing, and a bolt of heat went straight to his groin. He still couldn't believe the way she'd writhed when he'd kissed her—or what she'd said. *The best. Ever.*

How could that be true? Simon wasn't anything special. Not like she was.

It must have just been…something to say. Something to get him to come harder.

"Leona…"

"What is it?" Her voice was soft, affectionate.

Simon forced a smile. "I'm sorry about your floor."

She laughed. "I told you to do it, didn't I?"

"I couldn't have held out much longer, anyway."
"You liked it?"
"Yes." He kissed her belly. *Like* wasn't the word. "Wish I had another round in me."

"Maybe tomorrow," she said mildly. Frowning, he buttoned his fly with clumsy fingers, wishing he knew what that meant to her.

"How about that crepe, finally?" She smiled at him, her eyes full of sweetness.

"Sure." He should go home—he knew that. Just a few more minutes.

Simon went hunting for his T-shirt and pulled it on. He found some paper towels and gave her floor a quick once-over before sitting down at her kitchen table. Leona handed him a glossy red plate with a rolled-up crepe in the center, sprinkled with powdered sugar.

"Pretty," he said.

"Thanks." Leona smiled again.

He'd been expecting something like a pancake, but it was much springier and more delicate, with the cherries in the center adding a surprising mix of tart and sweet.

Simon was still licking powdered sugar from his fingers when they finally headed downstairs. Only the moonlight trickling in through the windowpanes lit the small stairwell. He reached for her, but after their intense night together, kissing her goodnight seemed so inadequate.

"Can I see you tomorrow?" he asked.

Leona touched his shoulder. Through his thick coat, her fingers were as intangible as the moonlight. "Actually, the crafts fair is tomorrow. It goes 'til nine, if you wanted to stop by with me after work? I'm sure that's not the most exciting way to spend a Saturday night for you, but—"

"It sounds great," he said, with a rush of surprise and delight.

They made plans to meet at her shop at the end of her shift, and after a quick kiss, Simon went out into the snowy night still flushed with warmth. On his walk home, her scent lingered in his clothes and on his skin, cutting through the clean, earthy smell of the frozen brook underneath the covered bridge.

Inside his apartment, he poured himself a whiskey on the rocks and brought it into bed with him. He imagined he could still smell her, taste her. He wished he could fall asleep next to her instead of lying here alone, listening to the murmur of his tenants' television through the walls.

She hadn't turned him down when he'd asked her out again. She hadn't even hesitated, the way she normally did.

But she was almost thirty, and she'd said herself that she'd never truly dated. Not ever. The closest she'd come to dating was with that man she'd met at some kind of BDSM party, Liam. Why would she change now, for Simon of all people? Even if she did like him, the most he could hope for was probably the occasional dinner, or a crepe or two between rounds of sex.

He ought to be able to recognize that as being for the best. God knew he wasn't any good at relationships. He was too intense, too neurotic, too married to his job.

He still wanted more. As irrational as that was. Where Leona was concerned, he wanted so much more.

Nursing a cup of coffee at his desk, Simon flipped through a stack of papers he'd gone through a dozen times before. He'd come into the office at seven, even though his shift didn't start for a few more hours. It was easier to go into work than to keep fighting his constant, months-long inability to sleep.

Around midday, Mrs. O'Shea's ex-husband, who lived in Oregon, returned Simon's call about a phone interview. Penelope had described her father as a good man, and even Simon had to admit her description seemed accurate. He came across as kind, patient, and down to earth. He had a solid job working in IT, a brother in California, a sister in Toronto. His divorce from Nancy O'Shea had been amicable, and he'd been mostly single since.

After the interview, Simon reluctantly turned to the photos, first of the accident site, then of the autopsy. He rubbed his jaw, thinking about Mrs. O'Shea grinning at their class as she'd lit a strip of magnesium on fire. It had burned bright white. He wished he could remember the point she'd been trying to make, but he'd never been any good at chemistry. His vision blurred with fatigue, and he thought, again, how much he wished this hadn't happened.

Simon set the autopsy photos aside and slid one of the accident site photos back into their place. It was a dangerous turn with hardly any shoulder, and people did take it fast.

Then again, he thought, angling the photo, any unimpaired driver would've seen Mrs. O'Shea jogging at least as early as this road sign. They could've swerved, or at least braked. He was no collision reconstruction expert, but still, looking at this photo…how could the driver not have at least *tried* to brake?

Keene would say Simon was still feeling a little jumpy from the bombing. He'd tell him to let the state police handle it, wait on the report he'd been promised, and try not to let it bother him.

Simon wondered what Penelope O'Shea would say.

"Sir?" Their newest officer, Jack Miller, stood in the doorway, sweeping his free hand through his hair, which he wore just a little too long to be regulation. Jack had joined them last July, only a few weeks after the bombing. The Chief had assigned Simon to train him, but calm, methodical Jack practically trained himself. And, if he was honest, Simon hadn't had a lot of time or brainpower for their new recruit.

"This came in for you," Jack said, holding up an envelope.

Simon held out a hand, and Jack brought it to him. "Thanks."

Jack nodded and left the office before Simon could think of what else to say to him. *How's it going, are you feeling settled in now, what else can I do to help you?*

With a sigh, Simon tore open the envelope. Mrs. O'Shea's bank records. He'd been looking forward to getting them, though he didn't expect to find much here. She'd been a schoolteacher for thirty years; she wasn't going to have a lot going on financially.

As Simon skimmed the numbers, the back of his neck began to prickle.

Deposit: $25,000.

Deposit: $25,000.

Deposit: $25,000.

Every three months, going back for as many years as there were records. They came from a trust account held with a different bank.

Simon flipped back to the first page and willed the numbers to say something else, anything else, but the string of unexplained deposits didn't change. It didn't make sense. Mrs. O'Shea had never lived like a wealthy woman. Her farmhouse was nice but nothing out of the ordinary for this area. She'd always driven an old beater. As far as he knew, she'd never taken expensive vacations, and she'd had no expensive hobbies.

He could've sworn Penelope would've told him about her mother's money, if she'd known. Penelope seemed like an honest woman, and exceptionally savvy, too. A woman it would be hard to keep secrets from. She would've realized that wealth could have made her mother into a target, especially if that money came from something—he hated to even think it—illicit.

He'd always known that any intentional act could be played off as an accident. But despite his occasional suspicions, he had not actually thought... Something like this, in Grenton...

It had to have been an accident. As terrible as that was, the alternative was so much worse.

Chapter Eleven

THE VASE WAS A BLOWN-GLASS monstrosity made of admittedly lovely sparkling blue and purple swirls. Leona wrapped both arms around it, barely able to touch her fingertips together, and heaved it into the air.

"Oh, my goodness, do you need help?" Margie paused mid-stride by the door into the back room. Her hair was in disarray, and she had shadows under her eyes.

"I've got it now," Leona said, tottering slightly. "Thanks, though. You feeling any better?"

"A little." Margie smoothed her hair self-consciously, and Leona felt a pang of worry for her. They'd known each other for years, but Margie was as private as Leona.

"That shirt looks fabulous on you," Leona told her, letting some of the vase's weight sink against her hip.

Margie gave her a wan smile. "You better go set that down."

"Let me know if you need any coverage, all right? Or anything else."

Margie nodded and slipped away into the back room. Leona, peering over the top of the vase, headed out onto the floor, where two of the tourists who'd wandered in from the crafts festival were waiting for her.

"What do you think?" Leona asked, setting it down, very carefully, on the table next to its green and blue mate. "They make a terrific set, don't they? Very..." *Back-breaking*, she thought. "Eye-catching," she suggested.

"Yes! *Very* eye-catching," one of the women exclaimed. "But how on earth would we get them home?"

"We can ship—"

The door to Leona's shop opened, and she lost track of what she was saying. Simon walked in, still in uniform, his face tight with exhaustion. She'd thought he was doing crowd control for the crafts fair all afternoon, but there was no way that could have made him look so sad.

"We can ship it to you," Leona said to her customers, "at a small additional expense, well worth it for a beautiful set. I'm—I'm so sorry, I'll be right back." They were still admiring the vases and hardly noticed her leave.

"Sorry I'm late," he said, before she could speak. "I still have to change, too, obviously, but—"

"What's wrong?" Leona asked.

"It's—wait, aren't you pissed off?"

"What do you mean? What would I be pissed off about?"

"It's six o'clock. I'm an hour late."

"I didn't even notice."

"You worked an extra hour without even noticing?" Simon's mouth twitched into a ghost of a smile. "You really need to buy this shop."

"Hang on, be right back." Leona's customers were now smiling at her expectantly. Plastering a big smile on her face, she hurried back over to them. "I'm sorry about the delay. How do you feel about the vases?"

"We love them," one of the women enthused. "Is everything okay?" she added, with a glance at Simon, who was standing in the middle of the store, one hand resting on his gun belt. He was obviously trying hard to look interested in a display of hand-made miniature Christmas trees, but it was spectacularly unconvincing. Leona had another one of those funny little moments of affection for him, mixed in with worry.

"Everything's fine," she assured her customers. "He's not here on police business or anything. He's my…" Boyfriend? They were trying out a couple of dates; that didn't make him her boyfriend.

On the other hand, he wasn't just her lover, and he certainly wasn't her sub.

"He's my friend," she concluded lamely.

The two women both beamed at her. "Isn't that nice," one of them said, just as the other said, "What a charming little town!"

Leona blushed, which was a first for her. She heaved one of the vases over to the counter, where Paul was working on the register.

"I see your police officer friend is here again," Paul said, as she set the vase down on the counter. He waggled his eyebrows at her over the top of the vase.

"Oh, Lord," she said. "First the customers, and now you."

Paul grinned. "I never get to meet your beaus. This is a new experience for me."

Me, too, she thought. Last night, she'd been so happy, so eager to spend more time with him, it hadn't even occurred to her that people in town would see them together and make assumptions.

"He seems nice," Paul added, with a thoughtful

glance at Simon. "Is he good enough for you, Leona?"

"Of course he is," she said, indignant. "If anything, he's too good for—"

Paul's grin widened, and her face burned even more. "You tricked me," she said. "That's low, Paul."

He chuckled, but she did not. She walked back to the second vase, telling herself to calm down. She should be glad Paul liked Simon. She *was* glad.

After she brought the second vase to the counter, she went, inexorably, back to Simon. He smiled sadly at her. Her embarrassment fell away, leaving warm, heady feelings that were even more foreign.

"I have a couple things to tie up really quick," she told him, reaching for his hand before she realized what she was doing. "You could go home, get changed, meet me at the fair?"

"All right." Simon tightened his fingers around her palm and wrist and drew her in toward him as if he were going to kiss her. Did she mind if he kissed her in her shop, in front of Paul and Margie and all of their customers? She probably *should* mind.

Instead of kissing her, Simon stroked the curve of her palm with his callused fingertips. He released her slowly, his eyes fixed on her, and turned to leave. Leona watched him go.

Eventually, she finished up her work, said a quick goodbye to Margie and Paul, and headed out onto Cascade Street. Fluffy white tents filled the street, underneath an explosion of decorations. Christmas music warbled from speakers set up beside each tent. Thank God Paul never subjected her to that in the shop.

Once she started browsing through the tents, she stopped paying attention to the horrible music and even stopped worrying about Simon. Looking at art was the only time she truly liked humanity. What people came up with never ceased to amaze her.

She found a couple of artists she thought Paul would like to talk to for the shop, so she picked up their business cards and a couple of their works: measuring spoons engraved with butterflies and bumblebees, a dazzling dichroic glass paperweight, a set of hand-blown martini glasses in reds and pinks. She also found a bud vase made of frosted glass and steel that fit perfectly with one of her own collections, so she bought that, too. But best of all was the jewelry booth, where she found something for Simon. She slid it into her purse, her skin tingling with anticipation.

Halfway to the next tent, she noticed Simon talking to one of Grenton's other cops, Bryan Keene. Back in high school, Keene had been a macho gym rat, and, judging from the size of him, he still was. He had the loud, cocky personality to match his size, but Leona had always suspected he didn't mean to come off as strong as he did. In a way, she could sympathize.

Though Keene was in uniform, Simon had changed into jeans. Underneath his dark brown coat, which he hadn't bothered to zip up, he was wearing a tight, stretchy T-shirt. Leona wanted to lick it.

Simon glanced over at her, and his serious expression softened into a smile. She crossed the street toward them, her pulse racing.

"Leona fucking Chaisty," Keene said, with a flirtatious grin, taking in her short dress and black tights. He'd always casually flirted with her in high school, too, but only when there were other people around. Another macho, meathead thing, maybe.

"Bryan fucking Keene," she said. "How's it going?"

"Can't complain," Keene said. "How about you? Haven't seen you around in a while."

"I like to cultivate an air of mystery."

Keene laughed. "No shit."

Simon cleared his throat. "Want to look around?" he asked Leona.

Keene's eyebrows shot up. "You two here together? No fucking way."

"All right," Simon said sharply.

Keene lifted his hands in a gesture of surrender. "Okay, I wasn't implying anything." His grin widened. "Have fun tonight." He clapped Simon on the shoulder and strolled off into the crowd.

Simon frowned after him. "I swear he means well."

"I know. It's all right." She also knew that even the best of intentions wouldn't stop Keene from gossiping about them. Pretty soon, the whole town would know. They'd wonder why Simon was slumming it with her; whenever he finally ended things, they'd wonder what took him so long.

Looking at Simon, and the worried notch between his eyebrows, she decided she didn't care.

"You okay?" she asked. "What happened today?"

"I can't tell you. I wish I could."

"Something to do with Mrs. O'Shea's case?"

"Yeah."

"You told me about it once before…?"

"Yeah, but I told you the same information that we released to the press. The stuff from today is confidential."

"So it can't go beyond the station," she said.

"Right."

"Got it." She hoped some of the other cops were a little more like Simon. Keene was an all right guy, but he wasn't thoughtful like Simon was.

"What did you buy?" Simon asked, glancing at her many shopping bags.

While they wandered through a tent filled with handmade wooden wind chimes, she told him all about everything she'd found so far—leaving out what she'd gotten for him. Tonight, though, telling him stories about her day wasn't good enough. She wanted him to talk to her.

"Okay," she said, as they moved onto the next tent, "if you can't tell me about your case, can you tell me about some other part of your day?"

Simon thought for a minute. "Nope."

"All right. Something about your week, then."

"What about it?"

"I don't know. Anything."

He slanted a glance at her. "Well…my sister's coming home for Christmas break tomorrow."

"I forgot you had a sister!" she exclaimed. "Where is she? She's younger than you, right?"

"She's twenty-five. She's in grad school at University of Vermont."

"She didn't catch the law enforcement bug from you and your dad?"

"No, Julia's going to be a scientist." He smiled. "She's a lot smarter than I am."

"I doubt that," she told him. "I'm sure she's smart, but you're—"

She paused, distracted by a table crammed full of tiny wooden whirligigs, including a fisherman tipping back and forth in a boat and a fairy drifting up and down on top of a flower. They were delightful. She wished she had an excuse to buy one, but they weren't quite right for the shop or for any of her own collections.

"I'm what?" Simon asked from behind her.

"Oh, wicked smart, obviously," Leona said, watching the fairy sink back down onto her flower again.

A little boy, maybe two or three, suddenly darted in front of Leona. He was running toward the whirligigs, clearly intent on grabbing as many as he could. The whirligig artist went white, his eyes widening, as the boy's hands grasped wildly for the table.

Leona bit back a laugh, while Simon made an alarmed sound and reached for the boy. Before Simon could grab him, the boy's father swooped in, snatched him up into his arms, and carted him away, apologizing to the whirligig artist over his shoulder. The little boy's face scrunched up in dismay. Leona smiled at him sympathetically. If it had been up to her, she would have let him play with them…though not all of them at once.

"Did you see that artist's face?" she asked Simon as they walked toward the next tent. "He looked petrified, poor soul."

"That's how I feel in your shop," Simon said wryly.

"What, petrified? Or do you mean you want to touch everything?"

"Both."

She laughed. "That's what I like about fine crafts. Unlike regular art, it's usually okay to touch it. With a certain amount of caution, obviously."

"'Touch with caution.' You should put that on a sign in your shop."

She smiled sidelong at him. "Maybe I will."

The next tent was all Christmas ornaments, which meant Leona was bored. Simon wandered through the tables while she trailed behind.

"Leona," he said, picking up a pinecone frosted with fake snow and frowning at it, "what do you do for

Christmas?"

She held back a rush of nerves. Other people in the tent streamed around them. Christmas music warbled on in the background, just audible enough to annoy her.

"Oh, you know, the usual Christmas stuff."

"Like what?"

"You know, dinner…presents…that kind of thing." It wasn't a lie. She did make herself a nice dinner, usually something tropical as befit her Cabana Christmas theme. And she *did* exchange presents with a few people, just not on the day of.

Still, she didn't want to tell Simon about Cabana Christmas. He wouldn't think it was funny the way Iris did.

"When you were a kid, it was just you and your parents?" Simon asked.

"Yeah. Fun and games."

"No grandparents? Aunts? Uncles?"

"Nope." She shrugged. "Well, I met my dad's parents once, I guess. They didn't like my mom and weren't particularly interested in me, either."

His jaw hardened. Leona tried to look away and ended up staring directly at a truly hideous ornament of a glittery, pink-cheeked caroler.

She inched toward the exit, and Simon, mercifully, followed. Outside the tent, he paused by a snow bank. "Is that…something that you'd want, someday? You know, a family? Of your own, I mean."

A few years ago, she would have laughed in his face. Today, she didn't know how to react. She finally understood why deer froze in place when they saw car headlights, their bodies telling them a hundred contradictory escape plans at once.

"I don't know anything about families," she managed.

"I think you do."

She shook her head, her throat tight with inexplicable sadness.

"I've seen you with Paul," Simon said. "He's family to you."

"Not *really*—"

"In every way that counts."

She couldn't argue. Paul *was* family to her. At least, Leona felt that way about him. She didn't know how he or Mellon felt about her. She didn't like to make assumptions.

"Have you eaten?" she asked, hugging her arms tight to her black pea coat. "I think there's some food trucks, up this way. I've heard rumors of a wasabi truck, though honestly I'm not sure what that entails… Wasabi sandwiches? Wasabi soup?"

Simon stopped her again, this time with a hand on her arm. His touch resonated across her body, like ripples across the surface of a pond.

"Do you go to Paul's? For Christmas?"

His pale eyes were focused on her face. Leona decided he was probably extremely good at interviewing crime suspects.

"I…yes," she said, a painful ache in her ribs. "I go to Paul's. It's not exciting. Just me and Paul and Mellon."

This time, when she turned away, he let her go.

"I'd rather hear about what your family does," she said, and that, at least, was the truth. Fortunately, Simon obliged her, telling her all about his cousins' kids descending on his parents' house to run amok and terrorize the dog.

They reached the food trucks, where the wasabi

truck turned out to be a myth. Instead of wasabi soup, they bought minestrone and ate on an empty park bench sprinkled with snowflakes. To their left, Cascade Street ended at Wyatt Park, which at this time of night was little more than shadows. To their right stretched the cobblestone road between the artists' tents, sparkling with new snow.

Leona didn't want the first day of the crafts fair to be over; that meant there was only one day left, and she'd have to wait an entire year until the next fair.

"We should probably go," Simon said. "You must be frozen."

"I'm all right."

"Your cheeks are pink." Shifting closer to her on the bench, he thumbed her cheek.

"The cold is ruining my gothic aesthetic," Leona said.

He grinned. His thumb brushed her lip, and, slowly, his fingers slid underneath her hat into the hair at her temples. His hand engulfed her cheek, keeping her face turned toward him, keeping her open to him, while his pinky finger strayed down to the sensitive skin of her throat. His eyes were intense and searching, as if he were staring right into her black heart. His questions about families had already left her feeling vulnerable and exposed. She *should* go home, to her safe, silent apartment.

And yet…she wanted his gaze, his hands, his power over her.

"Simon," she said, "I bought you something."

―◆―

Simon watched, puzzled, as Leona drew a small paper

bag out of her purse. She stood up, facing away from him, and pulled her long, red scarf free from her black pea coat. He caught it as it drifted down toward the bench. It smelled like her ginger perfume.

Leona sat back down next to him on the bench. The top two buttons on her black pea coat were open. A choker necklace made of red pearls and black lace clung to her white throat. He'd never seen her wear anything like it before, and he couldn't stop staring at it, while blood roared through his veins.

"Do you like it?" she asked. "It has snaps in the back." She slid a fingertip underneath the back of the necklace, pulling it tight against her throat. "So, it's like a collar. It can't tighten on its own. At most, you would break it."

Simon's chest tightened. "I can't—we—we're in public."

"There's no one around."

She was right: the food trucks a block away were packing up, and the last few stragglers from the crafts fair were wandering off in the other direction. But it was still a public space, and that meant everything he wanted to do to her right now was off-limits. He clenched his hands into fists, telling himself to look away, to ask her to take it off.

He thought about the way she'd pressed his hands against her throat last night. *Tell me I'm yours.*

She was so exquisite, with the snowflakes clinging to her black hair and the red pearls shining against her pale skin. If only he could—

He forced his eyes closed. "Just because it has snaps," he said through gritted teeth, "it's still—"

"I know you could hurt me, Simon."

"Then why—?"

"Because I know that you won't."

He shuddered so violently that his teeth chattered. His desire for her was a tangible, physical thing, like a monster trying to tear its way out of his chest.

"Touch me, Simon," she whispered.

His eyes opened against his will. A snowflake caught on her long lashes and slid down her cheek. His hand rose to wipe it away, but instead found the necklace.

"It's all right, darling." Her voice a hypnotic murmur in his ear, she brushed her lips against his jaw. With a ragged exhale, he bent his head and kissed her throat, sliding his thumb underneath the choker. She gave one soft small noise of pleasure and tilted her head back, inviting him in, yielding to him. He stroked her skin under the necklace with his thumb, as his fingers curled loosely around her neck. The line he'd toed all his life blurred and vanished.

He didn't deserve this, didn't deserve her, but he couldn't stop himself. He drew the tip of his tongue along the border of the choker. Her pulse ticked in her throat, and his own heart raced as he drew his tongue upward to the line of her jaw. Her eyelashes fluttered against her flushed skin. She looked as delirious and drugged as he felt.

With his free hand, he drew her legs in toward him and slid his palm underneath her short dress. He needed to know if she was wet for him. He needed to—

"Simon?"

A man's voice came from behind him. Simon froze. Shit. He'd completely forgotten he was on a public bench.

He disentangled himself from Leona and glanced up at the rookie, Jack Miller, who had been sent out to do crowd control with Keene this evening.

"Jack," Simon said. He wanted to stand up, but that would only make the situation worse. "We were…just leaving."

"Okay. Great." Jack's normally smiling face was studiously neutral. Simon was his superior officer. He was supposed to be setting a good example.

Leona smiled at Jack. With her lips and cheeks flushed, and snow sparkling in her hair and along the tops of her breasts, she looked like a depraved snow queen.

"Did you have a nice time at the crafts fair?" she asked Jack, her smile becoming more a baring of teeth.

"Uh," Jack said, "yes, ma'am. Thank you."

"*Lovely.*"

Jack scratched the back of his neck, bumping his hat forward. "Well…see you tomorrow, sir. Ma'am."

Simon nodded. Jack walked away, but he didn't stray too far, making a show of looking at the poles on one of the tents. Simon was sure Jack was waiting for them to leave, so he could feel like he'd done his job properly.

Simon ran his hands through his hair. A knot of worry and humiliation formed in his chest, taking the place where the monster had been. Jack had seen him with his hand up Leona's dress, literally *licking her throat*. For the love of God. If Jack had walked over a couple minutes later, he would've seen Simon doing a lot more than that.

The timing was too much of a coincidence. Jack must have been hoping Simon would get a hold of himself before he had to intervene. But there was no getting a hold of himself where Leona was concerned.

He stood and zipped up his coat. "Let me walk you home."

Leona rose to her feet beside him. Out of the corner of his eye, he saw her slip the choker off and drop it into her purse.

As they walked back along the now-silent street, Leona slung her red scarf across her shoulders and toyed with one end, as if it were a feather boa. When they reached her apartment building, Simon hesitated, torn between wanting to apologize to her and wanting to yell at her.

Leona leaned against her front door, the flared hem of her pea coat swaying in the breeze. "We were just making out. It wasn't that bad."

"Yes, it was."

"You think Jack Miller's never felt a girl up in public before? Or wouldn't, if he had a chance?" She smiled. "I've seen him check out Emma's ass enough times."

Simon crossed his arms over his chest. "It's not that."

"He didn't see anything with the choker. If that helps."

"That's not the point!" he snapped, his anger and frustration rushing to the surface. "The problem is— it's too goddamned *much*." He paced the sidewalk in front of her building, his boots crushing snow. "I can't stop—" He was trembling again. Sharp bursts of cold air pricked at his lungs.

I can't stop thinking about you. He couldn't say that— she would think he was a goddamned stalker.

She was standing so still, she looked like she was holding her breath. Her light eyes were wide.

"This stuff—the choker," he said. "I don't understand how you can be okay with it. It's so fucked up. It freaks me the fuck out."

"I know it's a lot to wrap your head around, but these feelings, in the kink world, are totally normal. I promise. All this confusion you're feeling—everybody goes through it when they start out."

"Not you," he said harshly. "You were beating David Bourdon with a fucking cane at fourteen years old."

"I'm different." Her hands tightened around the handles of her shopping bags. Standing by her building in her pretty coat and hat, she looked less like a dark fairy or a snow queen and more like a girl in a Vermont postcard.

"Why are you different?" he demanded, though he wondered if he knew. She was so Dominant that even her surrender was wholly on her own terms.

She bit her flushed lower lip. Simon ached with that familiar longing for her.

"I just am. But I know a lot of kinky people, and almost all of them have said this is how it was for them. Denial and anger, and fear of what it said about them, as a person, to be into something like this—"

She never answered his questions. Never. "Damn it, Leona, *why are you different?*"

She threw up her hands in exasperation, making her bags crash together. "Don't you get it by now, Simon? Kink doesn't scare me—*everything else* scares me! I don't know how to *do* anything else. That's why I keep fucking this up—fucking *us* up. I don't know what the rules are."

"You're not fucking this up," he said, dismayed, stepping toward her. "If anything, it's me. I'm just—" He didn't know how to explain to her that he was a screw-up. "I've wanted you for so long, and you're so—"

"Experienced?" she suggested bitterly.

"That's not what I was going to say." He was going to say *amazing*.

His anger gave way to exhaustion. The rest of his day had caught up with him at last. He wanted to go upstairs and make love to her until they both fell asleep, but he had to get up early tomorrow to work on the case. He jammed his hands deeper into his coat pockets. "Leona, the thing is…I like you so much, it scares the hell out of me."

As soon as the words left his mouth, he regretted them. He didn't want to pressure her, but he couldn't have stopped himself from telling her that any more than he could have stopped himself from licking her beautiful neck on that park bench. He couldn't resist her—that was the problem. It didn't matter that she didn't date or that he didn't deserve her or that he ruined every relationship he was in. Clenching his jaw in frustration, he closed his eyes.

"Can I see you again soon?" he asked. "Maybe next week? I promise I'll get my head on straight by then."

"Of course," she murmured, and Simon, his pulse humming, drew her in for a chaste kiss.

"I have to go." He kissed her cheek lightly, the corner of her mouth. Her breath hitched, and that small sound made him want to push her up against her door and slide his hands back up her dress. No—he had to go home, actually sleep for once, and work on the case fresh tomorrow. And he had to give her space, at least for a couple days. They both needed some space.

Chapter Twelve

LEONA LET THE DOOR TO her apartment swing shut behind her and stalked into her kitchen as if she were going to get a glass of wine. She opened cabinets and paced and closed cabinets and paced some more. What the hell *was* that? He liked her so much that it scared him? He'd wanted her for so long? He obviously hadn't been referring to the last few days they'd been spending time together. He meant, what, since high school?

She tore off her coat, threw it over a kitchen chair, and kept pacing. Her skin still burned where he'd kissed her, holding her as if she were precious.

Last night, when he'd subbed for her, he'd meant every single word. He *actually had* fantasized about her since high school. He *actually thought* she had the prettiest smile he'd ever seen and eyes like fucking rain clouds.

No one had ever said anything like that to her. Even Liam had only complimented her as part of their play, or as a lead-up to it. At least, that was what she'd always assumed.

Still restless, she crossed the living room to one of her shadowboxes and picked up a tiny, round vase, with a blown glass pattern that had always reminded her of sea anemones. Liam had tried to give her one of these pieces. He'd actually apologized to her when he gave it to her, since he'd known she didn't like to exchange gifts with her lovers.

I'm sorry, Mistress. It was just so perfect for you.

Liam had dark Irish eyes, the opposite of Simon's light coloring, but in that moment, he'd looked at her the same way Simon did sometimes. That intensity had made her far more nervous than the gift.

The gift was perfect. He was absolutely right about that.

She had refused to accept it, though she'd thanked him—nicely, she hoped—for thinking of her. And Liam had let it go, the same way he always did. Never challenging her. Never contradicting her. He'd shrugged, turned away to hide the sadness in his smile, and never mentioned it again.

A few days later, after an exhaustive search, she'd found a similar one online and bought it for herself. He'd never know, since she never invited him to her apartment. Sometimes, after she got back from an evening with him, she'd look at the sea anemone vase and think about him.

Even now, years later, she kept it in the center of her shadowbox, exactly at eye level. She didn't know if she wanted to be reminded of Liam or if she wanted to be reminded of how often, how badly, she had hurt him, every time she'd refused his small kindnesses, until eventually she'd ended things altogether for reasons she still didn't fully understand.

She didn't want to treat Simon like that. She wanted to do better, to *be* better, for his sake, and for hers.

After the crafts fair, the Christmas shopping season officially began in Grenton. They kept the store open late every night to draw in the after-work crowd as well as the tourists who came into town to blend skiing and holiday celebrations.

On Tuesday night, when it was finally time to close, Emma shepherded the last few customers from the store, waving a cheery goodbye. As soon as they were gone, she collapsed against the glass front door. "Finally! Who are all these people who are so desperate for fine crafts they want to buy them at ten o'clock on a Tuesday? Don't they have lives?" Emma went back to the counter, where Leona had begun closing out the register.

"Well, it is—"

"'Fucking Christmas'?" Emma suggested.

Leona smiled wryly. "Exactly."

"It isn't Christmas for another two weeks." Margie, who was straightening up the miniature Christmas tree display, looked even more tired tonight than she had the day before.

"I can handle things from here, if you guys feel like taking off," Leona said. "All that's left is the money stuff, anyway."

"I'm all right," Margie said. Leona didn't want to single her out in front of Emma, so she let it go.

"*I* have a date," Emma announced, "so I'd rather go if you don't mind."

"A date?" Margie looked up with a wan smile. "At ten at night?"

"Well, just a movie and some canoodling with Leif,"

Emma admitted, ruffling her bright blue pixie cut. "But it still counts! He's been working so much I've hardly seen him in weeks."

Poor Jack Miller, Leona thought.

Suddenly, Emma slapped her hand down on the counter. "Speaking of dates! Paul said you have a new boy toy, Leona."

"I do not have a *boy toy*." She looked up from the register to see Emma and Margie with identical sly grins. "*What?*"

"Call it what you want," Emma said, shrugging. "I'm sure he knows how it is."

Leona rolled her eyes. Ridiculous. Whatever Simon was to her, a boy toy was not it. He had to know that, if nothing else.

"All right, you," Leona said to Emma. "Go to your canoodling."

Emma saluted, grabbed her stuff from underneath the counter, and left in a flash, leaving Leona and Margie alone in the store.

"Who's your new man?" Margie asked.

Leona hesitated. But this was Margie. And everyone knew already, anyway, or would soon. "Simon Labelle."

"Oh." Margie took a step back. "The cop."

The front door opened, and Leona looked up to say *I'm sorry, we're closed*, but the words turned to ash in her mouth.

Two men in ski masks. Guns in their hands. She blinked. Real guns? In Grenton? She must have been transported into an action movie. It had to be a joke. Across the counter from her, half turned toward the two men, Margie paled.

Leona stared at them. *Ski masks*. She didn't know people actually wore those during a robbery. One of the men moved forward. Toward Margie.

"Where is the fucking money?" His voice was deep and cold. He didn't have a Vermont accent.

Margie stared at the floor and didn't answer him. Leona could actually see her shaking.

"I have the register open, right here," Leona said, raising her hands. "I can hand it over to you."

The man who'd spoken turned toward her. Her pulse quickened.

About six feet tall, she thought. Simon's height. She couldn't see his hair under his ski mask, but he was wearing a short-sleeved black T-shirt, and the hair on his arms was dark brown, threaded with gray.

"I don't want the fucking register," he spat. "What do you think this is?"

"A robbery?" Leona suggested, raising an eyebrow. "It sure looks like a robbery to me."

"You think I want, what, a couple of hundred dollars? Or any of this shit?" With a hard bark of a laugh, he slammed the butt of his gun down onto an assortment of vases that Leona had arranged the day before. Glass splintered, spattering across the display and the floor. Leona twitched with anger.

"Hey," she snapped. "You break it, you buy it, buddy."

He laughed again and pointed his gun directly at her chest. "You think you're funny, bitch?"

West Coast accent, Leona thought. *California*. She was sweating through her top, thinking about what a bullet from that gun would do to her ribcage.

The second man was watching her, his arms crossed loosely over his chest, his posture relaxed. He had a tattoo of a snake on his right forearm. He was hired muscle, maybe? Also white, about six two. Most importantly, he was not looking at Margie. *Run for it, Margie.*

Call the police. Call Simon.

"I prefer to be called 'witty,' in general," Leona said. "But funny works, too, if 'wit' is not in your vocabulary."

"I don't care what you *prefer*," the first man growled. He stepped closer. Only the thin, flimsy counter separated them. He had green eyes. Smile lines. He wasn't smiling now. The gun rose higher, the barrel pointing at her face. She'd never seen a gun up close before, apart from Simon's, but Simon's was always in his holster. This one was dark gray and black and looked every bit like a machine created in order to kill human beings.

The tip of the gun pressed against her forehead. The metal chilled her skin. Leona's eyes closed, and she thought fleetingly of Simon. And Paul. Thank God she had sent Emma home.

"Tell me where the money is, Margaret," the gunman said.

Nobody in Grenton used Margie's full name. Did that matter? Maybe Leona was hysterical. It was hard to think with the muzzle of a gun indenting her skin.

"Tell me, or your pretty little friend's brains will be all over that back wall."

Bullshit. She recognized a power play when she saw one. He wasn't going to shoot her. Not yet, anyway. He needed to get Margie to talk, that was all.

"It's in the back," Margie said. "I hid it back there."

"Terrific," the gunman said coolly. The pressure of the gun disappeared. She opened her eyes again, and the sight of his smirk, visible through the jagged mouth opening in his ski mask, filled her with fury. How dare he come into her shop, break her shit, and order Margie around? She wanted to pistol-whip him with his own gun, but she had to stay calm so she could stay alive, and keep Margie alive, too.

"If you gentlemen would care to join us in the back," she suggested icily, "we just got in a new shipment of Bill Campbell pottery. The patterns are *very* surprising—"

"Shut up, bitch," the gunman said. "Walk." He gestured at the back room with his gun. Margie glanced at Leona, her eyes filled with fear. Leona gave her a reassuring nod and walked toward the back. She hoped they couldn't see her ankles trembling in her high-heeled boots.

Margie followed Leona into the back room, which was its usual cheerful chaos of empty boxes, packets of blank labels, and bottles of sticker adhesive remover. Narrow shelves, crammed full of fine crafts, lined the walls.

The two men paced in behind them. Hired Muscle held his gun by his side. Up close, he looked much more alert than she'd thought at first. Like a lion, watching his prey.

The first man moved into the center of the room. "Where is it?"

Margie pointed at the shelves lining the left wall. Margie had kept her stuff on the lowest of those ten narrow shelves every shift for the last six years.

"Get it," the gunman barked.

Shadows bridged the undersides of Margie's eyes, and her skin had a greenish tint. Her purse slumped against the wall behind the shelf, but otherwise, the shelf was empty. Except for…

Leona squinted.

Empty except for *Margie's phone*, half-hidden behind her purse.

"I'll do it," Leona said. "If you tell me where to look,

Margie."

"Why?" the gunman snapped.

"Because she's shaking like a fucking leaf," Leona snapped back. "You've terrified the poor thing."

The gunman's smirk reappeared. "But not you."

"Not me, obviously." A cannonball of ice rolled in Leona's stomach, and she was still sweating through her top, but she felt alert. Ready.

She had to get to Margie's phone.

"Come on, Margie," she said, extending a hand. "Come with me and tell me where to look."

Margie reached out, and Leona clasped her fingers. *It's okay*, she told Margie silently. *We will get through this.*

"Get moving," the gunman said.

Leona pulled Margie toward the shelves, and they both got down on the floor. The gunman stood about six feet behind them. Leona could sense his gun trained on them, while they kneeled with their backs to him, execution-style.

"The money's under this shelf," Margie said.

"Okay." Leona wiped her sweaty palms on her pants. She had to act quickly. "I'll just lift the shelf up." She leaned across the shelf, hiding Margie's phone with her body. With both hands, she reached for the edge of the shelf, then dropped one hand down and slid the phone behind Margie's purse.

"It's stuck," Leona said, jiggling the end of the shelf. With her free hand, she swiped Margie's phone to the emergency call screen. She might be a Luddite with a landline, but she wasn't completely oblivious.

"Get it unstuck." The gunman's footsteps creaked on the wooden floor behind her. The hair on the back of her neck stood up. How close was he? Did he have his finger on the trigger?

Come on, Leona, she thought. *You can do this.*

She jiggled the shelf again. With her right hand, she hit the 9 button. Then the 1.

She played with the shelf again. "Almost got it." Behind her, the gunman released an impatient breath.

1.

Thank God. Thank God.

A faint, tinny ringing came from the phone.

"What's that sound?"

"What sound?" Leona jerked the shelf off its bearings and sent Margie's phone and purse tumbling against the wall to the floor. She jammed the shelf upward against Margie's things to muffle the sounds from the phone, and prayed that knocking it over hadn't ended the call.

Underneath the shelf, there were three wooden cigar boxes.

"That's it," Margie said softly.

"Bring them over here and open them."

Leona stacked the boxes and got to her feet, her limbs twitching with effort. The gunman pointed to the center of the room. Leona walked forward and set the cigar boxes on the floor. She flipped the first one open and stared, puzzled, at the jumble of papers inside.

"Watch them," the gunman said to Hired Muscle, who nodded, his eyes glittering.

The gunman crouched down and rifled through the papers in the first box, then opened the second, and the third.

Leona glanced back at Margie in surprise. Some of the papers looked like money orders, and there were bundles of cash, too, held together by rubber bands.

Margie didn't look at her. She was still sitting on the

floor by the shelving unit, with all emotion drained from her face.

The gunman counted under his breath as he went through the money in the boxes. Strange how meticulous he was, Leona thought. Not what she would've expected from the average criminal.

He reached the end of the third box after several silent minutes. Where were the police? The station was only two blocks away, but maybe they hadn't gotten the call? Or maybe, since no one had spoken, they thought it was a wrong number and wouldn't bother coming.

No—Simon would never let that happen. He'd never let his station blow off any 911 call, and for *her*... She was pretty sure Simon would walk through fire for her. God only knew why.

"Where's the rest?" the gunman demanded. He turned on Margie. "This is forty-five thousand. Where's the rest of it?"

Forty-five thousand dollars? Here in the shop?

"That's all of it."

"There should be hundreds of thousands." His voice rose dangerously.

Margie, still sitting on the floor, flinched. "I didn't know that."

"*Where is it?*" He advanced on Margie, seized her by her shirt collar, and dragged her to her feet. Leona's heart sprang into her throat.

"I am so sick of this bullshit!" He shook Margie by the collar of her pale blue top. Margie whimpered.

"Let go of her!" Leona cried. "You're hurting her!"

Still holding Margie in one hand, he swung his gun around to point it again at Leona's face. This time, there was no smirk, no showmanship, just a man who wanted to get rid of her. No time to run, to fight—he'd shoot her before she had a chance to draw breath.

Her only plan had been to cooperate and to somehow call for help. She'd done both, but it wasn't enough. She would die in her shop, the only place she'd ever thought of as home, and her blood and brains would ruin their newest shipment.

Blue lights flickered across her line of sight. *Some kind of anxiety response*, she thought. Hallucinating light spots. Blue light spots.

"Boss," Hired Muscle said. "Boss."

"*What?*"

"We've got to go."

"Shit." The gunman threw Margie away from him. She sprawled on the floor, slapping her head on the hardwood. He snatched up the cigar boxes, and both men bolted for the back door.

Blue lights, Leona thought again. Her bones were icicles; if she moved, she'd shatter into thousands of pieces.

In her center, though, a slow thaw began. She knew what—who—they had just run from.

Simon.

Chapter Thirteen

THE LIGHTS FROM HIS CRUISER cast an eerie glow across Leona's shop. Simon pushed the unlocked front door open and stepped inside, his boots crunching on a spray of shattered glass. The store was abandoned, silent. His hope of seeing Leona's ironic smile as she apologized for accidentally calling 911 vanished. Fear flooded through him in its place. He didn't know for sure that she was working tonight, but he still had to blink away horrific visions of her hurt. He had to focus. Dispatch had told him only that there was a call. There was no information on the nature of the incident. *A robbery*, he thought, glancing at the open cash register—except that all the money was still in the drawer. And if it was a robbery, where was Leona now?

Quietly, he radioed for backup. He had responded to the call alone, since he'd been the only one on duty when it came in. He wasn't supposed to be working this evening, but he'd volunteered for a double so O'Malley could go home sick. Simon didn't want to go home, anyway, where he'd think about Leona all night and how he'd promised himself to give her some space.

But now…

Drawing his gun, he moved silently toward the back room of Leona's shop, strategizing the best way to take down whoever was back there. If they had hurt her, he would kill them.

He stepped through the door, gun raised. In the center, Leona. Standing. No visible injuries, thank God. About four feet from her, a woman he recognized as one of her co-workers sat on the floor, clutching her head and crying. At the far side of the room, there was an open door, and through it, in the dim light spilling out of the store, a flash of skin and dark fabric, rapidly moving away from him.

Leona glanced at him, her expression frozen. "Simon. I am really…*really* glad to see you."

"Are you hurt?" he barked at her. She shook her head, and he swallowed his relief, his desire to grab her and not let go.

"Was it a robbery?" he demanded. "Armed?"

She nodded. Blood pounded in his ears.

"Simon, wait!" she called after him. "They're dangerous—"

He was already sprinting out the door into the tree-lined parking lot. *There*. A flash of movement in the woods. He ran across the lot into the trees, where the light from the shop did not reach. The darkness was heavy, oppressive. He could shoot his own foot off like this if he wasn't careful. Using his flashlight would only make him into an easy target, and his weapon had no special equipment. It was just a pistol. He'd never actually needed it before tonight.

The sound of their footsteps grew fainter. He slammed his fist into a tree branch. They were going to get away.

No. He'd cut through the woods to the street and

head them off. As quietly as he could, he radioed in with his new location and asked for two cars to come up Bow Street from opposite directions. Both sides of Bow Street connected with Cascade Street. It formed an almost perfect half-circle, cutting through the middle of this patch of woods before the woods turned into a state forest. It was their only chance at catching those fuckers. He wished he could smoke them out onto the street with gunfire, but there were a couple of houses tucked away in here. He couldn't risk it.

He felt his way branch by branch in the direction where he'd last heard them. All of his senses were on alert in case of new clues to their location, though the woods seemed as dark and endless as the night sky.

A car engine purred somewhere ahead of him. One of the cruisers?

Or did the suspects have a car stashed somewhere?

Damn it. Branches whipped at his face and tore at his uniform as he jogged toward the sound. He stepped out of the trees onto asphalt, with open air yawning all around him. Bow Street. To his left—northeast?—tail lights.

He radioed it in. The radio crackled with the sound of Russo cursing. "I'm still on Cascade."

"I'm on it," Keene said.

The next voice was Jack's. "Witness describes the suspects as two white males. One approximately six feet tall, average build, green eyes, brown hair. The other is six two, eyes and hair both brown, snake tattoo on right forearm."

Jack had to be at the shop with Leona and her co-worker. Simon was glad they weren't alone anymore, though the thought of Jack talking to Leona, comforting her, filled him with jealousy and possessiveness.

A cruiser hurtled by him, lights and sirens on full blast as it careened around a curve in the road. Keene always drove his cruiser like a lunatic. For once, Simon was glad, even though he wished he were driving that cruiser himself.

"I see them," Keene reported. "No—God damn it, there was a blind corner. I'm at the intersection with Mill Road, and I don't know which way they went."

"Officer Keene, go north on Mill Road," the Chief said. "Russo, take the southbound side. Labelle, is your vehicle still at the scene?"

"Yes, sir."

"Come back here. You and I are going to take a look around."

———◆———

Simon and the Chief drove around the town line for about two hours, checking in with Russo and Keene, the sheriff's office from their county and from the two neighboring counties, and the Vermont State Police. So far, nobody had seen a car with two men matching Leona's descriptions.

"That young lady, Miss Chaisty, gave us one of the most level-headed eyewitness accounts I've ever heard," the Chief said. "But it doesn't seem to be doing us a lot of good. Think it's time to call it a night."

"They've got to be here somewhere," Simon said.

"Could be halfway to Canada by now. Anyway, this is up to highway patrol. Outside our jurisdiction." Leaning back in the passenger seat, the Chief frowned out the window. "What do you think this is all about?"

"I don't know, sir," Simon said.

Jack had interviewed Leona's co-worker, Margie Smith, at the station, and had radioed the Chief with her statement. She'd told him the money was a gift. She'd decided to keep it at the shop instead of at home, but she'd refused to explain why. She'd also insisted she had no idea who the robbers were, or how they'd known about the money.

"Forty-five grand is a pretty big gift," Simon said. "And to keep it in cash, in the shop? Why not put it in a bank account?"

The Chief made a thoughtful sound. "Domestic situation, probably? Seen that plenty of times. Wife wants to leave, but he doesn't want her to go, so she stockpiles cash and valuables somewhere where he won't think to look."

"You think her husband figured it out and hired the robbers?" Simon asked. "Why not just take the money back himself?"

The Chief shrugged. "Give her a scare?"

That seemed like unnecessary theater to Simon, but he supposed he didn't know Richard Smith. Reluctantly, Simon turned onto Cascade Street, heading east toward the station. "This is the third serious crime in Grenton in less than a year."

"It's been a bad year."

"Do you think they could be connected?"

"I don't see how. I bet you anything that girl's boyfriend is the one who tried to blow her up. Even if the State's Attorney says they can't prove it in court. And Nancy O'Shea was just jogging with headphones on, on a dangerous road. Same damn thing I tell my daughter not to do all the time."

Penelope had pretty much said her mom hadn't thought of the road as dangerous, even though it obviously was. And earlier today, the task force had traced the deposits in Mrs. O'Shea's bank accounts to a trust account belonging to her ex-father-in-law, who'd passed away a few months ago, shortly after the last deposit. Simon had followed up with both the ex-husband and with Penelope, and they'd both claimed to know nothing about it. They'd just said that Nancy and her former father-in-law had been close, as if that were perfectly normal.

More gifts, Simon thought, running a hand through his hair.

The Chief could be right: Mrs. O'Shea's death might not be anything more than an accidental hit and run. That was certainly tragic enough.

And yet…Simon couldn't help feeling like he was missing something. This was too much money for quiet, blue-collar Grenton—first with Mrs. O'Shea, now with Margie Smith. He didn't see a connection between the two cases. As far as he knew, the two women hadn't even known each other. But he still couldn't shake the feeling.

As soon as Simon put the car into park, the Chief was halfway out the door. For such a quiet, patient man, his movements were quick and decisive. Simon trudged after him into the station.

Leona slouched in one of the chairs lining the wall in the main room, bouncing a tennis ball against a metal filing cabinet like some kind of teenaged delinquent. Jack glanced up from his desk against the far wall and nodded at the Chief. "Sir. Margie Smith's husband came to pick her up about a half an hour ago, but I have her contact information here if you'd like to get in touch." He glanced at Leona, then at Simon. "Ms. Chaisty wouldn't leave until you came back."

Leona smiled lazily at Simon, still bouncing her tennis ball. The Chief discreetly went back to his office, and Jack meandered into the break room, leaving Simon and Leona alone.

All his fears for Leona came rushing back, as if he were retracing his path through the empty shop, his boots crunching on broken glass. He thought of her frozen expression, and how she had stood so still in the center of the shop's back room.

She had to have stayed at the station for this long because she'd been waiting for good news—if not an arrest, then at least a *lead*, for Christ's sake. Yet again, they had nothing. *He* had nothing.

"I'm sorry," he said quietly. "We couldn't find them."

"Is that what you think this is?" She stood up and poked him hard in the chest. "You aren't wearing a vest, idiot."

He had completely forgotten about his bulletproof vest, or lack thereof. They so rarely wore them in Grenton. "What does that have to do with anything?"

She rolled her eyes in exasperation, but he could see the strain in her smile now, the tension in her eyebrows. A slow, dopey grin spread across his face. "Leona Chaisty, were you *worried* about me? Is that why you were waiting?"

"I'm human," she said indignantly. "I worry about things—I mean, *people*. I worry about people."

"Very convincing." Simon took her elbows and drew her close. After what she'd been through tonight, he wouldn't have blamed her for forgetting about him completely. Instead, she'd stayed at the station for over an hour after her interview, waiting for him in one of their awful folding chairs.

"And you…" he said, searching her face. "Are you

okay?"

"Of course I'm okay." Her lips curved into a sardonic smile, but her eyes were haunted. "It takes more to upset me than someone p-pointing a fucking gun in my face."

His hands tightened around her arms, crushing the soft fabric of her sweater. "They threatened you?"

She glanced down at the station's threadbare carpet.

"Leona…I'm so sorry." If only he'd gotten there a few seconds faster, he could have grabbed them before they ran into the woods.

"Don't be sorry, Simon," she said. "Really. You—you saved my life, you know. They ran off because they saw your police lights. Otherwise…."

"You think they would've hurt you, even after getting Margie's money?"

She shrugged. "I was pissing them off."

Of course Leona—indomitable, impossible Leona—had mouthed off at them, even while she'd cataloged every detail of how they looked and spoke and acted. He admired the hell out of this woman. What would he have done if something had happened to her? Just the thought of them threatening her enraged him, and if they had hurt her… Screw his jurisdiction. He ought to go back out there and hunt them down himself.

Leona's hands slid underneath Simon's unzipped police coat. Even through his duty shirt, her fingers were cold. Under her bravado and bravery, she was as exhausted and upset as anyone else would be. He pulled her into a tight, all-consuming hug and kissed her hair, absorbing her scent, the sweet intoxication of her presence. "I'm going to take you home."

"Okay," she murmured into his collar, her breath warm against his neck.

"Just got to let Jack know. All right?"

She nodded and pulled away from him, passing a hand over her mouth. He ducked into the break room, where Jack was leaning against the table by the vending machines, staring at his phone, though the screen was dark.

"I'm going to take Leona to her apartment," Simon said, "but I'll be back in a little while in case there's—"

"Don't do that," Jack said at once.

Simon glanced at him in surprise.

"You don't need to come back here," Jack clarified. "I'm the officer on call for the overnight shift tonight. I can handle it, Simon."

"It's not that—"

"You should be with Leona."

Simon *wanted* to be with Leona, even more than he wanted to catch the assholes who had threatened her. He didn't want to let her out of his sight, but would she let him stay? Did she want him there?

Simon took off his hat and ran a hand through his hair. "Okay. You're right. Thanks, Jack."

"I'll call you if anything comes in," Jack said. "Good night, sir."

Simon nodded and went back to the main office with his heart in his throat. Leona was buttoning up her coat, her eyes distant. He looped an arm around her waist and together they headed out to his cruiser. She drew her shoulders back when they left the station, and a shadow of her usual wry smile appeared as she slid into the passenger seat of his police car.

"Funny to sit in the front of a cop car, instead of the back," she remarked.

"Tell me that's a joke," Simon said.

She grinned at him.

He leaned over and caught her chin in his hand, kissing her on the lips. "Impossible woman."

"You like it," she breathed, kissing him back.

"You know I do." Too much.

He turned the key in the ignition with every bit of his concentration. A minute later, they reached her apartment. Simon pulled into the parking lot, where Lulu shone beautifully in the pale gold of the back porch light.

Simon turned off the car and cleared his throat. "You know, when I was a rookie, my dad was still Chief of Police. And my first year or two, I had a couple of bad calls." Each one had branded itself permanently into his memory—not because they were the worst, but because they were first: a car accident in which two little kids were badly hurt. A domestic violence call. A dead body.

Leona's eyes slowly focused on him, her eyebrows knitting together with curiosity.

Simon gripped the steering wheel to steady himself. "Each time, I went back to my folks' house, and my dad made me a drink, and we talked about it. And that used to help, you know, as much as…"

As much as anything ever helped him.

Leona didn't need to hear about that ugly side of him—the side that consumed him, sometimes, after a bad call, that made him so tired he could hardly muster the energy to walk or talk, though he never slept. Nobody needed to hear about that side of him.

He turned to her in the darkness, his heart thudding. "Want to talk?"

A corner of her mouth lifted. "Make me a drink first?"

He kissed her. "Deal."

There was something surreal about a man in a police uniform fixing her a drink. The fact that it was Simon only made it more surreal, not less. She couldn't wrap her head around him wanting to comfort her. Then again, she couldn't wrap her head around anything that had happened tonight.

After he'd run out the back door into the night, gun drawn, Leona had gone after him. Jack had found her shivering uncontrollably in the parking lot, trying to figure out which way Simon had gone. A moment later, Simon's voice had come through on Jack's radio. He was safe. Angry that he'd lost the robbers, but safe.

It made Leona crazy that he hadn't worn a vest. He hadn't even thought about it, hadn't even hesitated.

Why? How could any sane person *not even hesitate*?

Simon set a beautifully made Old Fashioned on the tablecloth in front of her. Their eyes met. She took a shaky sip.

Sitting across from her at the kitchen table, he swigged his own drink. "So," he said, his voice rough with fatigue. Light played across his glass, warming the swirl of amber within.

Now that they were here, she didn't know how to begin. What could she say, besides *why the fuck did you risk your life for me?*

"Why don't you start by telling me what happened?" The question came out like a cop interviewing a witness—something Leona had now personally experienced, even if Jack didn't have half Simon's intensity.

Simon noticed it, too, with a self-deprecating laugh. "I'm sorry, I didn't mean it like that. I just thought it might help if we talked about it as...friends. Or whatever. Here—maybe this will help."

Standing, he stripped off his gun belt and set it on the floor by his chair. Then he pulled his uniform shirt loose, worked through each button, and shrugged it off. Underneath, he wore one of his stretchy black T-shirts.

"Is that better?" he asked, sitting back down. "Less... official-looking?"

He still looked like a cop, even in a short-sleeved T-shirt that clung to his muscles. He could have a beard and shoulder-length hair, and he'd still look like a cop. It was in his bearing, his expressions. She'd teased him about that before. She must have thought it made him harder to relate to. She didn't feel that way anymore.

So she talked. She started out with facts, the same way she'd processed the situation as it unfolded and the same way she'd described it all to Jack. He flinched when she told him more details about the gun, but he didn't speak. He just listened, one hand wrapped around his glass, his blue eyes somber.

Gradually, the story shifted into her concerns about Margie. She didn't know why Margie had stashed money in the shop, but she was sure there had been a good reason. "I'd noticed that there's something up with her. She's usually really talkative. I think she's had an unhappy home life for a long time, and maybe it's gotten worse lately. I've met her husband once or twice," Leona added, "and I don't know why, exactly, but I don't like him."

"You think she was hiding the money from him?"

"Maybe. I don't know where she got all that money, but if I was her, I wouldn't keep it at home, either."

"Huh." Simon leaned back in his chair.

"I'm worried about her," Leona admitted. "Her husband picked her up at the station tonight, and he looked pissed, like she was putting him out."

Margie's husband was definitely not making her drinks and keeping her company in the middle of the night, after working all day.

"You must be exhausted, Simon," Leona said. "You should go home and sleep."

His gaze slanted away, his lips pressing together. "What about you? You have to be tired, too."

Leona could still feel the cold muzzle of the gun pressed to her forehead. Still see the look in the gunman's eyes when he discovered some of the money was missing.

"I'm okay." She'd never sounded less convincing, even to her own ears.

"Leona," he said, standing again, "you are tough as hell, but even you are not okay right now. Come on." Taking her by the arms, he pulled her to her feet.

"What's this?" she asked, as he steered her toward her bedroom. "What's going on?"

"I'm putting you to bed."

She wanted to joke that he was treating her like a little kid, but, of course, no one had ever put her to bed when she was a kid.

In her bedroom, he sat her down on the edge of the mattress and turned on the dim lamp on the nightstand. Slowly, he knelt on the floor at her feet.

Her stomach tightened. She didn't know if he meant to echo the other night in the kitchen, but now it was all she could think about. The way he'd kissed her, held her. The way he'd touched himself for her. She wanted to do so much more with him—*to* him. She wanted him completely at her mercy. Completely hers. But she still didn't know if that was what *he* wanted. He'd asked for it once, but that could have been simple curiosity.

His touch gentle but efficient, he unlaced her first book and tugged it off. He actually was putting her to bed, just like he'd said. He wanted her, she was sure of it, but he was also looking after her, because he was a good man, and that was what good men did for people they cared about.

Her eyes stung.

Simon slid off her second boot, drawing his fingertips down along her tights. Rubbing her ankles, he kissed the inside of her knee. She licked her dry lips.

He drew her legs up onto the bed, laying her down on her back.

Her hair splaying out across her pillow, she looked up at him, disoriented with desire and exhaustion and a strange, heavy grief.

"I don't want to leave," he said. "But if you want to be alone, then I'll go. Just tell me."

She'd never actually invited a man to sleep over before. She had almost never invited men to her apartment at all; she preferred to go to them, so she could leave whenever she wanted. With Simon, that had been different from the beginning.

"Stay the night. Please."

He nodded, his expressive grave. He toed off his boots and shucked off his work pants. Standing before her in his clingy T-shirt and his boxers, he was already a little bit hard—from taking off her shoes?

Climbing into bed beside her, he drew a strand of her hair away from her cheek. "If you want to just sleep—" he began, his voice husky.

"I want you," she said, turning to face him. "I want you so much more than I want sleep."

He kissed her, long and slow. Gradually, their clothes came off, piece by piece. They lay facing each other on her bed, still kissing, while she ran her hands over his muscular back. No matter how much she touched him, it would never be enough.

She slid her palm down his flat, ridged stomach to his cock and wrapped her fingers around his length, trying to mimic the way he'd held himself for her the other night. With every stroke of her hand, a flush spread across his throat and chest. She ducked her head and followed the flush on his chest with her mouth. His breath catching, he murmured her name.

Shifting her hips toward him, she drew him in between her legs, and he, seeming to know what she wanted, dragged his cock between her thighs, rubbing her sex. What would it be like to have him inside her like this—naked, no barriers? She couldn't remember the last time she'd had sex without a condom. Not since David, probably. It would be weird to ask Simon about it now, wouldn't it? She didn't know how long people normally waited.

It was embarrassing to realize how very little she knew.

Before she could decide what to do, Simon drew back and reached one arm behind him to her nightstand, pulling a condom free from the box. He tore it open and rolled it on, kneeling above her, his eyes filled with longing and tenderness. Last night, while they were standing outside her apartment, he'd looked at her like this.

I like you so much, it scares the hell out of me.

He scared the hell out of her, too.

She brought his mouth back down to hers, needing his lips, his tongue, his taste, scented with whiskey. He slid inside her. "You're so—" The words melted into a groan as he thrust into her, each stroke as long and slow as the kisses they'd shared earlier.

How could she ever have thought missionary with Simon would be boring? Every inch of their skin touched, thrummed with the electricity between them; and the way he kissed her made her feel like she was being worshipped, even if it looked different. He was dazzling.

"I want to see you come," he murmured, his mouth moving to her ear. "You're so beautiful. I need to see you."

Resisting her body's needs was already so much more difficult where Simon was concerned, and tonight, she had no resistance left. She rolled him over onto his back and straddled him in the middle of the bed, sliding his cock deeper into her. He gripped her thighs, hard enough to leave fingerprint bruises, as she slid a hand down her stomach to her clit. His heavy-lidded eyes tracked the motion of her hand. He pumped his hips harder, keeping time with her as she rocked against him.

"My pet," she murmured, her voice hoarse and trembling. That was the only endearment she had ever used, but tonight it was wholly inadequate. He wasn't her pet, and he wasn't her boy toy, either, whatever Emma and Margie might think. "Darling," she tried again. Almost right. "Dear heart."

Her heart.

Taking her free hand in his, he kissed her fingertips, her palm. "Sweetheart."

Sweet? No. She *wasn't* sweet. That was the problem. That was the gulf that separated them—that he was a good man, and she was not good, not sweet, not right for him in any way.

Her eyes were stinging again, and her hand seemed to be failing her.

His movements slowed, and he blinked up at her, his eyes dark in the low light. "Come here, sweetheart. It's all right."

Bundling her into his arms, he drew her down onto his chest, kissing her face and throat. "It's all right." The words were the gentlest whisper in her ear. "I've got you."

And he did. He tilted them both back onto their sides, one strong, capable hand sliding between them.

"Oh, fuck, your hands," she moaned, her eyes fluttering closed. He chuckled, still kissing her cheek. Pleasure throbbed through her as he traced his fingers in slow circles.

"How are you so good at this?" The question came out slurred. He'd hardly begun to touch her, but already she was on the brink, standing on the edge of a chasm filled with fireworks.

"You give me too much credit," he said. "But I'm glad I can make you feel good."

His cock slid deep into her again, and his hand… Oh, God, she was falling, falling.

"Anything to make you feel good. That's all I want." He shifted inside her, and that sent her into the depths of the abyss, or maybe it was voice, his breath, the friction of his skin against hers. She dug her nails into his shoulder and pressed her face into his neck, crying out. Simon. Simon.

"So gorgeous," he muttered, wrapping his arms around her, clenching fistfuls of her hair where it fell along her back. Groaning her name, he drove hard into her, until, suddenly, he shuddered, his orgasm soundless except for a final, trembling breath.

As his muscles relaxed, he didn't let go of her. He kissed her again. Every inch of their skin still touched, and it hummed, like electricity. Like magic.

Chapter Fourteen

SIMON WOKE UP WITH LEONA'S back nestled against his chest and her waist tucked under his arm. If this was a dream, it was an incredibly realistic one. His senses were full of her: the ginger scent of her hair, the soft sound of her breath, the silk of her skin.

Propping himself up on his elbow, he drew his fingertips down her bare shoulder. Her mouth curved into a smile at his touch. Even in her sleep, her smile was wicked.

Memories stole through him. Leona, crying out against his neck. Riding him. Sitting with him at her kitchen table, staring into her glass as she told him about the robbery.

The robbery. He sat up, painfully awake. He had to go into the station, see if there was any news from last night, even though he knew, logically, the chances that the robbers had been caught were slim.

His jaw tightening, he looked down at Leona again. Her tousled hair clung to her neck and skimmed her breasts, she had dark smudges under her lashes, and she was, by far, the most beautiful woman he'd ever seen. He scrubbed a hand across his face. He was hopeless.

Across the room, Simon's phone rang. The station. He rolled out of bed and fished his phone out of the pocket of his work pants. Instead of dispatch or the Chief, it was his sister, Julia.

Simon tugged on his boxer shorts and pants one-handed, and headed out into Leona's sunlit living room. "Hey, Jules. You all right?"

"Did I *wake you up*?" She sounded amused. "It's ten o'clock, Simon! Usually, you've been at work for like, four hours by now."

Leona's kitchen clock said ten, too. Simon shook himself, amazed. He hadn't slept this much in years.

"What's up, Jules?"

"We-ell," she drawled, "Mom and I are downtown, so we thought we'd stop by to see if you wanted to hang out and grab some lunch later, but you don't seem to be at home *or* at work. So, where are you, Simon?"

He could hear her smile. In the background, his mother said something that sounded suspiciously like "with a girl."

"Who is she?" Julia insisted. "Mom says you haven't brought anybody home."

This was a disaster. "It's all kind of new. I'm not…" He could not have his mom and Julia descending on Leona today, of all days.

"Don't you want us to meet her?" Julia asked.

"Of course." He glanced at the dark doorway leading into Leona's bedroom. "Of course I do," he said again. "Look at a damn newspaper, Jules. We had a rough night."

"There's nothing in the paper. What happened?"

"There was a robbery late last night."

"And you're not at work right now? You must really like this girl."

He grimaced. As if he needed a reminder. "I've got to go."

"Wait—I'm sorry, Simon. I really want to meet her. How about tonight? Maybe we could grab a drink after dinner? I've been home a whole day and I haven't seen my big brother yet. Even you can't work *all* the time."

"I guess I can ask her," Simon said, though every instinct warned him against it. "I've got to go."

He hung up just as Leona stepped out of her bedroom, shrugging on her microscopic robe and rubbing her eyes. His heart constricted at the sight of her.

"Who was that?" She smiled up at him.

"My sister, Julia. She's a pain in the ass."

Leona laughed as she headed into her kitchen. Simon padded after her.

"Do you like French-pressed coffee?"

Of course she drank something fancy. "No idea," he admitted. "I actually should—" He was going to say *go to work*, but, watching her putter around her kitchen, he couldn't. Not yet. "I'd love to try it."

"It puts hair on your chest," Leona told him, "at least the way I make it."

"Do I…need that?" he asked, with a self-conscious downward glance. He'd never had a lot of body hair. Maybe he should grab a shirt.

"You," Leona said, "are perfect." She fetched a teapot and began filling it with water at the tap.

Perfect?

"So…my sister is in town." Simon took a deep breath. "She says…"

He'd practically invited himself over last night, and now he was going to ask her to meet his family? He had to be insane.

"She says what?" Leona asked, spooning coffee grounds into a glass container.

He had to ask. If he didn't, Jules would have his head. And he really did want them to meet.

"She wants to meet you. And grab a drink tonight, if you're free."

She glanced at him, her brow creased, then stepped away toward the stove to fetch the hissing teapot. "Meet me?"

"Yeah, you know…because we're sort of…seeing each other. You and me."

Leona looked up from pouring the hot water from the teapot into her glass container. "Oh."

He must have imagined that sense of closeness last night. The way she'd touched him, moved with him, it had been like…

"If you don't want to…" His stomach ached. "I know it's kind of sudden."

"I want to."

He couldn't believe he'd heard her right. "You do?"

"Of course." She cast him one quick, nervous smile before she turned back to her coffee and pushed a metal filter down into the glass container.

"Okay." He was stunned, lightheaded. "Tonight at eight?"

"Sure. Coffee?" She poured him a mug and handed it to him. He took it, looked at it, then set it down on her table, sloshing coffee onto the tablecloth.

"Is there—?" she began, but he interrupted her by taking her roughly by the shoulders and kissing her hard on the lips. He expected her to pull away, laugh him off, but she purred and sank into him, running her hands over his bare chest.

He couldn't start this right now, as much as he wanted to. Struggling to compose himself, he broke the kiss. "Fuck," he muttered.

"What was that for?" she asked, with a little smile. "Are you excited about the French press? I was pretty excited my first time."

"It was obviously not about the French press," he said, with an exhaled laugh. "I'm just—glad you're all right. Yesterday was…"

Leona's hands slid to his waist. She traced her thumbs over his hipbones. "Simon…thank you. For last night. For everything you did for me last night. I know it comes naturally to you to be so kind, but it's not… I don't know, it's not normal for me. I don't usually have anyone looking after me."

She had him now, for as long as she wanted him. He only wished he hadn't wasted so much time being afraid to pursue her. Pulling her in close, he kissed her forehead. "Are you going into the shop today?"

"I told Paul I'd help him clean up all that glass this morning. And we're getting a guy in to install a panic button." She shrugged. "We've always had a alarm, but it's not much good if they walk in the front door… It never mattered before, you know?"

"I know." He rested his cheek against her temple. What was happening to Grenton? And why couldn't he seem to stop it? "I should go," he said, sighing.

"Me, too."

"It's brave of you to go in. You're sure you'll be all right? Paul can—"

"I want to go. It's my shop, too, whether I own it or not."

He drew back to look at the resolute set to her mouth. "I know."

He felt the same way about Grenton. It was his town, and he'd look after it, no matter what.

Later that night, Simon met her outside her apartment. She could tell from his expression that he hadn't had any luck looking for the robbers. She didn't ask, just touched his arm lightly through his coat, hoping tonight could be a happy occasion for them both.

They walked over to Piper's Pub, no longer touching. Leona had gone to Piper's countless times, beginning on her twenty-first birthday. It was the townie hangout, and the only bar within walking distance of her apartment. She and Iris used to go every couple weeks. They'd play darts while Iris flirted shamelessly with the bartenders—any of them. Iris wasn't picky.

Since Iris had left for Europe on her Grand Tour, Leona hadn't gone back. Until tonight. With Simon beside her. She remembered seeing him at Piper's a handful of times. If she was drunk enough, she'd admired the way he looked, playing pool with his cop buddies. She'd even seem him with a girl once or twice. Back then, Leona and Simon had never done more than nod hello, though sometimes she'd imagined he was looking at her.

That might not have been her imagination after all.

He put his hand on her upper back and steered her toward a high top table by the bar, where a young woman waved at them, beaming. She had the same light brown hair as Simon, though it fell in loose waves to her shoulders. She had his straight nose, too, and a fuller version of his mouth. The big difference was in her eyes. They were light blue like his, but instead of intense and serious, hers were cheerful and inquisitive.

"Simon!" The young woman stood and threw her

arms around her much taller brother. "You didn't tell me you were dating *Leona Chaisty*." She pulled away and looked at Leona, her eyes widening. "We all thought you were just the *coolest*."

"What?" Leona asked blankly.

"In high school!" Julia exclaimed, easing back onto her chair and gesturing for her and Simon to do the same. "You were just *such* a badass. I was only a freshman when you guys were seniors, but I still remember that time you wore a really slinky top, and then it rained, and everyone could see that you had pierced your nipples!"

"Jules!" Simon blushed bright red.

"Oh, man, I thought that was *so* cool," Julia said dreamily. "I really wanted to get mine pierced after that, but Mom and Dad would've flipped. They didn't even want me to get my ears pierced! Do you still have them?" She grinned sidelong at Simon, who turned even redder.

"I let them close up," Leona admitted.

"Aw, why?"

"Oh, you know, one goes through phases."

"One does," Julia agreed. "Phases in which one wants one's nipples pierced."

"Exactly." Leona smiled.

"I always wondered about you two," Julia said. "Simon was always mooning over you, you know."

"I was not *mooning*—"

Julia patted his shoulder. "Of course, brother, dear."

"I wish I'd known that back then," Leona said.

"Would you have mooned right back?" Julia asked.

Leona had no idea what she would've done. Even in high school, Simon had been gorgeous, with a lean, rangy body and a face so elegant it was almost pretty.

He'd also been quiet and serious, and, though he'd hung around with the popular crowd, he'd been one of those popular kids who was actually nice to people. Popular *and* nice. That was two strikes against them getting together.

And, if Simon's dating history was anything to go by, Simon would not have been interested in hooking up. Another strike. Leona wouldn't have been interested in anything else.

When had *that* changed? He had spent the night at her house. They had told each other things, been through something together. She was getting drinks with a member of his family.

She couldn't remember if Liam or David even had a little sister. It had never come up; it had never mattered. So why did it matter with Simon? Why was she so pleased that Julia seemed to like her?

"Why don't I grab us some drinks?" She needed a second to clear her head. "What can I get you two?"

"I'm good with my rum and coke, thanks!" Julia tapped her glass. Simon agreed to a beer, so Leona squeezed through the crowd to the bar and frowned at the beer taps without quite seeing them.

"Leona, right?" the bartender asked, drying a glass with a bar towel. "You used to come in with that girl all the time. The blonde."

"Iris." Leona set her purse down on the bar. "She moved to Europe last summer."

"Damn," the bartender said. "She was really good at darts."

Leona laughed. "She was."

"Cute, too," the bartender added, "but mostly I noticed the darts."

"I'm sure." Privately, she wished he hadn't remembered Iris. It just made Leona miss her friend even more.

"When's she coming back?" the bartender asked.

"I don't know." Leona hadn't heard from Iris in months, and since Iris was basically vagabonding across Europe, Iris didn't have an address or a phone. Not as far as Leona knew, anyway. "I'm not sure she's coming back."

The bartender frowned sympathetically as he handed over their drinks. "She just left you all alone, huh?"

Leona shrugged, but he was right. They'd been best friends since they were little kids, but that hadn't stopped Iris from leaving her. When Iris had said goodbye, she'd rationalized leaving by saying Leona would never abandon the shop. The truth was Iris just didn't need Leona as much as Leona needed her. She never had. Iris had always had other friends, a few halfway-decent family members to rely on, a life outside of Leona that Leona could never have outside of Iris.

She paid the bill, trying to ignore the sadness creeping through her. Drinks in hand, she made her way back through the crowd to Simon and Julia. She passed Simon his pint glass across the table. He thanked her and raised his glass, but paused with it halfway to his mouth, frowning at his sister.

"Since when do you drink rum and coke?" he asked.

"Since always!"

Even Leona could tell Julia's ready smile was a bit too ready this time. Simon narrowed his eyes at her.

"I thought Dad raised you as a beer drinker."

"I still like beer…"

"Let me see that." He reached for her glass. She swatted at his hand, but he shook her off and took a sip. He set her glass back down, his eyebrows creasing together.

"Jules…"

Julia cast Leona an apologetic look.

No, no, no, Leona thought. If this was what she thought it was, she most definitely should not be here for this conversation.

Julia turned to Simon, who had his cop face on. "Don't freak out."

"If you have to say that…"

She winced. "Okay, fine."

She took a deep breath, but didn't speak until Simon said *Jules* again, his voice low and stern.

"I'm pregnant," Julia said.

No, Leona thought again. She couldn't be a part of this.

"For fuck's sake, Jules," Simon said, pressing his palm to his temple. "Who's the father?"

"Aaron Hardy. He works in the lab with me. Simon, he's awesome. We love each other."

"Yeah? Is that why I've never met him?"

"We haven't been dating for very long, but I *do* love him."

"Do Mom and Dad know?"

"Are you kidding me?" She sighed. "I'm going to tell them. This weekend, when I'm officially three months along. I didn't want to tell anyone before then, just in case."

"So you thought it would be a good idea to meet me at a bar?"

"I didn't know you'd try my drink!" she snapped. "You jerk. Anyway, I had to get away from Dad. I think he suspects. He's just like you, you know."

"Smart?" Simon suggested.

"*Suspicious,*" Julia shot back.

Simon folded his arms across his chest and glared at

her.

"Leona," Julia said, with a pleading look in her direction. "Tell him he's overreacting."

Leona took a fortifying sip of her beer. Her usual witticisms escaped her. "Well," she said finally, wrapping her trembling hands around her pint glass, "you're what, twenty-five?"

Julia nodded.

When Leona was twenty-five, she was still doing drugs and drinking too much with Iris and Iris's friends. Iris, a compulsive traveler even then, used to convince Leona to go on long road trips, sometimes halfway across the country, with only a few days' notice and no supplies apart from booze and cigarettes. They'd had no one to care about but themselves, so that was what they did. At least the damage they did to themselves was relatively temporary.

Bringing a child into that world would have been like…well, it would have been like what her parents had done to her.

Leona looked back up into Julia's imploring blue eyes. Even after only a few minutes of conversation, Leona knew Julia was nothing like her. She was a smart, responsible woman, and if she was anything like her brother, she was a good person. She would love and care for her child more than anything in the world.

"I think you're completely capable of making your own decisions," Leona said. "And if you're happy about your pregnancy, then I'm happy for you, too."

Julia blinked back tears. "Thanks."

Simon glanced from his sister to Leona, a frown furrowing his brow. "I—it's—you're right. I'm sorry, Jules. I'm being an asshole. I *am* happy for you, I'm just worried."

"I know." Julia sniffed, and her mouth crooked into a smile so much like Simon's it made Leona's heart ache.

Leona clenched her hands into fists on her lap. As much as she didn't want to be here for this, she couldn't ruin this moment for them. Simon was going to be an uncle, and once he realized it, he would be—

"Holy shit," he said softly, the corners of his eyes crinkling with joy. "A baby."

"I know!" Julia said again. This time, she gave a tearful, hiccupping laugh. Simon slid off his bar stool and wrapped his tiny sister in a bear hug.

For the second time in as many days, Leona's throat hurt. She was obviously still overtired from the robbery, and from cleaning up shards of glass in her beloved shop. Paul had hugged her twice today and had apologized to her with tears in his eyes. The memory still made Leona cringe, hours later. He shouldn't feel responsible for her. She was responsible for herself.

Simon released his sister, kissed her cheek, and sat back on his bar stool. Glancing at Leona with a smile, he found one of her hands where it lay clenched in her lap underneath the table. The warmth of his touch flowed up through her body, and she smiled back, hoping, for his sake, that she looked happy instead of sad.

Chapter Fifteen

THEY LEFT PIPER'S AFTER A couple hours. Julia mocked him mercilessly for asking her if she felt up to driving herself home. "I'm pregnant, not drunk. Or an invalid."

Standing with Leona on the sidewalk, Simon watched Julia get into her hybrid car and wondered when she would start to show. She hadn't even finished her first trimester. So many things could go wrong before the baby was due—and afterward. Julia and the baby's father were both still in grad school. How would they support themselves and a baby? And how could Simon be sure that the father deserved his little sister?

Still…Leona was right. Julia was an adult—a brilliant adult. She would be a wonderful mom.

He slid an arm around Leona's waist and kissed her knitted hat. "Can I walk you home?"

She agreed, and they walked down Cascade toward her apartment. They passed by the covered bridge, where, underneath the white Christmas lights, a teenaged couple stood nose to nose, whispering to each other between kisses. If Simon were on duty, he'd tell them to go home, but he wasn't on duty. And even if he had been, he'd made out in the shadow of the bridge with Mallory enough times to feel like a hypocrite for telling them off. Kissing under the covered bridge was practically a Grenton teenager tradition.

Thinking back on it now, it didn't seem fair that he used to make out with Mallory in public all the time but he'd flipped out at Leona that night on the park bench. Obviously, there were differences. He was older now, and a cop, but Leona was right—no one had seen them except for Jack, and Jack didn't really care. If anything, Jack seemed to think Simon should be pursuing Leona.

Simon had been too hard on her about it. His own issues had gotten in the way, just like they always did.

At her front stoop, he reached for her gloved hands, expecting to kiss her goodnight.

"Want to come up for another drink?" she asked. "Is that a normal thing to ask?"

"Of course," he said, pleasantly surprised. "To both those questions."

As soon as they got upstairs, he pulled her in for a kiss. "Thanks for coming out tonight. After yesterday, especially." He slid her hat off and smoothed her hair. "I hope it wasn't too awkward for you, with Julia's big announcement." Leona had seemed a little nervous. Even without life-changing news, Julia could be overwhelming. And it was only one day since the robbery.

"It was fine." Slipping her hands underneath his coat, she traced his spine through his shirt. Desire for her expelled the cold from his limbs.

"I wish I'd been there that time in high school," he murmured, "when your shirt got wet and everyone saw your nipple piercings. I never knew you had those."

Julia's description alone had been enough to send blood surging to his cock, despite the incredibly inappropriate time and place. He'd never thought of himself as being into piercings, but on Leona...

"What would you have done if you'd seen them?" she asked, with a playful smile.

"Had a hard-on for days, probably." Days? More like months, years. "I would've been too afraid to say anything."

"Afraid?" She arched an eyebrow. "Of little old me?"

He grinned. "Can you blame me?"

She grinned back, but instead of teasing him, she pulled away to shrug off her coat and hang it over a kitchen chair. Opening the fridge, she bent down to peer inside. The hem of her dress hitched up to reveal the gentle curves of her inner thighs, silhouetted in her black tights. An image of her flashed into his mind, and he blushed, unzipping his coat with trembling fingers.

"Do you have any...outfits?"

She pulled a couple beers from the fridge and turned back to him, brow furrowed. "Outfits?"

Even with his tongue loosened by a couple of drinks, he struggled to get the words out. "You know, something...sexy." Something tight and black and revealing as all hell, worn with stiletto heels and a riding crop.

Her mouth quirked up in mischievous amusement. "Why, Officer Labelle, are you asking me if I have any Dominatrix outfits?"

With an embarrassed chuckle, he rubbed the back of his neck. "I know it's not really a good time—"

"The answer to your question," she said, walking up to him with the two beers in one hand, and with the other hand drawing a line down his jaw, "is yes."

"Okay," he breathed.

"Though I feel like I should point out that there are as many different kinds of outfits as there are Dommes. A T-shirt and jeans, pajamas, a princess tiara... It doesn't matter."

He swallowed, his embarrassment rising back into his throat. "Makes sense."

"But since this is *me* we're talking about…" She winked.

"Can I see it?"

Her arms fell to her side. "Simon…I want… Can we talk first?"

Never a good sign. He'd been pressuring her, after everything she had gone through yesterday, and after she'd been generous enough to meet his sister on such short notice.

"Come here, dear heart." Taking his hand, she pulled him into her living room. She sat him down on her couch, setting their beers down on the coffee table in front of them. Joining him on the couch, she frowned at her lap.

Was this it? Was she going to end this, whatever it was? He should leave, run away before she dropped the ax, and try to spare himself some of the pain that was to come.

"My darling," she murmured, "I want you at my mercy."

Holy shit, Simon thought, the fire in his blood searing away his fear. This was what she wanted to tell him? "I want that, too."

"Do you?" She tilted her head, her eyes thoughtful, before glancing away again. "I have to tell you… I lied to you, Simon, when I told you I liked variety. I *do* like it. I loved last night with you, and our night together after the Thai place. But the truth is that, in my heart, I'm a Domme. That is never…" She sighed. "That is never going to change."

"Don't you think I know that?" Simon said, surprised. "I've—Jesus, I've probably always known it, since we were teenagers."

A name for the energy that drew him to her had always escaped him before, but he knew it now. She was Dominant not just in bed, but in every way. She was strong and fierce and courageous, and she did whatever the hell she wanted, and he loved that about her.

On impulse, he slid off the couch onto the floor, kneeling between her legs on her geometric carpet.

"Leona," he said, resting his hands on her thighs, skimming the fabric of her tights with his thumbs. "It's true that I'm still figuring stuff out. It's all so new for me, and…and fucking terrifying."

Her hands went to his shoulders, kneading his tense muscles. He sank into her touch.

"The thing is," he said, "that night in your kitchen was the most amazing experience of my life." He hoped that didn't sound pathetic; he didn't know how else to describe how transcendent it had been for him. "I want to worship you again, and again, and again." With each word, he trailed kisses along her slender forearm. When he reached her elbow, he let his lips linger on that delicate skin. "And I want to let you do what you want to me. Cuff me, tease me…anything you want."

He had spent his whole life trying to resist her, knowing he wasn't good enough for her. Something about acting that out *with her* was intensely erotic. That night in his handcuffs, the show she'd put on for him…

Drawing her hand from his shoulder, he sucked the tip of her index finger lightly between his lips. A rosy flush stood out on her cheeks, and her eyes fell closed. It felt *right* to be here, kneeling before her, kissing her.

"Cuff me again." He kissed her rings. "Please."

"But—" She forced her eyes open, though her eyelids looked heavy and languid, and her pupils were huge in her light eyes. "But Simon, you *have* a Dominant streak. I can feel it. Even the way you beg me, it's like a command—"

"You don't like it—" he began, wincing.

"I do like it, actually." She gave a little gasp of a laugh. "I *love* it. It's so fucking sexy." Without seeming to realize what she was doing, she pressed her thighs tighter against his shoulders, letting her calves brush against his lower back, enfolding him within her legs. "I just—I don't want to hurt you," she said, her eyes growing sad. "I know some people are switches, or power bottoms, I guess. I just want to make sure that with *you*, that you're doing this stuff because you *want* to, and not because I'm pressuring you into it."

"I want to," he said, his voice husky.

"Then let's make a deal. When are you off work tomorrow?"

"Eleven. I'm second shift."

"If you still want to sub for me, come over after your shift tomorrow night."

"Not tonight?" he said, disappointed.

She smoothed his hair affectionately. "This is something you should think about with a clear mind. Not when you've been drinking, or right after you've gotten huge news."

"I've only had a couple drinks," he protested.

"I know, darling. But this way, you have time to think. To change your mind, if you want to."

He wasn't going to change his mind, but he could tell that she was set on doing things this way. She was looking after him, protecting him—from her desires, or from his own—and he was grateful that she cared enough about him to make this extra effort.

He kissed her knuckles again. "All right. Tomorrow night."

Letting the glass door swing shut behind her, Leona surveyed her shop. Yesterday, she'd only been here for a couple hours, and Paul had been with her the entire time. It was the shortest shift she had ever worked, and truthfully, she hadn't done much actual working, leaving Emma to tend to customers and ring up sales.

This morning, Leona would be alone in the shop for two hours before it opened to receive and unpack a new shipment. And that was fine. It was *fine*. It was her shop, and she would be damned if she would let some assholes in ski masks ruin it for her.

Behind her, a knock rattled the door. She flinched.

Emma waved at her through the glass, her short blue hair gleaming in the winter sunshine. A full-time breakfast cook at a local B&B, Emma usually only worked afternoons or the shop's occasional evening shifts.

Leona opened the door. "What're you doing here?"

"Paul thought you might want some help unloading the shipment."

"I can do it myself," Leona said, crossing her arms over her chest.

Emma shrugged. "I mean, if you *want* to unpack a hundred boxes all by yourself, be my guest."

With a sigh, Leona stepped back to let Emma pass and locked the door after her. "You better not tell anyone I let you help."

"Don't worry, Ice Queen, I won't. And I'm not going

to ask you how you're doing, or talk to you like you're five years old, or go on and on about the high rates of crime today, all right? So just relax."

Leona cast Emma a begrudging smile. They both signed in and walked into the back, where they began to clear space for the shipment. The delivery driver arrived a few minutes later. Soon, the back room was a maze of boxes, some as high as Leona's hips.

Leona and Emma unpacked the shipment in a companionable silence. Unrolling the packing paper and breaking down the boxes cut up Leona's hands and made her wrists tired, but she loved seeing their newest products in person for the first time, finding out the weight and balance of each piece, the way the light played on every surface.

"Think we'll hear from Margie today?" Emma asked.

Leona had been asking herself the same question. "No idea."

"It was insanely nice of Paul to give her the week off."

"I know." Leona bit her lip. "I was wondering if she might come in, anyway. Just to get away from her husband."

"That guy is a dick. I saw him at the grocery store the other day, and he was yelling at some poor employee about the meat selection, or something."

Leona should have asked Simon to check in on Margie today. Knowing him, he probably would, anyway.

"Are you pissed at her?" Emma asked. "I mean, they were coming for *her*, not you or the shop, you know? It was kind of her fault this happened to you…"

Leona squeezed one of the still-wrapped shipment pieces in her hand. The paper crinkled under her fingertips.

"I guess I would be pissed," she said slowly, "except that I don't really feel like it was her fault. I mean, I don't know where she got that money, but I don't think she would have hidden it here unless she had no other choice."

Emma pulled the last piece of tissue paper off of a plum-colored sugar bowl. "That's fair, I guess. I don't know. I'd still be pissed."

"Time for me to open the register," Leona said.

"I'll go with you," Emma said at once, and from her firm tone, Leona suspected Paul had told her not to leave Leona alone. She should argue with Emma about it. She didn't need to be coddled.

Leona just nodded and walked into the front room. As ridiculous as it was, she was glad Emma was here. Every innocuous moment with Emma was another stone in the wall between the present and the past. As the day wound on, Leona was grateful to every customer—even the ones who had a million questions about Christmas decorating—for the exact same reason.

Paul came in at two in the afternoon just as she finished ringing up a sale. He grinned at her guarded expression. "I promise not to hug you again. Don't look so nervous."

"I'm never nervous." She reached across the counter and squeezed his arm. He patted her shoulder, his eyes a little bright.

"There's my girl." He walked toward the back, shrugging off his big wool coat.

Leona rested her hands on the cash register, memorizing its smudgy contours. She was never nervous. Not about being in the shop after the robbery, and not about tonight.

At three o'clock, when Simon's shift was just beginning, Leona's shift ended. On her walk home, the brisk air was not cold enough to temper the fire growing inside of her.

Her apartment spilled over with pale afternoon sunlight and the scents of lavender and jasmine. She went straight into her bedroom and opened the doors to her closet, where she crouched down to poke through a storage unit against the interior wall.

She'd bought some new equipment about a year ago, and it had languished in her storage unit since. She was experienced enough to know that it was good equipment; the problem was finding someone worthy of its use.

She had found that person now, if he wanted it.

Leaving the ball in his court was the right thing to do. He needed to make the decision with a clear mind, not when he was already buzzed and horny and emotional. She couldn't bear the thought of him regretting his decision to sub for her because he'd decided to do it on an impulse. Better for him to think it through, and be sure. No matter how difficult it was for her to wait for him.

Would he come to her tonight? And if he did, then what?

He knew she was a Domme. He'd said he had always known. He might like it, want it, as much as she did. Not just tonight, but for—

Forever, whispered a small, closed-off part of her. She shivered.

She had never imagined a future with a man before—she never let herself imagine her future at all. To her, the future held even more loneliness than her past. Paul would leave her just like Iris had left her, and she would rattle around in the shop by herself for the rest of her days, too afraid and stunted to make any real changes.

Even when she'd agreed to her first couple dates with Simon, she'd expected him to realize, all too soon, that he should be with someone as good and upstanding as he was. Looking back, she'd needled him on purpose, building her armor against his inevitable realization that he was a better person than she was.

Except he hadn't realized that yet. He'd knelt at her feet and kissed her rings as if she were a queen—*his* queen—and he'd told her that subbing for her that night in her kitchen had been the most amazing experience of his life. Whatever their dynamic was, he liked it, and she liked it, too. So much. Just like she liked him, so much more than she should.

Chapter Sixteen

SIMON KNOCKED TWICE ON THE front door, frowning at the peeling paint and the battered wooden sign reading *home sweet home.*

Technically, he was not supposed to be doing this. The Chief hadn't assigned the case to anyone yet. Simon suspected the Chief wasn't sure what to do with it. The Chief was still convinced that Margie's husband was behind the robbery, but there was no evidence of that, and Simon couldn't imagine a husband—even an abusive husband—hiring the men Leona had described to scare his wife and steal from her. In his experience, abusers enjoyed doing their own dirty work. And from Leona's descriptions of the robbers, they'd been motivated to get that money for themselves—and furious when some of it had turned out to be missing.

So if they weren't her husband's buddies, who were they?

The door cracked open, and Margie Smith peered out.

"I just had some questions, ma'am," Simon said.

Margie paled, but she opened the door a little wider. "I already talked to that boy. Jack. Officer Miller. I don't have anything else to say."

"I had some follow up questions, that's all," he said.

"Can I come in?"

With a reluctant nod, Margie opened the door the rest of the way. Simon stepped over a mewling cat lingering in the doorway.

Two more cats slunk through the sunken TV room. Another perched on the dining room table, tiptoeing across stacks of catalogs and unopened bills. Margie's ranch, as careworn and tired Margie herself, didn't look like the house of someone with an extra forty-five thousand dollars.

"Is your husband home?" Simon asked.

"He's out back, up at the barn."

"Does Mr. Smith work?"

"Not anymore. He has a bad back." She jutted her chin out, defensive of the husband no one else seemed to like. But her eyes were nervous, her gaze flickering from Simon's badge to the floor.

"How does he spend his time now that he's not working?"

Margie gestured toward the window. "He likes to be out with the animals."

Simon crossed through the TV room to the dining room, where a window overlooked their back yard. A small red barn sat on a hill beside a paddock and chicken coop.

"We have chickens, goats, a couple of donkeys, and one old horse," she said.

"And you have the cats," Simon said. "Four cats?"

"Six cats and a dog. A mutt. He's out with Richard now."

Simon frowned out the window. "Where'd you get all of your pets?"

"All rescues from that awful kill shelter."

He glanced at Margie curiously. "You ever take your

animals to the vet's office here in town?"

"We've never needed their services for anything."

"You have all these animals and you've never needed a vet?"

"Richard is good with them." The defensive tone crept back into her voice. "He could've been a vet himself, if he wanted to."

Strange, perhaps, but not a crime. "What did you need that money for, Margie?"

"I didn't need it for anything. I already told Officer Miller that money was a gift. I didn't know what to do with it. I've never had that kind of money in my life."

"Who gave it to you?"

She shook her head, her lips pressed together. "I can't tell you that."

"Why not?"

Her gaze fell to the faded blue carpet under her dining room table. Sadness poured off of her, and Simon felt a twinge of guilt for questioning her about something that clearly pained her.

"Did the person who gave it to you get it illegally?" he asked quietly.

Her gaze snapped back up. "No. No. Nothing like that."

"Then you can tell me, at least, who gave it to you. If they weren't doing anything illegal, they won't get in trouble."

"I can't." Her lip trembled. "I can't."

"So why keep it in the shop? You didn't want your husband to know about it?"

"I can't talk about this," she whispered. "Please."

For the first time, Simon wondered if the Chief was right about what had happened. He scrutinized Margie for a moment, looking for injuries, but there was nothing on her face or hands.

"Did you know Kristy Woods, the vet tech?" he asked. "She was injured in the bombing."

"I saw her around a few times, before she left town. But we never spoke."

"What about Nancy O'Shea, the chemistry teacher?"

"I saw her around occasionally, but that was all."

"All right." He sighed, out of ideas for now. "Thanks for your time. I'm sorry to bother you."

He walked back to her door. She followed him, her steps slow and measured, her arms tight to her chest.

"Officer Labelle," she said.

He paused, his hand on the door, turning back toward her.

"Is Leona okay?" Margie asked softly. "I haven't seen her since and…I know you…"

"She's doing okay."

"I feel terrible she was… Leona and Paul, they've been nothing but kind to me. I wouldn't ever want… Leona, especially." Margie's eyes were bright. She pressed her fingertips to her cheek. "She's my friend."

"I know." He didn't trust Margie. There was too much she wasn't saying, and her silence had already put Leona in danger once. But he did believe that she cared about Leona, and he knew Leona cared about her, too.

He cleared his throat, his gaze flicking toward the window looking out at the barn. "Margie… If you ever need help…if you ever feel unsafe, you know you can come to me."

Margie gave a solemn nod, and Simon bade her goodbye, wishing he knew what she was hiding.

As he was driving back to the station, a call came in about a burst pipe flooding a street on the outskirts of town. He turned south toward the site, his hand falling to his pocket, tracing the shape of Leona's house keys through his work pants.

She'd given him a spare set of keys last night. No explanation, just keys, and the instructions to come over at 11:30, if he still wanted to.

Tonight, he'd be at Leona's mercy.

———◆———

At last, at 11:25, he drove to her apartment. On her front stoop, he reached for her keys. He'd waited for this all day, but now he couldn't believe it was finally happening. What if he disappointed her? What if it was too much for him?

What if he didn't like it?

Forcing the muscles in his neck to relax, he unlocked her front door and stepped into her dark stairwell. It was silent and mercifully warm—too warm, he thought, a moment later, as his racing heart picked up speed. She was upstairs, waiting for him. He couldn't stop trying to picture what she was wearing, or what she was going to do to him.

At the door to her apartment, he fumbled with her keys again. His hands were sweating underneath his gloves. He took them off and shrugged off his overcoat, but it wasn't enough.

Finally, he opened the door. A single candle flickered on her dining room table, casting threads of light into the corners of the room.

"Leona?" He licked his lips, hesitating in her doorway.

Seconds ticked by. He didn't know what to do.

"You came." Her voice was a low purr. "Good pet."

She stepped into the dining room, wearing her tiny robe with a pair of stiletto heels. The shoes had straps around the ankles, accentuating her long legs. All of his blood rushed to his groin.

"Tell me you're naked under that robe."

She lifted a finger and waved it at him. "No orders from you tonight, my darling."

"Okay." She was right. He knew the deal.

"The correct response is 'yes, Mistress.'" She smiled wickedly.

"Yes, Mistress," he said, the strangeness of the word heavy on his lips.

"Go into the bedroom and undress." She didn't need to speak loudly to imbue her voice with command. Some of the guys on the task force could have learned a thing or two from her. "What do you say?" she added, her eyes glittering in the candlelight.

"Yes, Mistress."

"Good." A splash of color stained her cheeks.

He sensed her eyes on him as he walked through her living room to her bedroom door, but she didn't follow him.

Inside her bedroom, three candles were staged around the room, illuminating the red silk bed. Now he was supposed to undress, right? What was she doing, while he did this?

He unbuttoned his shirt and slid it off. With each piece of clothing he removed, he felt even more exposed and vulnerable and nervous. He sat down on her bed, his limbs shaky, and his cock already hard and straight. A drop of moisture beaded at the head.

The door opened. Leona stepped inside, taking in the sight of him.

"Stand up."

He rose from the bed at once. A moment too late, he remembered what he was supposed to say.

"Yes, Mistress."

She prowled a lazy half-circle around him. "I love the way you stand. Did you know that, pet? You make standing look so energetic. So ready." She tapped a fingertip against her lips. "In fact, I'll keep you standing."

Turning away, she shut the bedroom door. Some kind of rig hung over the doorframe, with two straps ending in wide leather cuffs. Simon's stomach flipped over.

She took him by the wrist, and he let her position him with his back to the door. She raised his arms up over his head and slid his wrists into the cuffs, tightening the straps that held the cuffs in place. The leather hugged his skin. Considering that it was only slung over her door, it was very secure.

With his arms up over his head, his chest and stomach were open to her gaze, and she took advantage, letting her appreciation pour over him.

"You make a wonderful art piece," she said. "Let's make that the safe word tonight. Art."

Art. He smiled in spite of himself.

She walked away, leaving him strung up by the door, and vanished into a dark corner of her candlelit bedroom. A moment later, she returned with a wooden kitchen chair and, oddly, a glass of white wine. She set the wine glass on the floor by leg of the chair and turned back to him, still standing. Her hands moved to the belt of her robe.

His senses roared to life. "Yes," he groaned. "Please. Mistress."

The robe slipped from her shoulders. Underneath, she wore a tight black leather corset with lacing up the front, revealing glimpses of her stomach and the insides of her breasts. Apart from the corset, she wore absolutely nothing.

"Jesus." Simon couldn't take his eyes off her.

Her wide mouth curving into a smile, she perched on the edge of her chair with her legs crossed, facing him, and idly picked up her wine glass. "I like to appreciate my art at my leisure," she said, sipping her wine and licking a clear droplet from her lower lip.

"Leona…" The smooth curves of her hips and thighs, and the glimpses of her pale stomach through the lacings, were unbelievably tantalizing. He wanted to beg her to uncross her legs. He'd already waited twenty-four hours for her. He gripped the straps holding him in place, his knuckles whitening.

Her eyebrow rose. "Impatient already, my pet? How do you think I feel? I had to make myself come four or five times already today, thinking of you. And it's still not enough."

He tried to curse, but his mouth was so dry, the word cracked. He couldn't think about anything but Leona touching herself while she pictured him.

She uncrossed her legs, and his cock throbbed painfully.

"First, I made myself come like this." Her voice was hypnotic, her smallest movements mesmerizing. She drew her fingertips lightly down the lacings until she reached the end of the corset. Her fingers strayed lower, dipping into her sex. "I fucked myself," she murmured, sliding her fingers in and out, "thinking about your cock." Her fingers were wet. Simon desperately wanted to lick them clean.

"But then that wasn't enough." Setting the wine glass back down on the floor, Leona dipped her hand inside it. Her fingertips dripping wine, she trailed her hand up her leg, along the lacings, then across her chest. "I thought about you, coming on my breasts." She traced wine over the arc of her breast. With a sinful smile, she slid her finger into her mouth. His cock gave another painful throb.

"It still wasn't enough," she said.

Suddenly, she stood up. A drop of wine ran down the top of her thigh. The desire to lick it off overwhelmed him. He struggled against the cuffs, without knowing what he was doing, until the leather pulled on his skin and brought him back to himself.

She disappeared into the dark corner of her bedroom again, and when she returned, she was holding the choker necklace from the crafts fair.

"No," Simon croaked, dismayed. *Art*, he thought. *Please don't*.

Sweeping her long hair over her shoulders, she tightened the necklace around her throat. "*This* was what I needed," she said, "to come again and again and again."

It looked impossibly sexy on her, glimmering on her elegant throat in the candlelight, highlighting the expanse of her chest and the tops of her breasts over her black leather corset.

"Leona," he groaned, dizzy with desire for her. "Mistress." He didn't know what he was begging her for now—to take it off or to keep it on, to make herself come while he watched or to fuck him. All he knew was that he'd never been this turned on in his life.

"I slide my fingertips underneath it," she said, mercilessly, "and I imagine they're your fingers. I want your hands everywhere. Everywhere." She took a length of her hair in her fist and pulled it, tilting her head back. Her free hand slid up her breasts to the necklace, her fingertips slipping underneath the pearls just like she'd said. "Do you believe me? That this is what I want?"

"No," he said, without thinking. She was humoring him, that was all. Trying to turn him on. It was certainly effective.

Her eyes narrowed. "You think I'm lying to you?"

"No, but…" He trailed off as she stepped toward him, bringing the scent of ginger and wine and sex.

"You do, and for that, you will be punished. Turn around."

"I can't—" He glanced up at the rig holding him. He could turn, actually, now that he looked at it. The straps holding the cuffs were long enough to crisscross each other.

"Do it."

Simon turned around. The cuffs tugged his arms higher as the slack in the straps shortened. He rested his forehead against the door. Thoughts of a riding crop or a cane filtered through his head.

"You like to watch," she purred in his ear. Her body bumped against his back. Her breasts. The lacings in her corset. "But if you're going to doubt me, then you don't get to watch. I'll make myself come and go to sleep and leave you strung up like this all night."

The thought of her crying out behind him as she came, just out of sight… He shivered. "You wouldn't." Did he want her to?

"Wouldn't I?" She nipped his ear. "Maybe I'll make *you* come, whether you like it or not." Her hands slid over his hips to squeeze his cock, a little harder than he normally would have liked. Tonight, starved for her touch, it was perfect. Involuntarily, he pumped his hips, pushing his cock through her hands.

"Is this what you want?" she whispered.

"No," he moaned, "I want you to come first."

"Why?"

"Because it's…because…"

He'd always believed that the woman should come first, without exception, especially since he'd always known he wasn't much good in bed. He was too reserved, had too many hang-ups. At least if he could get his partner off first, she could enjoy some aspect of being with him. He didn't know how to explain this to Leona.

One of her hands released his cock to cup his balls, pulling on the skin hard enough for him to feel it, but not hard enough to hurt him. She was in perfect control of herself, even now. With her other hand, she stroked his cock, her grip loosening, her strokes long and thorough. He had no doubt she could make him come like this. She could make him do anything she wanted.

Her body pressed against his, pushing him into her door. The head of his cock bumped into the door each time she stroked him. "Mistress," he groaned, sagging forward, letting the rig support his weight. He could feel her pressed against his ass, and she was wet, and hot. Her hand on his cock ignited every droplet of his blood, every cell in his skin. "Fuck me, Mistress," he begged. "Fuck me the way you want me."

"Say it again," she groaned, her breathing harsh, "say Mistress."

"Mistress," he panted. His head was spinning. "My Mistress."

His stomach muscles suddenly clenched. White-hot light stabbed through him. He cried out as he came, his body seizing, his fingers gripping the straps holding him in place hard enough for the leather to chafe his skin. She held him steady, one arm wrapping around his waist, while the other cupped his twitching cock.

His mind reeling, he let his face rest against the door. He'd never had an orgasm like that before—like a sudden explosion.

"Let me make you come, Mistress," he said thickly, struggling with mingled exhaustion and urgency. "I want to make you feel good."

Without a word, she unbuckled the straps that held the cuffs on. His arms fell to his sides. Still standing behind him, she massaged his aching shoulders and kissed the back of his neck.

"Lie on the bed," she murmured. "On your back."

Simon took shaking steps to her bed and climbed into the center. What was she planning? He'd be hard again in a few minutes, definitely, but not just yet.

"Put this on."

Standing next to the bed, Leona handed him a strap with a leather-wrapped o-ring in the center. He had absolutely no idea what it was. "It goes in your mouth," she told him, running a fingertip along his lip. *Oh.* Lust flared back to life inside him.

He put the strap between his teeth, and the o-ring forced his mouth open, preventing him from speaking. She adjusted it for him before buckling the strap behind his head.

She had velvet fabric in her hands now; he had no idea where she'd gotten it. Obediently, he let her tie his hands and feet to all four bedposts, leaving him spread-eagled on her silky bed. He was even more vulnerable like this than when he'd been standing by her door, or when he'd been handcuffed on her floor the very first time they'd hooked up. He could not move, or speak.

"If you need it to stop," she told him, walking around the bed to check her knots, "snap your fingers, and I will stop everything and untie you. All right? Nod if you understand me."

He nodded. He trusted her, he realized. He was nervous, but not afraid. He trusted her completely.

She climbed up onto the bed beside him, distracting him from his thoughts. Her cream-white thighs straddled his chest. Their eyes met. Her expression was raw with lust. A drop of moisture landed on his skin, and he realized, with a jerk of desire low in his belly, that she had dripped on him.

She repositioned her legs on the bed, carefully moving higher to straddle his face. He groaned low in his throat, overcome with a mixture of longing and relief. He licked her clit through the o-ring, and she gasped, bending forward to clutch at her silky pillows. He couldn't hold her hips, or slide his fingers inside her. His tongue couldn't reach as much of her as he wanted, and he couldn't use the rest of his mouth.

It was driving him wild.

She sank a fraction lower onto his face, and he took his chance to thrust his tongue inside her. Her fingers tightened in the pillows above his head. He licked her inside and out, his strokes as firm and powerful as he could make them.

"Oh—*oh*, my darling—" Her body trembled, her thighs tightening against his cheeks.

His whole world was her scent, her taste, her soft skin. *My Leona,* he thought. *My Mistress.*

Her breathy moans grew louder as trembling swept through her body. She was still holding herself back, taking care not to press too hard against his face, watching his hands to make sure his fingers were loose, relaxed.

Suddenly, though, she cursed, and her hips bucked, her body twitching. The curse dissolved into a strangled groan, and her eyes squeezed shut, a flush spreading down her throat and chest.

As soon as her body stopped convulsing, she swung her leg over to kneel beside him. Leaning down, she unbuckled the gag holding his mouth open, pulled it free, and kissed him deeply. He kissed her back, wishing her could hold her, but thrilled, too, by his restraints.

"You're so beautiful when you come," he told her, between kisses. "So beautiful. Fuck me like this?" Like this: spread-eagled, at your mercy, yours.

Without another word, she reached across the bed to the nightstand for a condom and tore open the package.

He was hugely, achingly hard again, and when she rolled the condom down onto his cock, he shivered at her sweet, light touch.

"You feel so good, Mistress."

"How good?" She lowered herself onto him, tightening around him, and he swallowed, his eyes practically rolling back in his head.

"No one else compares to you," he said. "No one ever has, or ever will."

She was running her hands all over him: his chest, his bound arms, his thighs. His skin blazed where she touched him. He wanted to force his eyes back open so he could watch her ride him, but he couldn't. All he could do was rock his hips with her and hold on to the straps tying him to the bed.

He heard her curse and wondered if she was going to come again. He couldn't imagine anything better.

"Come for me," he said. "Use me to get off."

Her breath hitched in what was almost a laugh. "Giving me orders again, dear heart?"

"No, Mistress," he said, smiling. "I'm begging you."

"Then—then beg." One of her hands skimmed the side of his face. His eyes still closed, he turned his mouth into her palm and kissed it.

"Please, Mistress. I need to feel you come while I'm inside you. Please let me."

"Simon…Simon, I…yes, yes."

He drove into her harder and faster—he couldn't resist, as the sounds of her pleasure drove him to the edge. This time, she came with a choked scream, her fingernails digging into his shoulders, and he rolled over the edge a moment later, his climax crashing over him in long, slow waves.

Chapter Seventeen

IT TOOK A FEW SECONDS for Leona's head to clear. Looking down at Simon spread-eagled beneath her didn't help. She'd be thinking about how sexy he looked, tied to her bed like this, for the rest of her life.

Leona forced herself to climb off of him, slide off the bed, and take care of the condom. Going back to the bed, she untied his ankles and massaged his feet and calves. Next, she went to the head of the bed, untied his wrists, and massaged his hands and forearms. He cast her a sleepy, dazzling smile.

"Thanks."

"Of course." He was new to restraints. The last thing she wanted was to make his muscles stiff or sore. She got back up onto the bed beside him to massage his biceps and shoulders, but before she could, he pulled her down onto the bed and kissed her.

"Damn," he said, with another dazzling smile. "That was…insanely amazing."

She pushed herself up on her elbow to look at him, a flicker of hope in her chest. "You liked it?"

"It was, by far, the best sex I've ever had."

"Me, too." Saying it out loud, she realized it was true. She'd been nervous, especially at first, but his responses to her had been utterly exhilarating. The way he'd begged her to fuck him against the door, his powerful body supported only by the leather cuffs around his muscular forearms. The lust in his eyes when he'd realized what the ring gag was for.

"Did it bring up any feelings for you?" She had promised herself she'd do aftercare properly this time.

"Feelings?" He laced his hands behind his head, his blue eyes earnest.

"You know…were you afraid? Did anything bother you? Trigger anything for you?"

"I wasn't afraid. It was perfect. And I trust you."

She swallowed, touched. Honored. He hadn't just begrudgingly given her another chance after she'd screwed up the first few times. They had developed real trust, and that meant the world to her.

"And…" She took a deep breath. "The choker? That was okay?" That was the part she'd been most nervous about, and it was the only time she'd thought she saw real fear in his eyes.

"It was…" He sat up, facing her, and touched the tip of his index finger to one of the choker's pearls. "It's getting more manageable. I like it like this, with you calling the shots."

"All right," she said softly. They could work with that.

"You really do like it?" he asked, his brow creasing.

"Yes."

"Did you really make yourself come five times with it on?" A smile crooked his mouth.

She laughed. "Today? No."

"Other days?"

"Yes. Well, maybe not five times." She swept her hair back from her face. "But a few times."

"Damn." His gaze strayed from the necklace to her face.

"Can you blame me? I mean, look at you." *Know you*, she added to herself. "Simon…do you think, maybe…" She couldn't do it. She couldn't ask.

"What?" He brushed her cheek with the backs of his fingers. "What's on your mind?"

"I'm—I'm on the pill," she blurted out. "And I've been tested, recently, about six months ago, and I got a clean bill of health. I haven't been with anyone but you since, and I…"

I don't want to be with anyone but you.

She knew she needed to say it out loud, but she couldn't.

"I thought, if you were okay with it," she said, "maybe next time we don't need a condom."

"Oh."

She snuck a glance up at him. He looked dumbstruck, his mouth open.

"You mean it," he said.

She nodded, painfully aware of how awkwardly she had handled what should probably have been a straightforward conversation.

Simon leaned in close, cupped her face in his hands, and kissed her. "I would love that." He found one of her hands where it lay on her lap and squeezed. "I've been tested, too. A few months after Ashley and I broke up."

"Okay." She threaded her fingers though his. "Great."

"I have to be honest with you, though," Simon said gravely. "I might need a few hours before I'll be ready to go again."

Leona laughed, his mock gravitas setting her at ease. "I suppose I can let you rest."

He kissed her again. "Thank you, Mistress."

She shivered. She'd always liked the grand theatricality of that word, but from him it took on another world of meaning and context. Every time he said it, this strong, kind, thoughtful man offered himself to her.

No one else compares to you, Mistress.

She could get lost in their play forever. Already the lines were blurring, at least for her.

"Stay over tonight?" she asked. "Are you hungry? I can make us something."

"I'm honestly just tired. But I'd love to sleep next to you tonight."

She looked away, overwhelmed by her own happiness. Needing to do something with her hands, she slid off the bed and collected the ropes and the ring gag. She popped them all into the storage unit in her closet.

"Your corset," Simon said. "It zips in the back."

She laughed. "I know, it's totally cheating."

"Can I unzip you?" He stood and came over to her, still gloriously naked. When she didn't resist, he turned her away from him and swept her hair over her shoulder. Slowly, he tugged the zipper down. As the leather released her, she took an involuntary breath in. Simon pulled her backward into his arms, kissing her hair and the back of her neck.

"Come to bed, gorgeous," he said. "I want to fall asleep holding you."

"So bossy," she murmured, tilting her head so he could kiss the side of her neck.

"You like it."

"You know I do."

He unfastened the choker necklace's snaps and kissed the back of her neck again. "And last but not least," he murmured, kneeling behind her and unbuckling the ankle straps of her shoes. She stepped out of the heels, enjoying the stretch in her calves.

He set her corset and the necklace carefully on her nightstand, then took her hand and drew her into bed.

They lay awake, cuddling and kissing each other, until the last candle burned itself out and the room fell into darkness. Sleeping next to a man was a luxury she had rarely allowed herself, and nothing felt more indulgent than lying entangled with Simon, surrounded by his warmth and his scent.

Sometime in the very early hours of the morning, when the first gray light touched her windowsill, she woke up, sensing that he was awake. She could just make out the whites of his eyes, the silhouettes of his lashes.

"You're awake."

"Yeah, I never sleep well," he said, glancing at her. "Sorry if I woke you."

"Don't be sorry." She covered his hand with hers where it rested on his chest. "Are you thinking about something?"

"Yeah, I guess. The usual stuff. Work."

"I suppose thinking about work, for you, is kind of different than it is for other people. You aren't worrying about deadlines or spreadsheets."

He smiled. "Not usually, no."

"Do you want to talk about it?"

"I can't."

"Okay." She didn't know what else to say. He had a burden that she didn't have, and never would.

"Leona," he said, turning toward her, "I have to tell you something." He slid his hand into her hair, twining long strands around his fingers.

"What is it?" she asked, her heart skipping a beat.

"I…I'm…" He trailed off, his brow furrowing. "My family wants me to bring you to our Christmas party."

She blinked at him, startled.

"It's in two days, on the Saturday before Christmas. I told them I'd ask you, but I know it's a lot to ask."

"It's… I'm kind of a Grinch about Christmas," she confessed. "I wouldn't…" *I wouldn't have any idea what to bring, what to wear, how to act.*

She had never been to a Christmas party as an adult. A few times when they were preteens, Iris had dragged Leona to her extended family's parties. Leona didn't think she'd be getting high and sneaking shots of schnapps in the back yard at Simon's family party.

"If you don't want to come, I completely understand."

"I want to," she said, in a small voice. She did want to—but *why* did she want to? It could only go badly.

"We don't have to stay long," he said. "They just want to meet you."

It wouldn't take long for her to disappoint them. "Okay."

"Leona…thank you. I'm—I am…"

Whatever he was, he didn't tell her. He kissed her, his hand tightening in her hair. Soon, his kisses deepened, his tongue stroking hers. How could she want him so much, so soon? Being a little sore from earlier only made her want him more.

She breathed his name, and he rolled on top of her. "Are you sure you're ready? To go without a condom, I mean? I know it's—"

"Yes. God, yes."

His cock caressed her, gliding slightly in, then out again. Reaching between them, she took hold of him and brought him all the way inside her. His warm, silky skin, flush against hers, was surprisingly intimate.

He pressed his lips to her temple. "Is this good for

you?"

"It's wonderful."

Someday, she would tell him how little experience she had with vanilla sex, or how rarely she'd had sex without a condom—fewer times than she had fingers on one hand. But he'd probably already guessed. He knew her, all the way down to her black heart. God save him, he liked her, anyway.

The Christmas party came upon on her before she could figure out how to look forward to it. On Saturday morning, instead of going on her long-distance run around the lake, she made three dozen cookies. Simon rang her doorbell while she was still arranging them on a plate. She wrapped them with plastic wrap and stuffed them into a bag with a bottle of wine. Shrugging her pea coat on over a brand-new lilac dress, she hurried down her steps to Simon. She set the bag down by her high-heeled boots while she tugged on her gloves.

"You look beautiful," Simon said, watching her fasten the tiny buttons at her wrists.

"I didn't know if I should bring wine or cookies, so I have both." She frowned at the bag by her feet. "Is that weird? I can put one back."

"It's not weird." He caught her free hand and kissed her gloved fingers. "It's nice."

"We'd better go. I'll drive."

"My car's right here." He gestured at the street in front of her apartment. She'd seen Simon's personal car in his driveway, but she'd never seen him drive it. It was a little sedan in such a dreary shade of gray it was practically beige. It didn't suit him at all.

She wanted Lulu, her shiny red security blanket, but she couldn't think of any reason to take Lulu when Simon's car was parked right here. Arriving in Lulu would probably just make things more awkward, anyway. She was too loud, too flashy.

Reluctantly, Leona climbed in Simon's car, her muscles tight with unease. The interior was as miserably gray-beige as the exterior, and it smelled musty, probably because he never used it.

Simon started up the car. "It's going to be fine, you know. They'll love you."

Leona frowned out the window at the downtown sliding by. Her shop blurred past. Two traffic lights went next. They plunged into the mountains. It should have been picturesque. Normally, she loved how the snow turned the pine boughs into elaborate spun-sugar cages, but today it seemed over the top, like a theater set of Christmas in Vermont instead of her home.

Simon turned into the driveway of a quaint red house nestled in snowdrifts. Another perfect addition to their Christmas set. Simon fit in, too, with his handsome features and his collared shirt. The only flaw in their Christmas production was that worried notch between his eyebrows.

"If you aren't up for this…" he began.

She gripped the bag of stupid cookies. She could pretend, if only for the day, that she belonged. "I'm just nervous."

"Okay."

He parked behind the half-dozen cars already crowding the driveway and led her to a side door. Leona's heart pounded louder and louder with every step. *This is a mistake*, her heartbeat told her, but she ignored it.

Simon opened the door without knocking, as if he still lived there. Was that what people did, no matter how long it had been since they'd left home?

They stepped into a cheerful country kitchen. At least ten women were sitting or standing around a cramped kitchen table, talking over the sounds from the next room of a televised sports game and several shrieking children. All of the women looked up when they walked in, stopping in mid-conversation, their drinks or finger foods halfway to their mouths.

A petite, plump woman with auburn hair hopped up, squeezed through chairs and people, and threw her arms around Simon. "You made it! Merry Christmas, sweetie!" She turned to Leona. "And you must be Leona? I'm Simon's mom, Audette. I remember seeing you around the schoolyard occasionally, when you and Simon were kids. Funny to see you all grown up!" Audette's round, rosy cheeks dimpled.

Simon's mom remembered her from high school? That could not be good.

Placing a hand on Leona's back, Simon turned her toward the rest of the women clustered around the table. "Everyone, this is Leona. Leona, this is my aunt Beth, my aunt Melissa, my cousin Heather, my cousin Susan…" The list went on and on. No way would she remember all of their names. To make matters worse, Julia wasn't there. Leona had been counting on having her as an ally.

There were choruses of *nice to meet you* and *take off your coat and stay a while*.

"How did you two get together?" one of the aunts asked.

"We both live in town still," Simon said smoothly. "We ran into each other again, and that was that." The aunts and cousins all cooed with delight. *How nice*.

Leona balked. Her relationship with Simon wasn't *nice*. The way they had met—everything about their relationship—was so much more complicated and messier than that. So much more meaningful than something that was just *nice*.

Several little kids suddenly tore into the room, shrieking and fighting over something Leona couldn't see.

"No pushing!" one of the cousins yelled from the table.

"Look who's here!" another exclaimed, gesturing at Simon. All of the children, who couldn't be more than four or five, cried *Officer Simon* and mobbed him, wrapping their little arms around his jeans. He picked up the smallest and twirled her around, while she laughed and whacked him on the shoulder with a stuffed giraffe.

He made all of this look so easy, so natural. How did he know what to do, what to say?

The children wanted to show Simon the fort they'd made in the TV room. Simon, with an apologetic glance at Leona, let them lead him away.

"Why don't you sit down and have some wine with us, Leona?" Audette suggested, smiling up at her from where she sat at the head of the table and nodding at the only empty chair.

"Okay," Leona said. They weren't going to eat her. So why was she terrified?

She set the plate of cookies and the bottle of wine on an already crowded table and slipped out of her pea coat. They all stared at her lilac dress, their expressions bewildered. She'd tried so hard to wear something normal—not black, or slinky, or lacy—but even this dress was all wrong. It was too clingy, too revealing for this wholesome crowd and their wholesome kitchen.

"What do you do, Leona?" one of the aunts asked. Beth?

"I work at Grenton Fine Crafts Gallery," Leona said.

Another one of the aunts leaned forward, setting her wine glass down on the table. She was the only blonde. Melissa? "Isn't that the place that got robbed?"

Leona's stomach sank. "Um. Yeah. A few days ago."

"That was *crazy*," Melissa said. "A robbery, in Grenton!"

"Earl must have had a fit, Audi," someone else said. "Didn't Simon respond to the robbery?"

"He doesn't tell me anything," Audette said. "He's just like his father."

Everyone looked curiously at Leona.

"Simon was the first one there," Leona admitted.

"I heard that Margie Smith was working there that night," somebody volunteered.

They all glanced at Leona again, and Leona thought of the gunman, shaking Margie by her shirt collar. "Yes."

"Does that mean *you* were there?" Beth asked, peering at Leona over colorful glasses.

When Leona nodded, they clucked their tongues like a brood of mother hens. Pressure built up in Leona's throat. She didn't know whether she wanted to cry or to burst into hysterical laughter.

"What was it like?" Melissa asked. "Was it scary?" Simon's mom shot her a quelling look, but Melissa wasn't paying attention. "Did they have *guns*?" Melissa insisted, as if she were dishing on celebrity gossip.

"Yes," Leona said weakly. *I thought I was going to die. I'm still surprised I didn't.*

"Let's not bother poor Leona about this—" Audette began.

"It's okay," Leona assured them, then immediately broke into a cold sweat. Why had she said that? It *wasn't* okay. She didn't want to talk about it. But she also didn't want Audette's pity. She didn't want to be treated as if she were weak anymore than she wanted to be fodder for gossip, and she especially didn't want *both*. Wasn't that always the way? she thought bitterly. Suffering fascinated people who'd never experienced it.

"Where's Jules?" someone asked Audette, and Leona looked up hopefully.

"She went to pick up her man at the airport," Audette said.

"Isn't it nice to have both your kids paired off?" Beth said to Audette, who smiled. Paired off? No. Julia and her boyfriend were going to have a kid, and probably get married, and she and Simon weren't…he hadn't left her yet, but he wouldn't want to…

Leona suddenly realized all of the women's faces were cheerfully nonplussed. There were no giddy, knowing smiles.

Oh, no. They didn't *know* yet. Julia hadn't told them about the pregnancy. She had to be waiting for the baby's father to get here before she announced their big news.

The door to the kitchen opened, and Leona, with a rush of adrenaline, turned around, expecting to see Julia. Instead, two more strangers, laden down with presents and containers of food, came inside, ushering three more little kids along with them. Immediately, there were hugs, and laughter, and more useless introductions. Leona was standing in a sea of strangers who all knew each other. Trapped between the table and the kitchen island, she couldn't avoid the man who had just walked in.

"So you're Leona!" he said, with a friendly smile.

Had Simon told the entire world about them? How did he have the time? Did he send out a newsletter or something?

"I'm Bill, a cousin of Audi's," the man said. "Good of you to come. Your family doesn't mind sharing you with us this year?"

"My family? No, they don't. They don't."

"Do I know your folks?" he asked.

"I hope not," Leona said, without thinking.

He frowned, stepping back from her.

She flushed. "I mean…they're not good people. You're better off without knowing them."

"Okay," he said, still guarded.

"They didn't really do this kind of thing," Leona said randomly, with a gesture at the room around them.

"What, parties?"

That pressure in her throat, the confused urge to laugh or cry or both, got worse. "They did parties," she said, in spite of herself. "It was Christmas they didn't bother with."

By the time she was eight or nine, her parents had started going on Christmas cruises, leaving her on her own for two weeks at a stretch. The next-door neighbor was supposed to check in on her, but had never gotten around to it. Leona had ended up haunting her own fucking house, living off dry cereal and watching Christmas movies alone.

Years later, when she was twelve or so, she'd finally turned those movies off. She'd forced herself to accept that she could watch and watch but she'd never be able to break through the glass and have a Christmas—a family—like the ones on the TV. She'd started smoking pot in the back yard by herself, or, when Iris could get away from family stuff, with Iris. The loneliness had eased after that.

The door opened again. Another spark of adrenaline flashed through her body. This time, Julia stepped inside, followed by a young man with a close-cropped beard, who was smiling nervously. They were holding hands. Julia's face was full of anticipation.

Any moment now, Leona thought, her head starting to pound. She ought to be glad. If nothing else, it would take attention off of her. Until the comparisons inevitably came, encompassing the entire world of marriage and children and the future.

She had to leave. She couldn't do this—not at this time of year, not so soon after the robbery, any of it.

With everyone distracted by Julia and her boyfriend, Leona took her chance to slip through the crowd, apologizing in whispers. Just as Leona made it to the door, Julia turned, her eyes meeting Leona's and her eyebrows drawing together in confusion. Leona shook her head minutely and closed the door behind her.

The air, full with the promise of snow, chilled her skin through her thin dress. She didn't care. Anywhere was better than that hot, stifling kitchen.

Leona walked down a garden path to a snow-dusted stone wall and sat down, hugging her arms to her chest. Already the adrenaline in her system was burning itself out, leaving her oxygen-starved. She'd wanted so badly to be good at this, for Simon's sake, but she'd lasted less than an hour. The inescapable truth was that she didn't know how to be anything other than alone; she didn't know what to do besides act like a bitch.

It was her own fault. She could've learned how to deal with families and holidays from Paul, but after thirteen years of Christmas party invitations, she'd never gone to his and Mellon's place for Christmas. Even as a teenager, she'd known Paul was kinder to her than she deserved. She couldn't crash his grown-up, classy parties. And now that she was old enough to reconsider going, there was no point. Paul would retire soon. After he sold the shop to someone, he and Mellon would leave for Florida, or wherever retired people went. She'd never see them again, and that would be worse, so much worse, than living a lonely life unchanged from year to year.

Leona's hands tightened into fists in a futile attempt to warm her fingers. She had been a fool to get involved with Simon, or even to quit the scene two years ago. She should've known she couldn't be anything more than someone's lover. She ought to stick to what she was good at: low-maintenance, no-strings-attached, casual fun. Just like her parents.

Chapter Eighteen

JULES TAPPED SIMON ON THE shoulder. "I think Leona went outside for a cigarette, or something? Maybe you should go check on her."

"She doesn't smoke," Simon said, perplexed, looking up from the pillow fort that he'd been strong-armed into renovating.

"Well, maybe she just needed to get away from the Spanish Inquisition for a little while." Jules grinned.

"Oh, God." Simon stood, brushing off his khakis. He shouldn't have left her alone with his relatives for so long. He'd figured Leona would be fine, even if she'd been a little nervous. She never let anyone fluster her. But he might have underestimated just how nosy and gossip-obsessed his relatives could be.

He volunteered Auntie Julia for the pillow fort, then dodged through the crowd in the kitchen to the door. Outside, snow had started to fall. Leona was sitting on a stonewall with her back to him, her dress a blush of pale purple in a landscape of white snow and gray stone.

"Leona?" He walked toward her. "What's wrong?"

Snowflakes glistened in her long black hair. She shook her head, and his heart sank. He'd overwhelmed her, just like he'd known he would. He'd come on too strong with her from the beginning.

"You're not having a good time."

"It's…" She shook her head again, her throat working. "I'm no good at this kind of stuff."

"What stuff?" He dreaded her answer, but he had to ask.

"Relationships," she whispered. "And families."

In all the years they'd known each other, he'd never seen her look this vulnerable, with her eyes red and her lower lip swollen, as if she were going to cry.

"I'm sorry," he managed. "It was too soon for this. It's my fault. I shouldn't have—"

"No." She shook her head. "It's not you. Or your family. They're perfectly nice. It's me."

"I don't understand," he said stupidly, his fingers clutching air, as if he were going to hold her.

"I never wanted anything like this before." She frowned at the snowy lawn. "I was happy being independent. Choosing to be by myself was better than being ignored, you know? After twenty-nine years, it's a hard habit to break."

It was like she was having some other conversation. "I'm not sure…"

"Simon…" She scrubbed her face with her hands. Her fingers were shaking. "You can do better than me. Someone who fits in with your family, who they'll like."

"I'm sure they like you—"

"It's all right," she said. "I don't really expect it."

"I don't know where this is coming from. I'm sure they liked you, and they'll like you even more as they get to know you." Nervous energy hummed through him. He had to tell her the truth. He had to tell her how he felt about her. "You know I don't want anyone else but you. I've *never* wanted anyone else but you. I'm—"

"No," she said, flinching. "Please. Don't. You don't have to be nice—I can't bear it." Her arms tightened around her body, as if she were shielding herself from him. "I think I need to go home."

He swallowed. "Okay." If that was what she wanted. "I'll get our coats."

He went inside, his limbs heavy. He couldn't believe he'd bungled things with her so badly. He should never have rushed her. Last night, he'd come so close to telling her that he loved her, only to chicken out at the last moment and ask her to the Christmas party, as if that would be a less fraught step forward in their relationship. Of course it wasn't—not for her. She had Paul, but she didn't have a big, happy family to spend Christmas with the way he did. He'd been selfish, rushing her like this, when he knew she was skittish about families and not familiar with—not *interested* in—dating. He wanted her so much it had blinded him to what their relationship was actually about.

He found their coats and headed back toward the front door. Julia and his mom both tried to stop him, but he brushed them off, telling them Leona wasn't feeling well.

A moment later, they were getting into his car. They drove all the way back into town in silence. Parked on the street in front of her apartment, Simon turned to her, anxiety drumming in his pulse. *Give me another chance.*

"Maybe we can slow things down a little," he said.

Liar. He'd already tried to force himself to slow things down with her, after the crafts fair, and it hadn't worked. He wanted her to be his, immediately and forever.

"Yeah…slower might be better," she said. "I'm sorry… This is just…a hard time of year for me."

"Okay." *Slower might be better.* But it might not be. They might never have anything more between them. She would never love him. How could she?

She smiled, her lips quivering, and ran her fingers through the short fuzz of hair at his temple.

"I'm sorry I fucked up your Christmas party."

"You didn't." He wanted to take her hand, but he just clutched his steering wheel. "Don't—don't ever feel like that with me."

She nodded, her smile still in place, and got out of the car. She opened the door and disappeared inside her building.

Instead of going back to the party, he went home, where he poured himself a whiskey, collapsed on his couch, and stared up at the darkness. His mom called him, and Julia sent him a text, but he couldn't get up the energy to respond.

At work the next day, Simon sat in his office and stared, seeing Leona instead of the pile of papers on his desk. Leona in her corset and heels. Leona in her pale purple dress.

His coffee had grown cold, and he couldn't remember the last time he'd actually eaten. Yesterday, at the party, he'd grabbed a couple of crackers off a platter. There, he'd remembered.

"Simon, can I talk to you in my office?"

He looked up to see the Chief standing at the door of his office, his expression grave.

Shit. What had he done wrong now?

"Yes, sir." Simon forced himself to his feet. A dull ache starting in his temples, he followed the Chief into his office and winced when the Chief shut the door behind them.

The Chief took his seat behind his desk and gestured for Simon to sit. "What's this about you paying a visit to Margie Smith's house?"

Shit, he thought again, resisting the urge to put his head in his hands. "I had some follow up questions for her, sir, that Jack didn't get to in the initial interview."

"I haven't assigned that case to you." Despite the words, the Chief's tone was gentle—too gentle, as if Simon were about to snap.

"I know, sir," he said miserably, "but I thought it might be relevant to the O'Shea case—"

"What makes you think that?"

"Just a feeling I have." He knew it sounded lame, but it was the truth. "The money is suspicious. Two women, about the same age, both getting large, unexplained amounts of money—"

"The deposits into Nancy O'Shea's account were traced to her father-in-law's trust account in Washington state."

"Yes, sir, I know—"

"Then it's not unexplained, right? In her case." The Chief leaned on his elbow, his face etched with fatigue. "As for Margie, it seems pretty clear she's been hiding money away for a long time to get away from that husband of hers."

"But—"

"There's absolutely no evidence that those cases are connected."

Simon shook his head. "But who did she get the

money from? And who were the robbers, and how did they know it was in her shop?"

"Simon…"

"And Leona said that the robbers expected there to be *more* money, and Margie seemed genuinely surprised about that—"

"*That* is why I didn't assign the case to you," the Chief said, sighing. "You're involved with the witness, and I think it's… I won't say it's clouding your judgment. Your points are valid, and they're noted."

Simon frowned, his heart stuck on the word *involved*.

"But, since the bombing…you're here all the time, you clearly never sleep, you don't eat…"

Simon wanted to protest, but he thought about the crackers yesterday and stayed quiet.

"I know it's hard to have unsolved cases," the Chief said. "Your father was the same way, you know. Hard-driving. No stone unturned. But you aren't the only man working in this Department, and you can't act like you are. You've been here, what, six years?"

"Seven, sir," he said quietly.

"I've been here twenty-five," the Chief said. "You have to trust me, son. The Department is doing its best, all right?"

Rage and grief and frustration spiked inside him. It *wasn't* the Department's best, and it wasn't good enough.

"If I thought there was a connection between Nancy O'Shea's death and the robbery, believe me, I wouldn't ignore it," the Chief said. "But I just don't see how Nancy's death was anything other than a terrible accident. I'm not letting the driver, whoever he was, off the hook, I'm just saying that—"

"But the money she—"

"It was from her father-in-law."

"Her *ex*-father-in-law," Simon insisted, anger curling his fingers. He forced his hands flat against his legs.

"Who she had a great relationship with, even after she divorced his son. And, by the way, the divorce from the son was amicable. You interviewed him yourself and found nothing suspicious." The Chief sighed. "Look, I'm not trying to knock your instincts. You're a good cop. You need some time to cool off and rest, that's all."

"I don't want to rest." Resting only meant more time to dwell on the ways he'd failed himself and the people, the town, he cared about.

"You might not want it, but it's what you need. I'm taking you off the O'Shea case. And I'm going to unofficially put you on light duty for a couple weeks. Between us. All right?"

Simon's mouth opened, but he couldn't speak. First he'd fucked up his relationship with his dream girl, and now he'd fucked up his dream job. He'd be doing light duty shifts like a fucking invalid, even though he suspected that the O'Shea homicide was no accident, and he knew Margie's use of the shop's back room as her personal savings account was suspicious.

"Simon?" The Chief was watching him with concern.

Simon scraped his hands over his work pants. "Yes, sir. Whatever you say, sir."

He stood up, stumbling over the ugly seventies chair, and made it to the door despite the throbbing pain in his skull. He needed a drink, even though he owed at least half of his current headache to the whiskey he'd drank the night before, lying on his couch and obsessing about Leona.

In his office, he slumped at his desk chair, grateful, at least, that no one could see him behind his shabby wall, with its peeling paint and tacked-up flyers. The next three hours passed as aching, crawling self-loathing.

Back at his duplex, he went straight to his liquor shelf and poured himself a double whiskey. *Another night like this?* sneered a cruel inner voice. *Getting wasted alone, staring at the ceiling?*

Why not? He had nothing better to do.

His phone rang, but he couldn't be bothered to answer it. He found his couch and slumped onto it, his pistol digging into his side. *Coward's way out*, his dad had always said. Simon wasn't a fucking coward, but he'd be lying if he told himself he'd never thought about it. After his first few bad calls, and after the bombing case fell apart, he'd had these nights. Never told anyone, obviously. College, too, there had been some bad times. He didn't really remember what had made him sink so low then. It wasn't like now, when he'd lost both Leona and the respect of his Chief. This was the worst he had ever felt, because this time, he remembered exactly what it was like to be happy.

The next week passed in a blur, doing boring shifts patrolling at the lake or driving pointlessly around town while hung over as shit, and getting so drunk he passed out whenever he was home, no matter what time it was. His phone rang constantly, but he never checked it. Christmas was next week, and he didn't care. Didn't want to think about holidays or families or joy or any of that bullshit. None of it mattered anymore.

Chapter Nineteen

LEONA LINGERED IN SIMON'S DRIVEWAY, her hand brushing Lulu's shiny red paint. Simon's personal car was here, and so was his squad car. He was home. So why hadn't he returned any of her calls?

She'd turned into his driveway on an impulse on her way to the grocery store. His name had been pounding inside her head for days. She longed to see him, touch him, apologize to him, but he'd ignored all of her calls for the last five days. She'd expected their relationship to slow down; she hadn't expected it to stop completely.

Bracing herself, she walked up the stairs to his front porch and knocked on his door.

No answer.

She wished she knew what to do. After a minute, she knocked again, only to notice that his door was slightly open. Grenton was pretty safe, but leaving his door open seemed a little too trusting. Fear squirmed in her belly. What if something was wrong?

"Simon?" She pushed past the door and stepped into his kitchen. Light from the liquor store parking lot trickled in through the kitchen window's closed blinds, revealing the dishes stacked on the counters and the papers scattered across the floor.

She crossed his kitchen, her heels tapping on the linoleum. In his living room, clothes were strewn across his armchair. Empty liquor and beer bottles littered the floor by the couch.

She didn't realize he was in the room until she heard him inhale. He'd been lying on the couch, but he pushed himself up, bracing his elbows on his knees and rubbing his eyes.

He cast her a bleary look. "Leona? Fuck…you really here?"

She was too shocked to figure out what to say or do, other than stammer: "I'm here."

Last time she'd been at his place, it had been cheerfully disheveled, but not dirty or in darkness. He wasn't a neat freak like she was, but this was something else. Something bad.

Muttering a curse, he scraped his hands across his scalp. "What're you doing here?"

"You haven't returned any of my calls all week… I was worried." In her head, after she'd said this, he would tease her the same way he'd teased her at his station after the robbery, and everything would be all right again.

He didn't even look at her. "What do you care if I return your calls or not?"

"Of course I care," she said, stung.

"You should leave," he growled.

"I'm not leaving you like this. You're a fucking mess." The memory of Simon drinking by the lake popped into her head, and what had seemed quirky or a little unruly then seemed something else entirely now. She hugged her arms to her chest. "Are you drunk? Or hung over or something? It's seven o'clock, Simon."

"First of all," he said, his head in his hands, his tone

flat and cold, "I told you, you don't care. Second, I worked an overnight last night, so I can get drunk whenever I fucking want."

"But…why?" she asked. "Are you upset about something?"

"Besides you fucking dumping me?"

"I didn't mean…"

Had she meant to break up with him? If he asked her, right now, for a real relationship and all of the family responsibilities that went along with it, would she say yes? She wanted to be with him, but when she tried to think about the future…all she saw was him leaving her. Replacing her with someone better, more suitable. Someone more like his exes.

"It's over, Leona." Some of the anger left his voice, replaced by exhaustion. "Just leave. Please."

"I don't want to leave you like this."

"I don't care. I don't need your fucking kindness."

He stood up suddenly. His wrinkled T-shirt had ridden up around his waist, but he didn't fix it. He clenched his hands into fists at his sides.

"You don't love me." His voice was cold and relentless. "You will *never* love me. I think you've made that pretty fucking clear. So for God's sake, leave me alone."

The words slashed at her. She stumbled backward, her hand to her chest. He'd told her she was a nice person—he had told her that he liked her. Sometimes, when he'd looked at her… But that must have all been in the past. After the Christmas party, even Simon didn't believe she was capable of love. And why should he think anything else? He was right. Love was for people who'd had functional upbringings, or who were naturally warm and caring, like Simon's sister. Love did not belong to people like Leona. She didn't love anyone, and nobody loved her.

Her feet took her backward, into his kitchen. He didn't follow her. She ran out onto his front porch, slamming the door behind her, while what he'd said cut at her again and again.

She started up Lulu's engine. A few minutes later, she was back in her apartment, which was impossibly bright and clean after Simon's. Too bright, too clean, like a museum exhibition.

She went straight to her phone and her address book, where she had a bar napkin with Julia's phone number on it.

Julia answered on the second ring. "Leona?"

"Hey," Leona said, swallowing hard. "Can you go check on Simon? He's been drinking, or he was earlier, and he seems upset. He doesn't want me…"

He doesn't want me ever again.

"I was actually just thinking about going over to see him," Julia said. "He hasn't returned my calls since the party."

"Yeah, me neither."

"What happened? Did you guys have a fight?"

The painful shards in her chest sliced deeper. "I guess we broke up."

Julia made a soft sound of dismay. "But he's crazy about you."

Leona shook her head, even though Julia couldn't see her.

"There must be something else going on with him," Julia said.

The image of the wash of liquor bottles next to his couch came back to her. Leona bit her lip. "Do you think he has a drinking problem?"

"I don't know," Julia said, sounding shocked. "I've

never thought about it before. I know he's always had, like…bad spells, when he gets really down. Mom and Dad wanted to send him to a shrink while he was in college, but he said no."

Leona pressed her knuckles to her mouth, physically hurting for him. "I didn't know that." He'd always struck her as sensitive, even moody, but she'd never taken the time to think about the possibility of something more serious, like depression.

"I'm going to go over and visit him," Julia said. "Actually, my dad just walked in. I'll get him to come, too. He always knows what to say to Simon."

"Okay," she choked out. "Thanks, Julia."

"I'm just glad you called me. Hang in there."

"Let me know how it goes."

"I will."

Julia hung up, leaving Leona to pace her apartment.

You don't love me. You will never love me.

Had she triggered his depression, somehow? Wasn't it arrogant to think she could have that much of an effect on him?

She couldn't stand to be in her apartment a second longer. Grabbing her purse, Leona loped down the stairs and back to Lulu. She had to go somewhere, talk to someone. She'd never missed Iris as much as she did right now.

She found herself pulling into Paul's driveway, amazed she even remembered how to get there. She hadn't been to his house in a year or two, and even then, she had never done more than stop by to help him bring things over to the shop.

What the hell was she doing here? She was being totally irrational. Nobody went to their boss's house to talk about their relationship problems.

The door opened. Paul's friendly face creased in alarm.

"Leona? What's wrong?"

A big, hot tear pooled in the corner of her eye and rolled down her cheek, splashing onto her coat. The sensation was so foreign that she almost laughed. She hadn't actually cried in—what, twenty years?

Paul looked stricken. He took her hand and pulled her into their beautifully decorated Colonial house.

"Who's there, hon'?" Mellon asked from the kitchen, poking his head past the doorframe. "Leona?" Mellon hurried down the steps into the sitting room. Mellon wasn't as tall as Paul, but he had the same casual grace Paul had. They had always looked so *right* next to each other. The epitome of a happy couple.

Another tear rolled down her face.

"What is it?" Paul asked her again. "Did something else happen at the shop?"

Her throat too tight for her to speak, she shook her head.

"Is it—Simon Labelle? Did something happen with him?"

This time, she nodded. Paul and Mellon somehow got her to the couch. Paul sat down next to her, his arm around her, while Mellon took the armchair across from them, his eyebrows knitted together with concern.

"Do you want some tea or anything?" Paul asked. "A drink?"

"N-no," she stammered. "No drinks. Thanks."

Paul nodded. "Okay, sweetie. You take your time, all right?" He rubbed her back gently. At first, her muscles tensed. She never touched anyone, or let them touch her, except as a lead-up to sex, but of course that wasn't what this was. It was…affection. Kindness. And it was nice. Gradually, her muscles relaxed a little, and she sank sideways, leaning against Paul. Her chest still shook with the effort to breathe normally, but Paul's arm around her was helping.

"I went over to his place," she said finally, "just now, and it was trashed, and I think he'd been drinking… I'm so fucking worried about him." She told them what he'd said, and about getting Julia and Simon's dad to check on him. "I shouldn't have let him convince me to leave. I should go back."

"How did all this happen?" Paul asked, stroking her hair. "You two seemed like you were doing so well."

"He invited me to his family's Christmas party."

"Uh oh," Paul said.

"I know," Leona said. "What was I thinking? And it was awful, Paul. It was just—so overwhelming. They're all so normal and happy and functional. I just…panicked."

Mellon, unlike Paul, looked puzzled. "But you've always seemed so high-functioning to me, Leona. You've been on your own since you were eighteen."

"Longer than that," Paul said quietly.

"I'm not—I'm nothing like them," Leona said. "Nothing."

"Do you have to be similar to your in-laws?" Paul asked. "I'm not much like the Mellons. They're all accountants."

"I'm not that much like them, either, for that matter," Mellon said.

"That's the thing about your significant other's family," Paul said, still stroking her hair. "What you have in common with them is how much you all love your significant other."

"*Love*," Leona snapped, pressing the heels of her hands to her forehead. "What the hell do I know about that? As far as I can tell, loving people just gives them ways to hurt you."

Leaning back in his armchair, Mellon shrugged. "Maybe. But it's worth it, anyway, isn't it?"

More tears were splashing down her face, leaving little wet marks on their nice carpet. "It's *not* worth it." She wished she could stop fucking crying, but now that it had started, it was like she had twenty years' worth of tears stored inside her face. "It's not worth it because everybody just leaves you and then you have nobody, so you might as well just have nobody in the first place."

"Who's leaving you?" Paul asked. "Simon?"

"Yes. And Iris. And you."

"Honey, I'm not leaving you." Paul sounded a little choked up himself now, but she didn't look up at him to find out. "You mean because I'm retiring soon?"

"Y-yes."

"Even if we end up moving away, which we probably won't, we're not *leaving* you. We'll still see you as much as we possibly can. You're still going to be as important to us as you always have been."

"But Iris—"

"Iris is young and selfish," Paul said gently.

"She's my age."

"Well, you know what they say," Paul said. "It's not the years, it's the mileage."

Leona huffed a laugh, wiping her eyes on her sleeve.

"Sweetie," Paul said, "I love you. You're like a daughter to me. You're so independent, so self-possessed, I've always been worried about stepping on your toes. If I'd realized you didn't already know how much I care about you, I would've told you every day for years."

Somehow this just made her cry more. She didn't understand tears. Their lack of logic irritated her. At least now, instead of making her feel like she was drowning, they were freeing, like a dam inside her had finally burst open.

"Lots of people here love you, Leona," Mellon interjected. "You don't have to be normal, whatever that is, for people to love you."

"Simon said he didn't think I would ever love him."

"Leona," Paul said, "it was obvious you were in love with that boy the moment he walked into the shop during the crafts fair. It was written all over your face."

She snuck a glance up at Paul, who smiled ruefully at her.

"He probably just wants to hear you say it," Paul said.

"He thought I'd broken up with him," Leona said. "I asked him to slow things down, but I was just…afraid."

Mellon adjusted his glasses on his nose. "I would probably have thought I'd been dumped, too, in his place."

Leona groaned in frustration. "I'm so *bad* at this."

"You're not," Paul assured her, with an exasperated look at Mellon. "This stuff is just…tricky sometimes. For everybody. You should just tell him how you feel, and give him a chance to respond. Unless I'm getting senile in my old age, that boy adores you."

"That's what Julia—his sister—said, too. But I can't…"

I can't imagine anybody loving me.

But Paul had said he loved her. And he was an honest person. He wouldn't lie to her about something so important.

"I'm going to go back there," she said, standing. "I'm

going to tell him how I feel about him."

Paul stood up, too, and kissed Leona's forehead. "Good luck, sweetie. And no matter what happens, we're always here for you, okay?"

"Okay." Impulsively, she hugged Paul, her arms tight around his thin frame. The scent of his cologne was an old memory. It hadn't changed since she'd first met him at thirteen, and it had always comforted her. "I… um…I love you, Paul. Thank you for everything. You, too, Mellon," she added, pulling away from Paul and wiping her eyes again. "You guys are the best, and…"

And Simon was right. You're my family.

Steeling herself, she bade them a quick goodbye and went back outside to Lulu. Driving the handful of miles back to Simon's house, she rehearsed, again and again, what she would say to him.

I'm in love with you.
I want to spend the rest of my life with you.

As soon as she pulled into his driveway, she knew something was wrong. Simon's squad car wasn't in the driveway anymore. Julia stood on his front porch, twisting her fingers together.

Leona jumped out of her car and ran up onto the porch. "What happened?"

Julia's eyes were huge in the glow of the neighbor's Christmas lights. "He isn't here."

Leona's stomach plummeted. "Where is he?"

"I don't know," Julia said. "We got here maybe half an hour after you called, but he was gone. His gun's not here," she whispered, her voice breaking.

Leona rocked backward into the porch railing, overwhelmed by a surge of cold fear. *His gun's not here.*

How could that be? Where could he have gone, and why would he have taken his gun with him?

"My dad went to the police station," Julia said. "And they are going to look for him. Dad told me to wait here in case he comes back home." Julia wiped her nose on the sleeve of her coat. Tears glistened on her cheeks, but Leona's own tears had finally run dry. Every fiber in her body reverberated with fear and dread.

"Dad said it could be nothing," Julia said, sniffing, "because if he was going to hurt himself, he would've just done it in his house."

Leona paced the porch. She could go down to the station and demand that they fix this, that they find him, somehow. But she didn't want to leave Julia here alone, either. Their dad was right: someone should stay at the house in case he came back.

That left her directionless, turning in circles on his freezing deck, praying for him to come home.

Chapter Twenty

AFTER LEONA LEFT, SIMON TRIED to go back to sleep, or work up the energy to start drinking again, but he couldn't. Despite what he'd let Leona believe, he hadn't actually been drunk when she'd shown up at his door. He'd started drinking in the morning after he'd gotten off his overnight shift, only to fall asleep sometime midday. By early afternoon, he'd woken up stone-cold sober with a raging headache.

He hadn't bothered to correct Leona's mistake since the truth was probably worse. And she didn't care, anyway.

A knock sounded at his door. He dragged himself up, hoping, in spite of himself, that she'd come back.

Margie Smith stood outside on his front porch. Without speaking, she handed him a square of paper with a few numbers typed dead center: *9:00*.

"What is this?"

"I found it as I was leaving the shop, about a half hour ago." Her voice trembled. "Paul and I closed up at six, and when I went out to my car, it was there on my windshield."

Worry filtered through his hung over stupor. "You think it's from the robbers?"

"It has to be, doesn't it? What else could it be?"

"But what does it mean? They're going to break into the shop at nine p.m. tonight?" He rubbed his temples. The effort to think was only worsening his headache. "The shop is closed tonight, though, right? Paul hasn't kept it open late since the robbery."

"It's closed tonight. But I was supposed to go to my book club from seven to nine. Maybe that's what they mean."

"Book club," he echoed. "So you think it's a threat against you personally?"

She didn't answer, but he could see her shaking.

"Who are they, Margie?"

"I swear I don't know."

He shook his head, still not sure whether he believed a damn thing she told him. He was not at all capable of helping her with this. Not ever, and especially not now, when he was so hung over he could barely see straight. It was all he could do to keep standing upright. "We have to call it in."

"You don't understand," she said desperately. "It's not me I'm worried about. It's Rich. My husband." She swallowed. "I've been calling him all day, but he won't answer. I must've called him a dozen times since I got this note."

"Why won't he answer?" Simon asked.

"We had a fight."

No shit, Simon thought. "About what? The robbers?"

"Yeah."

"What about them?"

She shrugged.

He was sick of trying to get answers out of this woman. "I don't understand what you want me to do. Why come to me, instead of going into the station?"

"You said you could help me…and…I'm just worried about Rich. But…"

"You don't want anyone else looking in on him. Is that it?"

She nodded. Her eyes were hollow, her cheeks sunken.

Richard Smith was probably doing something illegal, then, or at least questionable. "Why not just go find him at home?" Simon asked. "You're afraid to go by yourself?"

She nodded again.

"Because of the robbers, or because of your husband?"

She flinched. "The robbers."

He supposed it was possible the robbers could show up at Margie's house, but that was pretty hard to say for sure based on a piece of paper with nothing more than a timestamp on it. The note could just as easily mean that they were going to show up at the shop again, whether at nine p.m. tonight or at nine a.m. tomorrow morning. Meanwhile, the robbers thought Margie was at her book club for the next hour and a half.

He swept a hand over his face. He could just drive over and see if Margie's husband was home. Conducting a wellness check while off-duty was overreaching, but he'd done it before, with Ray Waller and a few others. He'd overlooked the odd joint or needle, too, when it meant saving someone's life.

He wouldn't get into any more trouble at work than he was already in. And even if he did…his life was already a mess. What did he truly have to lose?

"All right," he said finally. "I'll drive by, see if he's home. A wellness check, that's all. And afterward I'll get both of you to a safe place, just in case."

"Thank you," she breathed.

"I am *not* promising you I won't call for backup," he snapped, shaking a finger at her. God help him if he did call the station right now, but she didn't have to know that part. "And you're going to tell the Chief about your damned note afterward, do you understand me? If those assholes ever threaten Leona again, because of you—"

"I know," she said. "I know. I can't stand to think of it."

"All right. Good. Stay here."

He went back inside, splashed some cold water on his face, pulled on a long-sleeved shirt, and strapped on his gun. After a moment of indecision, he decided to take his patrol car. If something went wrong with Rich Smith, or if the robbers did actually show up, then he wanted to have his radio and other equipment with him.

"Your car still parked at the shop?" he asked, back on the front porch with Margie. She nodded again.

"I'll take you to it. You got a friend or somewhere you can stay while I do this? Somewhere nobody knows about?"

"I want to come."

"I didn't ask you what you want."

"There isn't anyone," she said. "Just Paul and Leona."

There was no way in hell he was going to risk leading anyone to Leona or Paul. And he couldn't risk leaving her alone, either. God only knew what the woman would do. If he tried to bring her anywhere else before he checked on her husband, she'd probably throw herself out of the car.

"Fine. Come on." He directed her into the patrol car's passenger seat. "But you are going to do exactly what I say, and you are not getting out of this car, understood?

We're just going to drive by and see if he's there."

He went to the trunk of his patrol car, where he always kept a stash of equipment. He found a bulletproof vest that would fit her well enough and went back to the passenger-side door. "Put this on under your coat. Just to be safe."

He went back to the trunk to give her some privacy and to grab a vest for himself. As he strapped it on, he thought of Leona, poking him in the chest the night after the robbery.

You're not wearing a vest, idiot.

He'd never forget his odd discordant joy at seeing her worry about him, like she cared about him. With a sigh, he tightened the last strap. God damn it, he'd been such an asshole to her tonight. It wasn't her fault she didn't want the same things he wanted. He shouldn't have yelled at her.

In his patrol car with Margie, Simon turned right, taking them away from town and the safety of the station. Margie's street was to the southeast, tucked into the mountains.

Simon glanced sidelong at her thin, drawn face. Even after the reprimand from the Chief, and even feeling as physically run down as he did right now, he wanted to know what was going on with Margie and her husband. She obviously loved the man, but Simon had gotten enough domestic violence calls to know that didn't necessarily mean anything. On the other hand, Simon didn't know for a fact that Rich was an abuser, either. All he truly knew at this point was that Rich was an eccentric loner who would rather spend time with animals than with people. If that were a crime, Simon would have to lock up half of Vermont.

Still…the sheer number of animals they had was a

little strange. Lots of people in Grenton had animals, and plenty of them, but Margie and Richard were practically animal hoarders. It seemed…extreme.

What had she said, when he'd been asking her random questions about her pets?

We rescued them all from that awful kill shelter.

Huh.

Still lost in thought, Simon turned onto Margie's winding, wooded street. They passed one narrow driveway. Otherwise, Margie's street was all snow and trees and darkness.

"This is the driveway that leads up to the barn," Margie said, gesturing at a break in the woods. "The main driveway is around front. But…"

"But what?"

"Well, the barn light isn't on. And I don't see his truck."

"So he's not home?" Simon asked. "Try calling him again. We'll circle the place." If Rich Smith wasn't home, where was he? And why wasn't he answering his wife's calls?

She reached for her phone while Simon edged the car around a bend in the road. Margie's little ranch house was set back onto the slope of a mountain. Through the tree branches, a single light glowed inside the house.

"He's not answering."

"Think that's him?" Simon nodded at the lit window.

"It's not like him to sit inside. He's always out at the barn."

"And you didn't just forget to turn a light off this morning?"

"Never. We don't waste electricity." She was trembling again. "That shouldn't be on."

So someone was in Margie's house, and it wasn't her husband. Could it be the robbers? Even if they'd decided to show up early, they wouldn't exactly make themselves at home after breaking in, would they?

Then again, they'd been pretty brazen when they'd robbed the shop. Walking in the front door as if they owned the place. It could be them. The note could have been a misdirection, or they might have come early just to fuck with her.

He could turn around, take Margie to the police station, and come back here with backup. But what if this actually was her husband, and the robbers showed up after Simon left? He didn't think the Chief was right about the robbers being her husband's buddies. Margie seemed terrified that they'd hurt Rich, too, not just her.

"I'm sorry, Margie," Simon said quietly. "I have to call this in."

"No—please."

"I can't be in two places at once. I can't protect both of you by myself."

He expected her to argue with him, but she clenched her hands together in her lap.

Simon switched off the car's headlights and nosed the car onto the dirt track leading up to the barn, hoping that whoever was inside the house couldn't hear the tires rolling over old snow and rocks. He took a deep breath, his head still aching, and wondered if he was about to lose his job. He should've told Margie to go see the Chief and then slammed the damn door in her face.

He radioed dispatch and briefly explained that Margie had received a possible threat of violence; there was an unknown person in her home; and her husband's location was unknown. Beside him, Margie drew in on herself even more, her shoulders hunching, her lips pressing together.

After Simon replaced his radio, he frowned at her. "It would be safer for everyone if you told me what was going on."

Again, she didn't answer. She was worse than Leona, for God's sake.

The robbers were blackmailing her—but why? What could Margie Smith have done? Unless it wasn't something *she'd* done, but—

"Holy shit," Simon said, as all of the pieces clicked together. "Your husband bombed the vet's office."

Margie's face went ghostly white.

"The bombing wasn't about the vet tech at all, or her stalker ex," he said. "It was something else—something to do with the way they treat the animals?"

"They euthanize," she whispered.

"Holy shit," he said again. "So it's true? He blew them up as—what? Political protest?"

Without thinking, he reached for his radio again. Margie fumbled for the door handle, and before he realized what was happening, she pushed the door open and sprinted up the slope toward her house.

"No—Margie, God damn it—" Simon bolted out the door after her. Her winter coat was a smudge of gray between black tree trunks. He sprinted up the slope, twisting past sharp, snowy branches, and tackled her before she could reach the house, flinging them both down onto the ground, just underneath a low windowsill full of golden light.

"The fucking robbers could be in there," he hissed. "Are you trying to get yourself killed?"

She struggled to get free. "I have to warn him—"

Simon released her from his bear hug, but kept his hand clamped down on her thin wrist. "You have to warn him about the *cops*. Because he's the fucking bomber, isn't he, Margie?"

"I swear I didn't know he was going to do it," she gasped, her face contorting with grief. "We all used to be activists together—me and Richie and Nance—but never like that. Never anything—"

"Nance?" Simon said. "Nancy O'Shea? She was an activist, too?"

Tears seeped from her eyes. "Only at first. Rich and Nance had a falling out years ago. She thought he was getting too extreme. That's why she wanted me to leave him, and she started sending me all this money. But I never thought he would... He could've killed that poor girl, Kristy—"

"Then he should go to jail," Simon snapped.

With a sniff, she wiped her eyes with the back of her hand. "Rich and I have been married twenty years. Sometimes, I hardly know him anymore. But I still love him. I'll always love him."

A door hinge creaked, and around the corner of the house from them, light poured out into the night, illuminating the slope leading up to the barn.

"Thought I heard something." A man's voice. Too young to be Rich, and from his inflection, he wasn't a Vermonter.

Margie cast Simon a frozen, terrified look and mouthed the words *I'm sorry*.

Tightening his grip on her arm, Simon pulled her into the house's shadow, flush against the worn wooden siding.

"Must've just been an animal or some shit," the man said.

Someone inside the house spoke, the words an indistinguishable low hum, like the strumming of a bass guitar.

The man in the doorway laughed. "Oh, yeah. She'll be here."

Margie turned to Simon again, her eyes pleading. "What if they have Richard in there?"

Simon mouthed *no* at her, but she was already trying to pull away from him and crawl toward the window.

Another low murmur came from inside the house.

"Yeah, sure," the man in the doorway said. "Be right back." The hinge creaked again, and the golden light vanished. After some muffled cursing, a watery beam of pale light appeared. A flashlight.

Fuck, he was going to search the yard.

Simon's mind turned over one possibility after another, trying to come up with a way to keep Margie both quiet and safe. He needed a miracle, or at least backup, but neither was likely to happen before the man with the flashlight found them.

The flashlight beam sliced through the side yard about twenty feet from them. If the robber walked about five feet to his left, he'd see the second driveway. One more foot, and he'd see the nose of Simon's patrol car.

Mercifully, the beam turned away, sweeping up the slope toward the barn. Simon could handle that, but first he needed to make sure Margie wasn't going to do anything crazy.

He motioned for Margie to stay where she was. On his hands and knees, he crawled forward to the window glimmering gold above him, rendered magical by the still, silent night even though in the daylight it was nothing but grimy paint and old glass. Sitting back on his heels, Simon leaned his shoulder against the siding and peered into the window. A man sat in Margie's dining room with his feet up on her cluttered table. He wore a ski mask, and a gun lay on the table in front of him. His posture was relaxed. One of Margie's cats sat purring on his lap.

Apart from the man and the cat, the dining room and living room were both empty. Simon couldn't see into the kitchen. This was as good as he could do.

Turning away from the window, he shook his head at Margie. Relief and anxiety both flickered across her face. Simon gestured for her to hide behind a thick pine tree next to the house. After a moment's hesitation, her expression questioning, she crawled behind the tree. She'd be visible from the street like this, but hopefully hidden from the view of the robbers in the back yard. He just had to make sure the robber inside the house didn't go out the front door.

Only one way to do that.

Dropping to his elbows, Simon crawled through the snow underneath the windowsill, hoping the man inside wouldn't think to look out. Once across, Simon stood up, still in the shadow of the house, and drew his gun.

The flashlight beam bobbed halfway up the slope. Simon tracked it, moving from tree to tree. His boots crumpled the frozen snow underfoot no matter how lightly he tried to tread.

The beam lit up the barn's closed Dutch doors, then swung to the right, away from Simon, to illuminate the paddock. This close, the robber was a tall, hulking shadow, except for the eerie silhouette of his profile. His face tilted up as if he were smelling the air, like a wolf.

With the robber focused on the paddock, Simon seized his chance to creep to another tree, closer to the barn.

The beam of light wobbled suddenly, making the paddock flicker, and swung back to the barn. Behind the tree, Simon went absolutely still, apart from the bead of sweat trickling down his spine. Had the robber heard his footsteps? And if so, now what? Taking the first shot wouldn't do Simon much good without any decent cover. The second man could come outside at any time.

Light flooded the trees surrounding Simon, as bright as noontime sunlight after so much darkness. His heart pounding, Simon pressed himself closer to the tree trunk.

Simon's thoughts flitted randomly to Leona. He should've told her that he loved her, even if she didn't love him back. She deserved to know all the reasons he'd fallen for her. Sometimes, for all her bravado, she didn't seem to know how incredible she was.

"What the fuck?" Footsteps crunched in the snow, advancing on Simon, followed by an unmistakable metallic *click*—the safety coming off.

An ear-splitting shot rang out through the woods. Three more followed, zinging off the trees around him. Shredded bark and pine needles spiraled through the air.

Keeping as much of his body as he could behind the trunk, Simon turned and fired off several rounds from behind the tree. With the flashlight shining in his eyes, he couldn't see the robber at all anymore. He aimed at the light, praying for accuracy, and fired until his trigger clicked. Empty.

The light flickered and vanished, leaving Simon

blinking in the dark, utterly blinded.

He stumbled toward where he thought the barn was. Between the darkness and the spots flashing before his eyes, he couldn't see the barn at all. With his ears still ringing from the gunfire, he couldn't hear the animals, either. At least he could smell hay and molasses. Smell seemed to be the last sense he had left.

His outstretched hand connected with wood. The side of the barn. The open sliding doors were to his left… There.

Still blinking, Simon lurched inside and stopped for a moment to let his eyes adjust, wishing he could risk his flashlight and searching, instead, for his spare clip.

Finally, after the longest minute of his life, he could see again, thanks to the moonlight filtering through the ceiling beams. He crept across the barn into an empty stall that faced the house. In the corner of the stall, he slid the bolt free from the top Dutch door and nudged it open, absurdly reminded of an old cowboy movie he'd seen once, years ago.

The back door to Margie's house opened. Light streamed out into the back yard, silhouetting the figure of a man in the doorway, loading a pistol.

"Come out, come out, wherever you are," the man in the doorway called out, his deep voice grotesquely sing-song. "Is that you already, Margaret? You're a pretty good shot. But I heard you run out of bullets, you know. You might as well come out and play nice."

A dark smear stained the snow between the barn and the house. Blood. A trail of bloody footprints led toward the paddock, then vanished into a pile of rocks. The second robber was injured, but not bad enough to stop him. As soon as Simon fired at the first robber, the second would figure out that he was hiding in the barn. Still, he couldn't waste his clear line of sight to the first robber. He had to do this now, while he still could, and pray that backup would get here soon, for Margie's sake.

Simon jammed his spare clip into his gun. He spared one last thought for Leona, and then he fired.

Chapter Twenty-One

LEONA COULDN'T SIT STILL. WHILE Julia sat at Simon's kitchen table with tears sliding down her face, Leona did the dishes. After she finished the dishes, she stacked Simon's papers into a neat pile, picked up all the empty booze bottles in his living room, and brought all of his laundry to the hamper that she eventually found in his bedroom closet. She'd never been in his bedroom before, strangely. It wasn't trashed like the rest of the house. His flannel comforter lay untouched across his big bed. A book about community policing rested on his nightstand. She almost cried when she saw it, and had to go back into the kitchen to be with Julia, where she sank into a chair and let her forehead rest against her clasped hands.

Julia's phone buzzed. They both jumped. Julia snatched up her phone.

"Dad?" She waited, listening and nodding. "Okay. Okay. Thanks. We'll be right there."

"What is it?" Leona asked. "Did they find him?"

"He's been hurt. They're taking him to Fletcher Allen's E.R. in Burlington."

Leona gripped the edges of the table, afraid she might pass out. "Did he—?"

Julia shook her head. "No, nothing like that. Something to do with a suspect. Police work. Dad thought we might want to go see—"

Leona was already halfway across the kitchen. Julia hurried after her, pausing only to grab their coats and lock Simon's door. They ran outside to Lulu and made it to Burlington in half an hour.

In the hospital parking lot, Julia called her dad again, who met them outside in front of the hospital's long bank of glass windows. Earl Labelle's buzz cut was mostly white, and he had more weight on him than Simon, but he had the same pale blue eyes and the same quiet intensity. Leona would have recognized him anywhere.

Julia dashed up to him and threw her arms around him. Earl patted Julia's back gruffly. Pulling away from his daughter, he turned his assessing gaze to Leona and offered his hand for her to shake. "You must be Leona."

Leona shook his hand, though she was practically vibrating off the ground with her impatience to see Simon. As soon as Earl released Leona's hand, Julia seized Leona by the arm and pulled her close.

"Is he all right?" Julia asked. "What happened?"

"Apparently Margie Smith was being threatened, and she went to Simon for help," Earl said. "Simon apprehended the suspects, but..." His brow furrowed. "In the process, he was shot at a relatively close range."

Dizziness crashed over Leona. *Shot?*

"He had a vest on," Earl continued gently, "which stopped the bullet."

A vest. Leona's knees shook with relief and terror. *Thank you, God. Thank you.*

"There's some bad bruising," Earl said. "And he's cracked three ribs."

"Three ribs!" Julia echoed, her eyes wide.

"Just cracked," Earl said. "Not broken clean through. And the internal scans have come back normal so far. He'll be right as rain in a couple months." Earl patted his daughter's arm, though his gaze slid to Leona, concerned and questioning.

Leona couldn't speak, couldn't react at all.

He could have died tonight.

"I don't understand," Julia said. "He wasn't on duty… Why did someone come to him?"

"It sounds like Margie felt safe going to him because of his relationship with Leona."

"But why was Margie being threatened?" Julia asked.

"Pending investigation," Earl said. "But, between us, sounds like her husband is the one who bombed the veterinary office last year. And she was being blackmailed because of it."

Leona stared at Earl in shock. Margie's husband was the bomber? And Margie had tried to cover for him—even though it had meant endangering Simon's life?

"I'm going to kill her," Leona said.

"No need to undo all of Simon's hard work." Earl smiled sadly. "By Margie's account, Simon saved her life."

Leona pulled away from Julia, hugging her arms to her chest, and paced in the cold night air. She had known and trusted Margie for years. Even after the robbery, Leona had been more than willing to forgive her. Endangering Leona's life was one thing, but Simon's?

And what had Simon been thinking, going with her by himself, in the state he'd been in?

"We should go in," Earl said. "I persuaded the nurses to let us visit, but I don't want to impose on their good graces."

Julia took Leona's arm again and pulled her into the hospital after Earl. He led them down a hallway, nodding at a nurse walking the other direction as if she were the guest in his hospital. A few minutes later, they arrived at a white curtain, partially open. Inside, Jack Miller and Bryan Keene stood by a hospital bed, blocking her view. Jack glanced over his shoulder at them, his eyebrows drawn together. Stepping aside, Jack gestured for them to move closest to Simon.

Fury and relief and lingering panic clashed inside her as she walked inexorably toward him. He was propped up in bed, wearing a hospital gown and pants, with a thin blanket over his legs. His groggy gaze sharpened when he saw her. He licked his lips, and color rose to his pale cheeks, but he did not speak to her. She didn't know what to say, either: she'd never wanted to run to someone and away from them so badly at the same time. She trembled in place like a metal ball held between two magnets. He would hate her now, because of Margie. He would send her away again—if not today, then soon. Despite whatever Paul thought, Simon would leave her.

"The Chief got a call from the State Police while you were outside," Keene said.

Leona looked up at Keene in confusion. She'd forgotten he was there, forgotten anyone else was in the room at all besides her and Simon.

Earl glanced at Keene. "Did they find Margie's husband?"

"Yeah, halfway to Canada. How's that for the sacred bonds of matrimony, huh? He didn't even say goodbye to his old lady."

"Maybe he thought she'd be better off if he left," Jack Miller suggested.

Keene frowned. "What, like the blackmailers were going to go away? What a dick."

"Who were they?" Leona didn't realize she had spoken aloud until everyone looked at her.

"Don't know yet," Keene said. "They're both in critical condition and had no ID on them. Once they're in better shape, we'll find out. Come on," he said, punching Jack in the shoulder. "We should see if the Chief needs us. Labelle," he added, pointing at Simon, "no fucking working. You need to rest."

"I'm fine—ouch, fuck." Simon winced, his hand moving to his ribs, and sank back onto his pillows.

"You'll be fine when you can sit up without a bunch of pretty nurses helping you." Keene winked at Leona. "Or even one pretty nurse."

Simon shot Leona a concerned look, as if she were going to claw Keene's face off. She looked down, flummoxed.

"I'll walk you out," Earl said to Keene and Jack. "Gonna grab a coffee."

"Me, too. A decaf." Julia patted Leona's back and hurried off after her dad.

Alone with Simon, Leona shuffled closer to his bed, wishing she could touch him to reassure herself that he was here, and safe.

"I'm sorry you…saw me that way. Earlier." Simon winced with every word, every shallow breath. "It was…fucking shameful."

Leona shook her head, tears burning her eyes again. "No—don't say that. It's not like that. I could never be ashamed of you. I think you need help, Simon, with your drinking, and…depression, I think. I don't know."

"I know," he said quietly. "I know I need help. I've known it…for a long time."

"But I'm not ashamed," she insisted. "You're amazing. You saved Margie's life, even though she didn't deserve it."

He smiled, but he still looked sad, worried. Ashamed of himself. There was so much she wanted to say to him. Overwhelmed, she exhaled. "God, Simon, you scared the hell out of me tonight."

"I'm sorry." He stretched one hand toward her. That was all it took to set her free from the pull to run. Dropping to her knees by his bed on the grungy hospital linoleum, she pressed his palm to her cheek.

"Don't send me away again," she whispered. "Please." *Don't leave me.*

"I thought… I was trying…to spare you."

"*Spare* me?" Her tears slid down his palm onto his wrist, catching on his neon yellow hospital bracelet. She braced herself on the metal railing alongside his bed. "I don't want you to spare me from anything. I want to be there for your darkest moods, just like I want to be there for your brightest. I want every part of you, no matter how bad or scary you think it is."

He drew his palm away from her cheek and brushed her hair from her eyes. His brow creased.

Authoritative footsteps tapped on the linoleum outside Simon's curtain. "Officer Labelle?" A man in scrubs poked his head around the curtain. "Oh, I'm sorry."

"No, it's okay." Leona stood, brushing off her jeans and wiping her eyes on her wrist. "I'm in the way."

"Actually, I just wanted to let you know we're discharging you," he said to Simon. "Everything looks good. Just keep taking your painkillers, and make sure you take as deep a breath as you can, at least once an hour, to help prevent pneumonia, okay? We're going to grab you a wheelchair. You have someone who can drive you home, or should I call for a transport?"

"I can drive you." Leona glanced nervously at Simon. "If you want me to."

He smiled up at her, though his eyes were anxious, and he nodded.

A very kind orderly helped Simon out of the wheelchair and into Leona's car. Simon couldn't move, couldn't breathe, couldn't even exist without the pain in his ribs becoming so intense it practically blinded him. He forced himself to lean back against Leona's bucket seat while the orderly buckled his seat belt for him and patted his hand, wishing him a good night and a speedy recovery. Simon could only nod, gritting his teeth. Fortunately, the pain subsided to a more bearable level after a few minutes of stillness.

Leona slid into the driver's seat beside him, her face tight with worry. He'd been so shocked to see her in the emergency room that at first he'd thought he'd been dreaming. And when she had cried… What did it mean? How could she still want him, especially after what he'd said to her?

He had to tell her how he felt. It could be crazy—the painkillers could be dulling his reason—but telling her that he loved her now seemed like the most important thing in the universe. She had to know, even though she didn't feel the same way. She had to know she was special.

"Leona…" His tongue was heavy and awkward. Why was it easier to face two armed men than to tell this girl that he loved her? He'd said it to his exes, always after the appropriate amount of time. It had been easy, comfortable.

"What is it?" She maneuvered the car out of its parking space. "Tell me if I'm driving too crazily, by the way. Maybe you should've gone in your dad's car. Softer suspension. I could've taken Julia home—"

"I'd rather be with you," he said.

She broke into an anxious smile. "All right."

In the reflected glow of the parking lot lights, her lashes cast spiky shadows across her cheeks. The curves of her lips were swollen from crying.

"You're so beautiful," Simon said.

She laughed. "Painkillers kicking in?"

"Yeah." He grinned. "But I mean it, too."

She reached across the console and squeezed his knee, just for a moment, before she had to take her hand away to shift.

He didn't realize he'd dozed off until the car suddenly stopped moving. They were back at his duplex already. With a groan, he rubbed at his eyes, which felt like they'd been sandpapered, and wondered how he was going to get up the energy to stand. Maybe he should've had an ambulance bring him back after all. But then he wouldn't be with Leona right now, and he was determined, he was absolutely committed, to telling her how he felt.

Leona helped him out of the car and up onto the front porch, where his thoughts turned to Margie and—

"Fuck," he said. "I just remembered."

"What?"

"I've got to call Keene. Hang on." He dug his keys and his cell phone out of his pockets and dialed Keene's number as they made their way inside.

"What did I tell you about working?" Keene demanded, in lieu of hello.

"Yeah, I know." Simon needed to finish what he'd started while he still could. The Chief had stopped by the hospital room briefly, looking more worried than angry. Simon was no longer convinced he'd lose his job when his medical leave ended, but he might never be assigned to another investigation again, after his lapse in judgment with Margie. "I thought of something, that's all," he said.

He could practically hear Keene roll his eyes. "Course you did."

"Look, Nancy O'Shea's ex… He had a brother. I'm wondering if that's who's behind this. That one robber, the leader, has a California sort of accent…and that's where the brother lives."

Keene grunted. "You think he was jealous of his ex-sister-in-law, getting all this money from his old man?"

"Yeah, and he must've figured out that Nancy O'Shea was giving money to Margie, hoping it'd get Margie to leave her husband."

"So clever Mrs. O'Shea realized Richie was the bomber, after she saw it on the news," Keene said. "And since she and Margie were friends, she gave Margie this money to help her get out, not thinking it'd bring her brother-in-law all the way from California."

"Exactly," Simon said.

"All right. I'll look into it."

"Thanks, man. Let me know what you find out."

"Will do. Hey, about your girl…"

"Yeah?" Simon glanced at Leona, who was pouring herself a glass of water at his kitchen sink. *His* girl?

"Well…not that my opinion counts for shit, but I

like her. You two, together…it makes a lot of sense."

Simon laughed, then winced, as pain lanced through his ribs. "Are you giving us your blessing, Keene?"

Keene chuckled. "Shut up. You know what I mean. I'm just glad you're not dead, asshole. And you've found someone. It's not that easy."

"I know. Hey, thanks." Simon knew, better than Keene could imagine, how true that was.

They said goodbye and disconnected.

"Figuring out the case?" Leona said, glancing up at him. "You don't have to tell me if it's confidential…"

"I'm not sure what's going on still," he admitted. "But I think it's getting there."

She nodded and sipped her water, still standing in the middle of his kitchen. Simon blinked, suddenly realizing how different his kitchen looked from when he'd left.

"My kitchen…is really clean."

"I cleaned it," Leona said.

"What? Why?"

"Because I was waiting to find out if you were alive or not, and I needed something to do."

"I guess that makes sense?"

She smiled ruefully. "Come on, let's get you to bed." She led him into his bedroom, where she carefully turned him to face her. "Arms up."

With a pained grimace, Simon lifted his arms. Leona eased his coat off, one sleeve at a time. She untied his hospital gown next and slid it off, leaving him in only his absurd baby blue hospital pants.

Her eyes widening, she stared at the bruise on his chest. "Jesus Christ, Simon."

Even he had to admit the bruise was grotesque. It rippled purple and black across his ribs, with a pucker in the center, where the bullet had indented his flesh.

"How did it happen?" she asked.

Sitting gingerly on the edge of the bed, Simon told her about Margie running out of his car toward the house, and the man coming out back to search the yard. "I made it to barn, for cover, and…I got the first guy, the ringleader, in the leg, but the second guy followed me into the barn. I'd hit him in the wrist, earlier, but he'd wrapped it in something… He was holding his gun one-handed. Strong guy. Well-trained."

"Hired muscle."

"Yeah, definitely. I couldn't tell where he was. It was so dark, and he was fast, and silent… The force of the shot—it was like getting hit with baseball bat. It knocked me off my feet."

Despite the vest, he'd been consumed with panic and dread at first, expecting to find blood everywhere, expecting to be dying. It had turned out, once he'd a chance to think about it, that he had not wanted to die after all.

"He came up to finish me off," Simon continued. "Don't think he realized I had a vest on… He probably thought I was as good as dead already. I'd dropped my gun when I fell, but I rolled for it and grabbed it, and I got him in the shoulder."

The sound of his own pistol had been so loud that afterward his ears had rung like church bells. He'd gotten to his feet, still high enough on adrenaline to ignore the pain in his chest, and had cuffed the semi-conscious man slumped against the wall before he'd even realized that he was hearing sirens as well as ringing. Backup, at last.

Leona sat down next to him on the bed and took his hand in hers, bringing his knuckles to her soft lips.

"I'm so…" She cast him a nervous glance, her shoulders tense. "I have to tell you something. I should've told you before, and now it's just…"

Concern for her broke through his exhaustion. "What is it?"

The tip of her pretty nose bumped his, and her breath warmed his skin. Nothing had ever felt better than this.

"Simon… I'm in love with you."

He froze, the rest of the world forgotten. "Are you—?" He shivered, though it worsened the soreness in his chest, and looked away. "If this is about pity, or guilt—"

"Pity!" The word was a pained gasp. "No. Not at all." She took his face in her hands and turned him gently back toward her. The intensity in her eyes was shocking. "I didn't know it at first," she said. "I never thought I'd love anyone. Not like this. But I love you, Simon."

He stared at her, too astonished to reply. She still wanted him, after he'd rushed her into meeting his family, after what he'd *said* to her, after she'd seen him at his lowest, his most despicable? No—she didn't just want him, she *loved* him? How could that be?

She bit her lip. "I know I'm pretty fucked up. If you don't believe me…that I'm capable of it…"

"You're not fucked up. You're wonderful." He knew she could love any man she chose; he just didn't know why she would choose him. "I love you, too. You have to know that. I've always loved you."

"I know." She pressed his forehead to hers, her eyes closing, her body trembling. He surrendered to her touch. All these years, he'd never dared to imagine this. What had he done to deserve her? He had saved Margie's life—but only by endangering it first. He wasn't a hero.

She kissed him, tenderly at first, but the kiss soon

grew more passionate as her tongue slipped between his lips. Despite the storm in his mind, her kiss was all-consuming, and he succumbed to the sweetness and warmth of her mouth, desperate for her comfort.

Carefully, she laid him down on the bed. He winced as the weight of his body readjusted, but after a moment, lying down was easier on his ribs than sitting had been.

"I'm not going to try anything, don't worry," she said, with a sad little smile. "I just want to see you."

He let her strip off his shoes and socks and pants, leaving his boxers on. She sat on her heels next to him, still in her usual tights and black dress, and ran her fingertips up his leg, his hip, his arm, as if she had to reassure herself that he was all there. He watched her wonderingly. Tomorrow or the next day, she would come to her senses, and she would realize she deserved a better man than him. Until then, he'd take every touch, every kiss.

Eventually, Leona curled up next to him on the bed, taking care not to bump or jostle his chest, and dropped one kiss after another along the top of his shoulder. "I love you, Simon," she whispered, moving her mouth to his neck. "I love you so much." She kissed his ear, his cheek, and, finally, his mouth. Each kiss, each word, filled him with happiness until, in spite of everything, he overflowed with joy.

Chapter Twenty-Two

LEONA HAD NEVER DOTED ON anybody before and was surprised to realize how much she enjoyed it. After a few days of rest and pain meds, Simon could get around a little better—or was already restless enough that he was willing to suffer through the pain. She made him elaborate meals, anyway, and helped him dress or shower when he would let her. She hoped he didn't mind that she stayed over. He seemed happy to have her there, and she couldn't bear to leave him on his own. Every time she closed her eyes, she pictured the liquor bottles strewn around his couch, or, worse, Julia standing on his front porch, outside an empty house.

Whenever Leona had to go into work, she called Julia or Earl to take over from her. Julia was always her bright, cheerful, loveable self. Earl was brusque and, in the mornings, a little grumpy, but Leona found Earl's grumpiness inexplicably endearing. Since Earl was secretly a coffee snob, Leona always made him a couple of extra cups in her French press before she left.

Between Earl, Audette, Julia, and Leona, Simon wasn't home alone much. It wasn't something they discussed; it was just something they all did, and that Simon accepted.

Then, suddenly, it was Christmas Eve. Leona and Paul closed the shop at noon. After promising Paul many times that she would see him at his party on Christmas day, she headed back to Simon's to drop off his presents before his family came over for dinner. Leona didn't begrudge them their family time, though it would be strange to spend the night at her own place.

Walking up the front steps of his duplex, Leona fished his spare key out of her purse. She stepped into the kitchen to the scents of roasting ham and sweet, spicy desserts. The kitchen was filled with light and music. Julia and Audi were giggling about something by the stove, while Julia's boyfriend, Aaron, stood nervously by the fridge next to Earl, probably being interrogated a little. A family trait.

Simon sat at the kitchen table, pale but smiling. Happiness radiated from him. Her heart caught in her throat. How strange to love someone so much that seeing him happy delighted her, and seeing him sad destroyed her.

"We didn't want to miss you, so we came early," Julia said, bustling over to give her a hug. "Will you stay for dinner?"

Disentangling herself from Julia, Leona waited for the feelings of panic and shame to rush over her. But she'd spent so much time looking after Simon with his family's help this past week, it was only natural to see them here, even if they weren't usually all here at once.

A smile blossomed inside her. "I'd love to. Thank you."

———◆———

Sometime after an extremely gluttonous dinner of

ham, mashed potatoes, and gravy, they all traipsed into the living room to eat cookies and chat, while the Christmas movies that Leona usually avoided like the plague played in the background. They didn't bother her as much like this.

Eventually, she peeled herself up off the couch to grab another gingersnap cookie from the kitchen. Earl followed her, stretching. "Seen that movie so many times I know every line."

"Which movie?" Leona asked.

"All of them." He poured himself a glass of milk and sat down at Simon's kitchen table, where he plucked a cookie off the platter.

Impulsively, Leona sat down across from him. She didn't know why, other than that she liked him and if she went back to the couch she was likely to fall asleep.

"You don't see your family at Christmas, do you?" Earl meditatively dunked his cookie in his glass of milk.

"Nope." Nervousness flickered through her. But this was Earl. She trusted him. He wouldn't raise the subject without a good reason.

"You see them at all?" he asked.

"Nope."

"Good."

She raised an eyebrow, startled by his response. "Good?"

Earl shifted in his seat with a pensive sigh that reminded her of Simon. "I remember your case from when you were a little kid."

"My case?" She had no idea what she could have done as a child that would have caught his attention. She hadn't gotten into any trouble—tagging, smoking weed, occasionally shoplifting—until she was at least a preteen.

"When your folks left you at that mall."

She flinched. "Ah. That."

"The department that picked you up told us about it," Earl said quietly.

"Of course," she murmured. Thinking about it now, it made complete sense. She still remembered how pissed those police officers had been, even though, at the time, she'd assumed they were mad at her for stealing a pretzel.

"I handled almost all the child abuse cases back then," Earl said, "but the Chief at the time told me he'd take care of yours. I figured he'd keep his word about investigating it." Earl's jaw tensed. He tapped his fingers on the table. "A few weeks later, I found out he still hadn't done a damn thing. I reported the case to social services myself."

"I don't remember any social services stuff," she said hesitantly.

"That's because they never even opened an investigation," Earl growled. "I don't know if the Chief leaned on them or what, to keep them quiet, or if they were just incompetent. There wasn't anything I could do for you, short of kidnapping you."

Something in his tone told her he'd considered it. "I don't understand," she said. "Why would the Chief have leaned on them?"

"I found out later that the Chief and your dad were gambling buddies."

"*My* parents were friends with the Chief of Police?"

He smiled grimly. "He wasn't Chief for long. He ended up resigning because of his gambling problems. Big scandal for a town like ours. That was how I ended up Chief myself, in fact."

"So that's something," she said, but Earl just shrugged,

breaking off another piece of his cookie.

"Is it? I saw a lot of child abuse cases go nowhere, during my time on the force. I still remember every single one of them, and yours… I don't know if it was the gambling thing or not, but yours stuck with me." His light eyes flicked toward her. "My own father was not a nice man."

"I'm sorry," she said softly. "You seem like such a great dad… Simon thinks the world of you." She'd figured that Earl had passed down to Simon the same things he'd learned from his own father, from fishing to how to ask out girls. Apparently not. Earl had done it on his own, somehow.

Earl grunted a laugh. "Audi gets all the credit for those two."

"I'm sure that's not true."

"Well, anyway…sorry to lay all this on you. Guess it's been a relief these past few days to see you all grown up and self-sufficient…to know you turned out okay."

She thought of Simon telling her she was wonderful, his voice raw with emotion. Maybe she had turned out all right.

Simon padded into the kitchen, his hair mussed, his arms bundled into the front pocket of his sweatshirt. "How's it going in here?" he asked, keeping his tone casual as he glanced from her to his dad.

"Good," Leona said. "Really. Thank you," she added to Earl.

"Nice girl you got here, son," he said gruffly to Simon, getting to his feet and clapping Leona on the shoulder. He shuffled back into the living room. Simon eased into the chair his dad had left open, pressing a steadying hand to his ribs.

"You okay?" Leona asked.

"Yeah," Simon said, through clenched teeth. "What was that about? Was he bugging you?"

"No, not at all." She frowned, trying to process everything Earl had just told her. In halting steps, she told Simon what Earl had said.

"What the fuck," Simon said. "I knew he didn't like his Chief much, but I never thought… That is really fucked up, Leona."

"It's crazy to think…" She swallowed. "It's crazy that your dad wanted to help me so bad. That he still remembers me almost twenty years later. That it bothered him so much, you know?"

Leona tried to picture Earl, then only in his late thirties or early forties and already second in command at the department, dwelling on her case, caring about what happened to her even though they were complete strangers. She couldn't picture it until she looked back up at Simon and saw the outrage and concern shadowing his features.

"Of course it bothered him," Simon said. "I only know about one incident and I'm fucking furious."

"Oh, Simon," she murmured, with a choked laugh. "You don't understand. Other people don't care the way you do."

"Fuck that," he snapped. "Just because your parents didn't—"

"No," she said, "it's true. You're different. You care about everyone, and you never hide it. I can't…"

He reached across the table, enfolding her hand in his. "There's a lot more, isn't there? That you haven't told me."

It was so hard to describe an endless spool of the same experience, reinforcing over and over again that she was forgotten, forgettable. She had been abandoned, in large ways and small, every day.

"More of the same," she said finally.

"I'm sorry."

"It's okay," she said, forcing her shoulders to relax. "You've—you've already helped me, more than I can tell you."

Christmas music warbled in from the living room, followed by the sound of Julia and Audi both giggling. Strangely, his family had helped her, too. Though they each expressed it in their own ways, they all were as caring as Simon was.

"I lied to you about going to Paul's," Leona said suddenly. "For Christmas. I've never gone."

He blinked. "You—what? You've never gone? What do you do every year?"

"My friend Iris used to come by for an hour or two. Otherwise…" She shrugged, looking away from him.

Simon's fingers tightened around hers. "I didn't know."

"I should have told you. I didn't want to admit how scared I was, and then, once we got there, I just…panicked."

"I rushed you. It was my fault."

"It really wasn't." He blamed himself for far too much; he could not seem to be kind to himself. He could barely stand to accept kindness from her, and he had to realize she wasn't going to bother being nice to anyone she didn't truly love. "I wanted it as much as you," Leona said finally. "To get to know your family, I mean. I just didn't know how to do it."

She wished she could have a do-over with his family's Christmas party, now that she knew his parents and sister a little better. "Your family's getting together tomorrow, right?"

"A few of my aunts and uncles are coming over."

"Could I…" She steeled herself. "Could I come with you? And maybe you could come to Paul's party with me?"

His eyebrows shot up. "If that's what you want, I would love it." He stroked her wrist with his thumb. "If you're sure."

She gave a tight sigh of relief. "I'm sure. Though I can't promise not to hang out with your dad the whole time."

Simon grinned. "You'd get stuck watching sports. Do you know anything about sports?"

"I know most of them are played on teams?"

He laughed, though it made him grimace with pain. He pressed his hand to his side. "I'm sure he'll fill you on the essentials."

She ducked her head, smiling, the weight on her shoulders lessened.

After his family left, they made their way to bed.

"Arms up." A smile played on Leona's lips. He raised his arms, wincing at the pain that sparked through his side. After she pulled his sweatshirt and T-shirt off over his head, her gaze fell to the bruise on his ribs. "It somehow manages to look worse every night, but I think that means it's actually getting better."

He glanced down at the mottled yellow, green, and purple splashed across the side of his chest. "Yeah. Think so. It doesn't hurt as bad anymore." He still couldn't bend or twist, and, even though he was supposed to take as many deep breaths as he could, the deepest breaths were dazzlingly painful. But it was improving nonetheless, and he was glad to be working his way out of his painkiller haze.

Leona started to turn away, since Simon could usually manage to take off his own jeans. Tonight, he took her elbows in his hands and drew her back toward him, studying her expression.

"You all right?" he asked her roughly. Trust his dad to drop a huge emotional bomb on her on Christmas Eve, when she was already on edge.

"I'm okay. Really. I'm glad he told me."

His fingers tightened around her arms. Bending forward as best he could, he kissed her. She responded immediately, her mouth warm against his, her hands sliding into the waistband of his jeans.

Sitting next to her on the couch tonight had been a form of erotic torture, with her leg pressed against his and her perfume spilling through the scent of cookies. They'd been intimate with each other once this past week, but he hadn't been able to move well enough to do much. She had gotten them both off, with her mouth on his cock and her free hand slipping down into her panties. He'd loved, it, but he'd also wanted so much more: to be claimed by her, just like that night when she'd fucked him up against her bedroom door. He wanted to call her Mistress. To worship her.

Sighing her name, he pulled her even closer, shamelessly bumping his erection against her stomach.

Her fingernails dug into his skin. "Your ribs…"

"I don't care." He kissed her. "I want you even if it hurts."

Her eyes darkened with desire, her fair cheeks pinking. "Take your jeans off."

With a breath of relief, he shoved his jeans and boxers to the floor. She pushed him backward toward the bed and eased him down onto the mattress, supporting his weight to bring him down gently. He clenched his teeth while his body readjusted.

"Hold onto the headboard."

The pain in his chest forgotten, Simon lifted his arms over his head and gripped the top of his headboard. She surveyed him lying naked on the bed, a predatory smile widening her mouth.

Climbing onto the mattress, she straddled his thighs. Her smooth skin pressed against his.

"Look at you." She traced one of the lines that ran along his hipbones to his groin and wrapped her cool, slender hand around his length. "Right where you belong."

"With you." For as long as she would keep him.

Her hand glided down his shaft. He wanted to pump his hips and push his cock through her light, teasing grip, but she was still straddling his legs, pinning him in place.

"Please," he groaned. "I need you."

She swept a bead of moisture from the head of his cock and slipped her fingertip between her lips with a little purr. "You don't want my mouth tonight, dear heart?" she asked, her tone as teasing as her touch.

"I want you to fuck me."

The tip of her finger stroked him, the lightness of her touch a dizzying, excruciating torment. The more she teased him, the more he craved her. "For God's sake, Leona."

"What do you say?"

"Mistress," he said, through gritted teeth. "Mistress, fuck me. Please."

Graceful as ever, she lifted up onto her knees. She took his cock in her hand and slowly drew her hot, wet folds up and down its length. Gradually, she lowered herself onto him, her inner muscles tight and hot around him, until, at last, he was fully sheathed inside her. Sweat dripped down his temples, as waves of agonized relief flooded through him. "I've missed you."

He tried to thrust his hips, desperate to move inside her, but she was still pinning him to the bed, permitting only the slowest, most circumscribed strokes. Careful not to touch his chest, she ducked her head and kissed him, her lips tight against his, her tongue sweeping inside his mouth. He moaned against her, wishing he could bury his hands in her beautiful hair. But she had told him to hold onto the headboard, so that was what he did.

"I love you, Simon," she murmured, kissing the line of his jaw.

Every time she said it, longing and fear and love tore through him. Tonight, after a day of quiet domesticity with his family, he wanted it to be true more than ever. He wanted to build a life together with her, living here in town, spending time with their families and friends, and someday having a family of their own.

Her mouth moved to the sensitive spot just under his ear, her cheek bumping against his. If he'd turned his head, he could have kissed her neck. "Tell me you believe me, Simon. I need to hear it."

He shivered, though his cock still throbbed with heat inside of her. As much as he trusted her, believing her required believing so much—about himself, about what he deserved from life. Happiness—since when did he deserve that?

"Say it, Simon," she murmured, nipping his earlobe. Adrenaline flickered in his chest. He gave into his urge to kiss her throat. She purred again, arching her neck and sinking into his kiss.

"You know—you know I love you," he said, breathing hard against her neck. "I'll always love you, but I can't expect you to…to feel like that, about me. Especially not—forever, the way I…"

"Yes, you can." She sat up, still straddling him, and his cock slid all the way inside her again. So deep, so exquisitely deep. "Let go with your right hand. And hold it up."

He wasn't sure what she was getting at, but he did as he was told, keeping hold of the headboard with his left hand and lifting his right arm up toward her.

"I want this, dear heart." Leaning forward, she placed her pretty throat into his open hand.

His heart skipped a beat. Their eyes met, and hers were as serious as he'd ever seen them. He stroked the side of her throat with his thumb. Her eyelashes fluttered, and her inner muscles gave a little squeeze.

"Jesus," he whispered, through dry lips.

She exhaled, pressing the soft skin of her throat more firmly against his palm. She set one hand on the mattress beside him to steady herself, but brought her free hand to his forearm, her fingers tracing the outlines of his muscles, so slowly, almost with reverence.

"I've missed wearing that necklace," she murmured, her eyes falling closed. "I didn't know if you'd still want me to wear it."

"Always," he choked out, without thinking. "As much as you want." The idea that she might want to wear it—that she actually might *miss* wearing it—awed him. He was so in awe of her.

"I love you, Simon. I will always love you. Everything about you."

He swallowed hard. "Even this?" His fingertips gently rubbed the side of her neck.

"Yes," she murmured, with a slight movement of her hips that sent pleasure rippling through his whole body. "Tell me you believe me."

He bit his lips, his eyes stinging. So many years of trying to hide this from himself, of hating himself for being unable to, of wishing he could be anyone else just to escape it. But he did believe her. Because he knew her. "I believe you."

"Promise me forever."

"I promise." His heart was slamming against his ribs. "I promise."

"Good." Still leaning forward, pressing her throat into his palm, she dropped her hand from his forearm to her clit, and rubbed her pussy as she rocked her hips against him. He thrust up to meet her, a tortured sound escaping his lips with every new rush of pleasure. Pain radiated up his side, but he was too far gone to stop now.

"Oh, I'm—oh—" Her inner muscles clenched hard around him. Her nipples tightened, and goose bumps broke out across her skin. She still didn't move her throat away from his hand. If anything, she leaned into him even more, and that trust broke him as much as each hot, wet thrust into her. He came with a hoarse groan, dimly aware of her lingering gasps.

I love you.

He didn't know if he said it, or if she did, or if it was just understood. Pleasure engulfed him, soothing his aching body, filling him with the lightness of surrender. He was free—free from the demons that possessed him, from the worries that burdened him, from the barriers he had built around his heart.

Leona carefully climbed off him and sank down

onto the bed beside him. He pulled her in for a kiss, letting himself touch her all over, as much of her as he could reach.

Chapter Twenty-Three

PAUL MET THEM AT THE door, wearing a hideous reindeer sweater and holding a plate of cookies. He kissed Leona on the cheek and, after some juggling of the cookie platter, shook Simon's hand. "I'm so glad you made it! Come on in and say hello to Mellon. You have to try the pie he made, it's phenomenal."

He ushered them inside, where a throng of people were listening to classy Christmas jazz and drinking cocktails. Leona recognized at least half of their guests from town, but others were from further afield. In addition to Mellon's work colleagues, their old school friends, and their families, there was a small number of artists who'd been selling their work to the shop for years, including an elusive glass blower who'd made some of Leona's all time favorite pieces. Being introduced to him was like meeting a movie star, especially after he agreed to give her a sneak peek at one of his newest lines the following week.

Eventually, Paul pulled them into the kitchen. Mellon, Emma, and Emma's boyfriend, Leif, were standing around the table, eating pie and talking. Leona said warm hellos, introduced Simon to everyone, and accepted a slice of pie.

Simon, resting a hand on the small of her back,

reached around her for a jug of apple cider on the table. Their eyes met, and Simon ducked his head in quiet acknowledgment. She hadn't seen him drink since he'd gotten shot. He'd started seeing a therapist and had joined an alcohol program. Leona squeezed his arm. It was a good start. She believed in him.

Soon, Emma and Leif pulled Simon into conversation, but Leona couldn't concentrate. Christmas with Simon's family had gone well—really well. Earl had, as predicted, taught her quite a lot about sports. Julia and Aaron had been happily overwhelmed with baby-related gifts. Leona had felt, for the first time in her life, that this family stuff was not so hard.

But now, standing in Mellon's quiet kitchen, Leona was suddenly overwrought. She couldn't help thinking about the last time she'd been at Paul and Mellon's house, when her life had seemed on the brink of total collapse. They had both been so kind to her. So unprompted, so generous, the way they always were. Just like the way Paul had offered to sell her the shop. He *wanted* her to have it, and yet she'd put him off for weeks and weeks, unable to believe Paul might still want to see her after they no longer worked together. Every second she didn't buy the shop—*her* shop— was a second she couldn't get back. And, since Paul wouldn't sell it to someone else unless she insisted, her refusal to buy his shop meant he was postponing a very well-deserved retirement with the man he loved, and all the wonderful adventures that came along with that.

Paul ducked away from the group to open another bottle of wine by the kitchen sink. On impulse, Leona followed him.

He smiled down at her. "What did you think of the pie, Jellybean?"

"Delicious. Mellon is a wizard." She smoothed an imaginary dust mote off of her sweater. "Paul, I've been thinking… I want to buy the shop." His face lit up. Before he could speak, she added: "That offer you made me was ridiculously low, though. I won't buy it for less than twice what you offered me."

Paul laughed. "If anything, my offer was high! I insist on halving it."

"Absolutely not!"

He shook his head, still laughing. "You know I'd give it to you for nothing. It's as good as yours, and always has been." Clearing his throat, he set the wine bottle down on the counter. "Are you sure this is what you want, Leona?"

"I'm sure. I've always been sure."

His brows knitting together, his smile faded. "I'm glad you brought this up today, actually. I need to tell you, Mellon and I found a place where we'd like to retire."

"Oh." Her heart sank. This was it. They'd be going to Aruba or wherever else, and she'd see them once a year, at most.

"I think you'll like it," Paul said. "You can come with us to the closing this weekend, if you want."

"I don't think…" Last-minute flights to Aruba couldn't come cheap.

"It's in the Green Mountains."

Leona stared at him, shocked. "You're not serious."

"Why not? Who doesn't want to retire in Vermont?" He winked.

"It's an hour away from where you live now," Leona said.

"Forty-five minutes," he corrected her. "Which means we've already done a great job of scouting out the neighborhood. We figure we'll sell this old place… Maybe to some deserving young couple? There's plenty of room for little monsters—"

Leona's cheeks burned. "Oh my God, too soon!"

He laughed again and pulled her into a hug. For once, she didn't resist.

"First day back! How's the ribs?" Keene stood in the doorway to the break room, sipping coffee.

"Absolutely fine," Simon replied, "as long as I don't sneeze."

"Learned that lesson the hard way?" Keene grinned.

"You have no idea." Simon paused in the middle of the shabby main office, absorbing the fluorescent light and the smell of old carpeting. Over the last six weeks, he'd missed this place down into the marrow of his bones.

"Glad to have you back, sir," Jack said, looking up from his desk in the far corner. "And I'm glad you're feeling better."

"Thanks, Jack. Any updates on the case?"

"Not since last week," Keene said. "The State's Attorney has it now. You know how that goes." Keene had been kind enough to give Simon regular updates on the progress of the case over the interminable six weeks of medical leave. Simon's hunch about Mrs. O'Shea's brother-in-law had proved correct. Penelope had identified her uncle while he was in custody. Since then, the task force, with Keene's help, had been piecing together a timeline of his activities, from when he'd discovered how much money his father had given to Mrs. O'Shea to when he'd realized that Margie had ended up with a substantial portion of it. Meanwhile, Richard Smith had confessed to the bombing, saying he wanted to let his wife move on with her life.

The Chief opened his office door and poked his head outside. "Simon, welcome back. Come on by when you have a second."

"Yes, sir."

The Chief vanished back into his office. Simon cast a worried glance at Keene, who shrugged a shoulder and smiled innocently at the ceiling.

"What's going on?" Simon asked.

"Go find out. It's not bad news, I promise."

Yeah, right. His body electric with nervousness, Simon crossed through the clusters of desks and filing cabinets to the Chief's office. The Chief waved him in. Simon sat down in the chair across from the Chief's desk, his skin prickling with uncomfortable memories. He took off his hat and set it on his knee.

"So, you're feeling better?" the Chief asked.

"Yessir. Thank you."

"Very glad to hear it." The Chief cleared his throat and shuffled some papers on his desk. "Simon, while you were out, we relied heavily on your notes for all three cases. I have to tell you, they were incredibly helpful. You have a very organized mind. And a lot of curiosity."

"That's a nice way of putting it, sir. I usually get called suspicious."

The Chief's mouth twitched. "The one I always get is stubborn, especially from my wife."

"Not necessarily a bad trait, sir."

"No, not necessarily. With you, though, I let my stubbornness get the best of me."

"You didn't…" If he meant taking Simon off the

O'Shea case—well, in retrospect, Simon would've done the same thing.

"What I mean is, your instincts were right, on every case," the Chief said. "You were doing great work before I interrupted you. If I'd supported you instead of hamstringing you, you might have been able to crack these cases without getting shot."

"I don't think—"

The Chief shook his head. "It's all right. You don't need to let me off the hook. For what it's worth, I'm not saying I approve of what you did. Going to Margie Smith's house the first time was bad enough, but the second time… Taking on two armed men by yourself? Bringing Margie with you? You could've gotten her killed, and yourself, too."

"I know, sir." Simon turned his police hat over in his hands. He still felt guilty about putting Margie in danger. If he hadn't been so hung over and miserable that night, he would've been able to think of some other way to keep her safe and check on her husband, too, he was sure of it.

"I do understand why you did it," the Chief said quietly.

Simon looked up, too taken aback to speak.

"But I still need you to promise me that you won't act like a one-man department again—that you will call us when you need us, and you will focus on safety first. And if you promise that, I will not write you up."

"Of course—"

"Good. Because I've been thinking, Simon, that what you really need is actually a little more autonomy. You're independent, a self-starter, and, if anything, hard-working to a fault." The Chief leaned back in his chair, tapping a pencil on the edge of his desk. "This is subject to various approvals, of course."

"Okay," he said, unsure of the Chief's direction.

"I was thinking of making you a part-time detective," the Chief said.

Simon's surprise from earlier ballooned into amazement. In the Academy, Simon had daydreamed about the possibility of becoming a detective, but when he got the call from Grenton PD, he knew he'd have to choose: working in his home town or focusing on a career as a detective. The choice was too obvious to dwell on.

"About half your time would be specifically for investigations," the Chief explained. "The rest of the time, you'd function as you always have, as a patrolman. If there was a lot of investigative work that needed doing, we could make it full-time later on."

Simon swiped a hand through his hair. "I'd be honored. No matter many hours it ends up being."

He'd been so thrilled just to get on the task force handling the bomb threats, and that was only in his capacity as a local patrol officer. A detective position, even part-time, would mean a little more respect, a little more authority, and most of all, more time doing what he loved, looking after his town in every way that he could. "I never expected anything like this, sir," he said. "Not in such a small department."

"Lots of departments in the area have started adding full or part-time detectives. Grenton's got to adapt, just like everywhere else. It's getting bigger. It's not isolated from the rest of the world like it used to be, when I joined up. Suppose I've been fighting that, this past year."

The Chief stood up, and Simon stood, too, automatically.

"By rights," the Chief said, meeting Simon's gaze, "the position should be offered to Russo or Keene first, since they've been here longer than you. But I spoke to them while you were gone, and they want you to have it. We all believe you're the right man for the job."

"Thank you, sir," he said, swallowing hard. "I appreciate the department's confidence in me."

Simon excused himself and walked back out into the main office, still dazed with shock. Kyle O'Malley and Jack both pretended not to know what had just happened, but Keene followed Simon into his office, sipping coffee and smirking. "Good news?" he asked, leaning against the doorframe.

"Keene," Simon said, tossing his hat onto his desk, "you're sure you're okay with this, man? You've been here, what, ten years?"

"Are you kidding me?"

"You're a smart guy. You could be a great detective."

"First of all, no, I'm not," Keene said. "Second, that's the last thing I'd want. I like my job the way it is. And you're going to be great. Seriously."

Still standing in the middle of his office, Simon looked down at his desk. "Thanks."

"No problem." Keene scratched his close-cropped buzz cut. "Congrats, my friend."

They discussed the case for a while, until they both had to go to their respective patrol assignments. Simon was thrilled to be back on his beat.

As soon as his shift ended, he walked down the street through the late afternoon snowfall to Leona's shop. She'd bought the shop from Paul last month, though Paul was still around a lot. Ostensibly, he was showing Leona the ropes, but Simon suspected they were just hanging out.

Simon paused outside her door, one hand on the glass. Leona stood at the counter, alone in the store for once, smiling to herself and writing something out on a notepad. Her hair fell loosely around her shoulders. A few long strands brushed against her pearl choker. She was exquisitely beautiful.

He pushed the door open and stepped inside, stamping the snow off his duty boots onto the welcome mat. Leona looked up.

"Hello, darling. How was your first day back?"

"Good." *Better than any man has a right to expect*, he thought. He took off his hat and gloves, jammed them into his coat pocket, and crossed the store toward her. She leaned across the counter to give him a kiss while he twined his hands through her hair. "Guess who's going to be Grenton's first detective?"

Her pretty, sinful mouth fell open. "No fucking way."

"Part-time, at least at first," he amended. "And part-time on patrol still. But I think it will let me do some good."

She gripped his arms through the heavy sleeves of his coat. "Of course it will."

"You think I'm up for it?" he asked, smiling.

"Dear heart," she said, "you're going to be fabulous."

The End

Author's Note

Thank you so much for reading *Breathe*! I know you have many choices when it comes to entertainment, and I'm truly grateful for your time.

Breathe is the first book in the Grenton PD erotic romance series. If you'd like to learn more about the series or sign up to be notified of new releases, visit my website: www.londonsetterby.com.

If you enjoyed this story, I hope you'll consider leaving a quick review. It makes a huge difference, and I appreciate it very much!

Thank you again for reading!

~London

P.S. Did you find a typo or other error? Please do let me know! I'll send you a free thank-you gift. You can reach me at setterby@gmail.com, or through the contact form on my website.

Acknowledgments

This book would not exist without Alexa Rowan and Isley Robson. Thank you both so much for sticking by me and for repeatedly convincing me not to throw *Breathe* into the sea.

Thank you to Becky Langdon for your unfailing kindness and support, and to Kristi Jones for your warmth and encouragement. Thank you to my fellow Wattpadders for being so delightful.

An earlier version of this novel appeared on the Radish Fiction app, and I am very grateful to everyone at Radish for taking a chance on me and *Breathe*. Thank you especially to every single one of my Radish readers. I'm so honored by how much you liked this story.

Last but not least, a huge thank you to my editor, Sarah Frantz Lyons. You made the book so much better. Especially that scene. You know the one.

About the Author

L. Setterby is a writer, lawyer, and life-long New Englander. She is apparently trying to write as many different kinds of romance novels as possible, including (as London Setterby) contemporary fantasy romances and Gothics. She also writes across the gender and sexuality spectrums. When not writing, she enjoys taking long rambling walks through various forests with her husband.

Also By L. Setterby

Set Me Free (written as London Setterby)

CPSIA information can be obtained
at www.ICGtesting.com
Printed in the USA
LVHW081255070219
606746LV00017B/295/P

BREATHE

Copyright © 2017 by London Setterby

All rights reserved.
Second Edition

No part of this book may be reproduced in any form or by any electronic or mechanical means, including information storage and retrieval systems, without written permission from the author, except for the use of brief quotations in a book review.

This is a work of fiction. Names, characters, businesses, places, events, and incidents are either the products of the author's imagination or are used in a fictitious manner. Any resemblance to actual persons, living or dead, or to actual events, is purely coincidental.

Cover image © conrado (via Shutterstock)
Cover fonts: DCC Ash by Draghia Cornel (via dafont) and Thinking of Betty by Stereo Type
Front cover design © 2017 London Setterby
Editing by Sarah Frantz Lyons

Copyediting by Laura Elliott

Interior Format